the
further
adventures of

SHERLOCK HOLMES

THE COUNTERFEIT DETECTIVE

the further adventures of

SHERLOCK HOLMES

THE COUNTERFEIT DETECTIVE

STUART DOUGLAS

TITAN BOOKS

THE FURTHER ADVENTURES OF SHERLOCK HOLMES:
THE COUNTERFEIT DETECTIVE
Print edition ISBN: 9781783299256
E-book edition ISBN: 9781783299263

Published by Titan Books
A division of Titan Publishing Group Ltd
144 Southwark Street, London SE1 0UP

First edition: October 2016
10 9 8 7 6 5 4 3 2 1

A CIP catalogue record for this title is available from the British Library.

Printed in the USA.

What did you think of this book? We love to hear from our readers. Please email us at: readerfeedback@titanemail.com, or write to Reader Feedback at the above address.

To receive advance information, news, competitions, and exclusive offers online, please sign up for the Titan newsletter on our website: www.titanbooks.com

the further adventures of

SHERLOCK HOLMES

THE COUNTERFEIT DETECTIVE

Chapter One

The summer of 1899 was a troubled period in the life of my friend, Sherlock Holmes. Since the turn of the previous year, he had been working on an occasional basis for his brother Mycroft, frequently disappearing for days at a time, only to return – filthy, irascible and near collapse – in the dark of night. Often, he would be injured in some manner that required my medical aid, but so great was his exhaustion that even as I stitched and bandaged his wounds, he would fall asleep in his chair, murmuring darkly to himself.

When he was not engaged in such clandestine activities, he sat before the fire in a thick haze of pipe smoke, saying nothing, but polluting the atmosphere to such an extent that I was forced to go out to my club more often than not. I began to fear that he was suffering from some form of mental imbalance, so morose had he become, and for the first time in several years I took to examining his arms for needle marks as I tended to his more mundane cuts and bruises. There were none, I was relieved to see, but that was no guarantee for the future, should his mental state remain so depressed.

I attempted to quiz him about his mysterious labours, of course, but he was tight-lipped on almost every occasion, and more than once lost his temper entirely, causing a cloud to descend upon our rooms. On the sole occasion he did speak of his work, all he would say was that it involved issues of state; though I naturally allowed the matter to rest at that point, I remained worried for Holmes's health and general wellbeing. The news from southern Africa, where the Boers seemed finally to have worked themselves into enough of a frenzy to threaten revolt against British rule, had done little to improve the general mood, while his increasingly thin and pale face reminded me painfully of the early days of our friendship, when cocaine too often wrapped him in its malignant fingers.

It came as something of a surprise, therefore, when he announced over breakfast one morning that he intended to leave for America as soon as could be arranged. He would elaborate no further, but as he had received a letter five minutes previously that he now held crushed in his fist, it was not difficult to guess the inspiration for his sudden travel plans, even if the specific reason remained unclear.

Determined to show that I was capable of exercising those powers of observation that my friend often claimed I lacked, I called him back as he rose from his chair. "Bad news?" I enquired, nodding meaningfully at the crumpled paper in his hand.

"You might well say so, Watson!" Holmes strode to the fireplace and back in a few paces, then repeated the action several times, waving the letter like a white flag. "Here," he said finally. "Read this. I would appreciate your opinion on the contents."

He handed me the missive. I smoothed it on my knee and,

as was my custom when Holmes and I considered a document together, read the contents aloud.

Dear Sherlock Holmes,

You will surely not remember but some years ago I briefly made your acquaintance when you were instrumental in proving my maternal uncle innocent of a minor theft from the house in which he was employed.

I paused and raised my eyebrows querulously at Holmes. "This is hardly the stuff of outrage, Holmes. This man and his family obviously remember you fondly and hold you yet in high regard, even if they consider you unlikely to be able to respond in kind." I frowned at a sudden thought. "Surely you are not so vain that the belief you might not possess infallible recall has placed you in so foul a mood?"

Holmes irritably waved away my suggestion. "Of course not, Watson. Vanity, I'm sure you would agree, is not one of my character flaws." He sniffed. "Besides, the letter is unsigned and gives no further indication of the identity of our correspondent. Even my deductive powers rebel when faced with so little information. But please, do continue. I am keen to hear what you think of the next section."

I picked up the letter again, and let my eyes run down the page.

Since then, I have emigrated to the United States and now make my home in the city of New York, where I have been fortunate enough to take a wife and start a family. In fact, I am about to move on again, to California of all places, where my wife's family have an interest in a thriving hotel, but before I left I felt it only proper to relate to you a peculiar incident I witnessed yesterday and, by so doing, perhaps partially repay my family's debt to you.

Yesterday morning I was walking from my place of employment to my home when I happened to pass by a boy selling newspapers. You must understand that I do not, as a rule, waste valuable pennies on what tend to be mere purveyors of scandal and gossip, but as I walked by on this occasion, something caught my eye. There, on the front page of the nearest newspaper, was the name Sherlock Holmes. I bought a copy, expecting to read of your fresh triumphs of detection, much as *The Strand Magazine* prints Dr Watson's tales. You may imagine my surprise, therefore, when I opened the 'paper to discover that Sherlock Holmes is currently working in New York, and has been for some time. More surprising still, the sketch that accompanied the article was of a man who, though similar to yourself, was most definitely not the Sherlock Holmes I had previously met.

I cannot tell you much more than that, Mr Holmes. The article mentioned this man's many grateful clients in the city, and hinted that a permanent move to New York might be imminent, but little else. Perhaps he works here with your blessing, but – remembering the service you did my uncle – I thought it incumbent on me to make you aware of what may be a terrible imposture, which could well have a damaging effect on your reputation.

A Well Wisher

Holmes cocked his head to one side in enquiry as I laid the letter to one side. "Can you believe the impudence, Watson?" he snapped. "The effrontery of this imposter…"

His words became lost in indistinct muttering, allowing me to pose an obvious question.

"Are you sure that this 'well wisher' is what he claims to be, Holmes? An anonymous letter is hardly the most credible of sources."

Holmes glared at me for a moment before speaking. "Of course I shall need to make enquiries by telegram before making any firm decision, but assuming all is as this individual claims, I intend to book passage to the United States and confront the blackguard who has stolen my identity!"

I rushed to placate him. "I would say that you must certainly do something to put an end to this sorry state of affairs, Holmes. Whoever it was sent you this letter, he is quite correct when he says your reputation could be damaged. We should go to New York and confront the villain!"

"Perhaps…" Holmes lit a cigarette and blew smoke angrily towards the ceiling. "I have completed all but a tiny fragment of Mycroft's many requests, after all. Moreover, why should I wait about for my brother to snap his fingers in the expectation that I will immediately come running? Enough is enough, Watson. I will tolerate his overbearing attitude no longer!"

Clearly, there was no need for me to say anything. Holmes's relationship with his brother was a complex one that I did not entirely comprehend, but his unexpected inferiority complex whenever Mycroft was involved played a major role in all of their interactions. I had watched with alarm over recent months as Holmes had worn himself out at the behest of Mycroft, and felt only relief that my friend had decided to put his own interests first.

As Holmes shrugged on his coat and hat and headed for the door, it was all I could do to keep up with him.

Three days later we stood on the deck of the RMS *Oceanic*, the world's largest ocean liner, and our home for the next six days, as it began its maiden voyage from Liverpool to New York. Already I could tell that the journey would be beneficial to Holmes's health. Colour had returned to his cheeks, and his eyes – which had for weeks been heavy with tension and lack of sleep – were clearer than for some time. His manner, too, would, I hoped, undergo a similar transformation. Holmes had been ill-tempered and irritable ever since he had taken on whatever mysterious task Mycroft had given him, but I was optimistic our voyage would restore him to normality.

For myself, I must admit that the change of scenery was equally welcome. The *Oceanic* was as luxurious and well-appointed as any first rate London hotel, and I had already taken a pleasant stroll around the library while waiting for the ship to leave port. Holmes, for his part, had spent the time walking the decks, his mind, I assumed, turning over the matter of the mysterious imposter who had stolen his identity. Now, we met up on the port deck and stood, watching the sea slip by beneath the smooth keel below us.

"So, Holmes," I began, "rather an impressive vessel, wouldn't you say?"

Holmes nodded, though with little obvious interest. "The largest afloat, I believe." His eyes flitted around as he spoke. "I admit, however, that the people on board are far more likely to maintain my interest for the next few days than a study of the fixtures and fittings."

Evidently any change in Holmes's mental, as opposed to physical, demeanour would be a gradual one, but I was encouraged by the fact that he was at least showing an interest in his fellow passengers. It had been some time since my friend had engaged with those around him, and if I only imagined a familiar glint in his eye as he scanned a group of crewmen manhandling a crate through a doorway, it was still enough to give me cause for optimism. Attempting to build on this possibly fragile improvement, I chided him that he had no way of knowing that his fellow passengers were of any interest at all.

He reacted as I hoped he would. "No way of knowing, you say, Watson? Why, from this spot alone I count two couples travelling with companions other than their legitimate spouses, a minimum of three former convicts amongst the crew, one of whom served a substantial sentence, almost certainly in an English prison, and a lady concerned about an expensive necklace, which she fears may be broken. That small selection will be enough to satisfy my curiosity for a while."

"I will not ask how you can identify a man in the company of a woman other than his wife, Holmes, but the others? What marks out the convict so clearly? How can you know the thoughts of a lady who is a stranger to you? Are you not exaggerating just a little?"

It would be an exaggeration of my own to say that Holmes bridled at this suggestion, but he was clearly vexed to be doubted. He took his cane and, in turn, pointed to the crewmen he believed to be criminals. "Wait a moment," he cautioned, "until one of them chances to walk past us. Look at his hands as he does so."

We had not long to wait. Within a minute, the nearest man picked up a heavy bag and, throwing it over his shoulder, made his way past us and down into the body of the ship. As he crossed in front of me, I glanced at his hands, but could see nothing of particular interest. I said as much to Holmes, who shook his head in mock sorrow.

"You failed to see four heavy black dots tattooed between his right thumb and forefinger? Their meaning varies from prison to prison, never mind country to country, but in every case they commemorate the criminal status and achievements of their owner. I have noticed similar markings on two other crewmen, suggesting that they too have been incarcerated in the past."

I shook my head ruefully. "The breadth of your knowledge continues to astound me, Holmes. But the length of his sentence – how can you gauge that?"

"Simplicity itself. The sailing man's life is an outdoor one, spent in the sun, rain and wind. It tans and weathers the face. The man who just passed us has skin as pale as a maiden's, though his face is as lined and creased as any of his colleagues. Hence, though long in experience on the sea, he has led a wholly interior life in recent years. He also has a faint stoop and his upper arms are slightly over-developed in comparison to the rest of his frame, such as is seen in long-term prisoners who have spent many years turning a punishment crank. The crank is no longer the fashion even in English prisons and was never popular in the Americas, thus I suggest a long sentence, covering many years, served in a British institution."

Holmes's logic was irrefutable, but I was determined that he should explain each of his claims in turn. "And the nervous lady, with the expensive necklace?" I asked.

In response, he subtly indicated a young woman standing to our right, watching the dock disappear in our wake. I looked across under cover of taking in the same view. She wore the most fashionable and expensive of dresses, cut daringly low and decorated with a white ruff collar of the sort that would have meant a great deal to my late wife, but merely looked uncomfortable to me. Her face was small and perfectly symmetrical, with large, round brown eyes and blonde hair that peeked out from beneath a pale green sun hat. An attractive young lady, in other words, but otherwise unremarkable. I said so to Holmes.

"It is the details that should concern you, Watson, not the broadest brushstrokes. Whether her eyes are brown or blue is immaterial. Much the same can be said of her hair. Such peripheral matters are of no consequence and should be discarded. Look again, but this time do more than simply admire the lady."

In the early days of our acquaintance, I might have taken offence at Holmes's tone. But after many years spent in his company, I had come to recognise that no insult was intended. The simple truth was that Holmes occasionally forgot that his mind was a unique one and that not everyone was as naturally observant as he. I crossed to the railing and considered the lady from the corner of my eye, feeling rather ungentlemanly as I did so. A minute or so sufficed for me to make every observation I thought pertinent. I returned to Holmes's side and reported my findings.

"The lady is around twenty-five years old, and of substantial means. She is carrying a monogrammed leather bag, with a heavy gold clasp and the initials JAD stamped in the leather. She is wearing diamond and emerald earrings and a matching bracelet, but no rings. There is a faded scar on her right wrist and a small mole on the back of her neck. Nothing else struck me, I'm afraid, Holmes." I knew even as I spoke that there had been more to see, and that Holmes would delight in telling me so. "I take it I have missed something of importance?"

"No, Watson," he replied, to my astonishment. "You have missed nothing. The pity is that, as ever, though you have seen, you have not observed." He led me by the elbow into the interior of the ship. "I did tell you that the lady is worried about her necklace, yet you did not think it pertinent that she is wearing no such item?"

I cannot deny that I was stung by so unfair an accusation, and was quick, therefore, to correct Holmes. "I did not mention its absence because I believed that to be the exact situation we were considering!"

"Come now, Watson," my friend chided, "there is no call to take offence so readily! You described the earrings and bracelet as matching; it is surely not too great a leap to suggest that there was once a necklace in the same set? Or that its absence is the cause of the lady unconsciously reaching up and touching her throat several times in the past few minutes?"

I thought I had spotted a flaw in his reasoning: "Even so, perhaps it was stolen, and not broken?"

"I would say not," replied Holmes firmly. "Judging by the quality of the remaining pieces, the missing necklace was a spectacular item. Its theft would raise a hue and cry on land, far more so at sea, where there is almost no chance of escape. No criminal would take so foolish a risk."

"It may have been stolen on land."

"And the lady chose to wear an incomplete set rather than buying new jewellery before boarding? You have been married, Watson. Does that strike you as at all likely? No, the necklace was damaged in some way today, soon after the young lady came on board – within the past hour, at most. She has not taken the time to go to her cabin to change because she wished to see the ship embark from the quayside. Doubtless she tucked the necklace inside the bag she carries, which, as you noticed, has a stout clasp."

Holmes's argument was convincing. "Very well done," I

exclaimed, slapping him on the shoulder in a fit of bonhomie. Then, determined to keep his mind active, I continued, "but now, having dealt with our fellow passengers and the ship's crew, have you had any further thoughts on the scoundrel we are crossing the Atlantic to confront?"

There was no doubting the change that overcame Holmes as he spoke of our current case. He pulled a folded sheet of paper from his pocket and handed it to me. I had no need to read it, however, for Holmes quickly explained its contents to me. "As you know I contacted the New York police force, who were able to confirm that Sherlock Holmes is, indeed, currently a resident of their city. Beyond that they would not elaborate, on the admittedly sensible grounds that they were unwilling to discuss the habits of Sherlock Holmes with Sherlock Holmes."

He smiled, the first such expression I had seen on his face for months. "Fortunately, that letter you hold is a note from our own Inspector Gregson to one Inspector Simeon Bullock of the New York constabulary. It appears that Bullock is a Yorkshireman by birth, and trained alongside Gregson when both were callow constables in England. They have kept in touch intermittently since Bullock emigrated to the United States, and the letter should serve as a useful introduction once we arrive."

"Well, that is a stroke of luck!" I exclaimed – and nothing made me more sure that this trip had been the tonic that Holmes needed than the pained expression which crossed his face in response.

"My apologies, Holmes," I replied with a small smile of my own. "I should have known better than to give any credit to mere Providence."

Holmes acknowledged my gentle barb with a raised eyebrow, but said nothing. He continued to scan our fellow passengers and such crewmen as were above decks, and I was reminded – not for the first time in our acquaintance – of a young boy considering an ant colony. I did not give voice to this observation, as I knew Holmes would not be flattered, but instead suggested lunch in the ship's luxurious dining saloon. Remarking that the sea air had left him hungry, Holmes agreed with my suggestion and, with a final glance around the deck, led the way.

I admit to having no great knowledge of passenger liners or of sailing ships in general, having until that point exclusively travelled in army ships, which are not vessels renowned for their luxury. Even I was in no doubt, however, that the dining saloon of the *Oceanic* was a wondrous sight. With seating for several hundred diners and a massive and ornate domed glass ceiling, reminiscent of a similar feature in the library, the room was also lit by a series of oversized portholes along each side of the ship that bathed the whole room in a deep golden late afternoon light. The maître d' hurried over as Holmes and I entered and quickly showed us to a free table. Around us, diners chatted loudly as at least a score of waiters weaved amongst them, lifting and depositing silver salvers and delicate china plates with complete aplomb. We ordered our meals and sat back in contented silence.

In this manner, we passed the first three days at sea. Every morning after breakfast I would stroll to the library, where I would spend my time writing up my notes on recent cases. Holmes, meanwhile, disappeared into the body of the ship without explanation. I would see him now and again via a window as he strode across the deck, or through the library door, as he made his way from one unknown location to another, and though I was aware that I should call his name and ascertain what he was doing, equally I cannot deny that the peace and quiet of solitude was refreshing in its own way. At exactly one o'clock we would meet in the dining room for luncheon when, in the absence of any news regarding Holmes's American double, we would desultorily discuss the weather and the state of the sea, then part immediately afterwards. Twice, I tried to bring up topics that I hoped would stimulate his mind, but he seemed uninterested and answered in monosyllables. Holmes, I feared, was bored and would likely soon descend once more into the dark mood that I had hoped this trip might alleviate.

In spite of my concerns, I would not have wished for the news that greeted me later that night, however. When a firm knock at my cabin door caused me to lay down my book and glass of whisky, the last thing I was expecting was to be informed of a murder on board.

I recognised the young officer who stood before me as the one who had greeted us on our arrival – Sub-Lieutenant Agnew was his name. He described the discovery of a crewman's body inside an otherwise empty starboard lifeboat, and the ship's own doctor being occupied with a passenger in First Class running a dangerous fever, he explained that the captain wondered if Dr Watson might spare the time to examine the body and provide some idea of the cause of death?

"The dead man is one of the crew – Fireman Thomas Bellamy – and, obviously, the location of the corpse suggests foul play," he continued in a suitably serious tone. "But nobody has touched anything and a professional opinion would be most helpful to the captain."

I immediately agreed to dress and go with him, asking only that he make his way to Holmes's cabin and apprise my friend of what had happened. "I'll meet you both at the lifeboat in ten minutes,"

I concluded, already casting my eye around my cabin, wondering where I had stored my medical bag. Although I was sorry to hear of the dead man, I cannot deny that I was also envisioning the improvement a case would bring to Holmes's disposition and, perhaps, even hoping a little that it would not prove to be a simple case of a drunken seaman falling and breaking his neck. I am not proud of the admission, but such was my concern.

Shortly afterwards, Holmes and I stood to one side as two crewmen rolled back the heavy canvas which covered one raised lifeboat. The night air was chill after the warmth of my cabin, and this section of the ship was gloomy and deserted, the sun having set. I shivered a little as we waited, but Holmes stood stock still with his head to one side, taking careful note of every element of the scene before him. Finally, the lifeboat was secured satisfactorily and I was beckoned forward.

I clambered up the ladder that had been propped against the side of the small boat and, with the sailor who was already inside holding a lantern above my head, leant forward and looked down at the bottom of the vessel. The wood was painted white and, in spite of the canvas cover, wet, curving down on either side, with benches stretching almost the entire length. The flickering light illuminated a dark, humped shape partially hidden by one of these benches, but it was impossible to make out any further detail without a closer examination. Moving to one side, my helpful companion laid down his lantern and, reaching out an arm to balance himself, pulled me over the side of the boat.

I heard Holmes scramble down beside me as I squatted and carefully rolled the body onto its back. A thick hank of dark hair covered the man's forehead, but nonetheless I could see enough of his face to know that he had suffered a fairly severe beating before he died, including one particularly vicious cut across his left temple. From habit alone, I felt for a pulse at his neck and, as expected, found none, though I did pull my hand away sharply as I felt the unmistakable wetness of congealing blood. I heard Holmes softly hiss at my side, then he took the lantern from the waiting seaman and brought it down close to the man's neck. In the yellow light a gaping razor wound, stretching from ear to ear in a crooked line, was hellishly obscene, though thankfully there was not a great deal of blood.

With such an obvious cause of death and in such poorly lit conditions, there was nothing more for me to do, and I said as much to my audience. "I cannot be absolutely positive until I examine this poor chap under more favourable conditions, but he has been dead for around three hours, I would say. The condition of the wound and the fact there was still a little unabsorbed water under the body supports such a timescale, as does the fact that this area of the ship will have been quiet at that time, allowing the hiding of the body in this lifeboat. I should add that he is unlikely to have been killed here. There would have been a great deal of blood, and as you can see, there is little such to be found."

I couldn't help but glance at Holmes as I laid out my conclusions, lacking though they were any solid medical basis, and was gratified to notice that he was smiling with obvious satisfaction at my recital.

My part complete, I moved back to allow Holmes access, and as I did so my foot kicked a small, hard object across the bottom of the lifeboat. "Hello," I said in surprise, "what's this?" I scrambled unsteadily across to the object, whatever it was, and picked it up. Held to the lantern light, it was plain that we had found the murder weapon – a commonplace shaving razor, with a wooden handle and a blood-encrusted blade. The letters "BP" were carved in the handle, a fact that caused our officer escort to give a sharp intake of breath as I handed it to him.

"If you will excuse me, gentlemen, there is a matter that I must urgently attend to," said Agnew. He made to leave, then, evidently remembering that we were passengers and not members of his crew, briefly turned back. "Smith!" he shouted to one of the waiting crewmen. "Look after Mr Holmes and Dr Watson until I return. Do not leave this area until you hear from me. Clear?"

With that, he made to leave, but before he could do so, Holmes called him back.

"You recognise the blade?" he asked.

"I believe that I do. If you will excuse me, sir, I will ensure that the owner is held secure."

I thought that Holmes would say more but instead he nodded his agreement, and we returned to the task at hand. Holmes knelt down beside the body, seemingly unconscious of the water soaking the knees of his trousers, bending so close to the dead man's face that they were almost touching. He examined the killing wound for a long minute, then inspected the hands and particularly the fingernails of the victim. Finally, he undid the man's shirt and, holding the lantern close to the skin, checked both sides of the torso.

"See, Watson," he said, "there is a mixture of old and new bruises extending from this man's waist to just below his collarbone. Nothing further up, excepting the perimortem damage to the face, which was part of the final assault, so before tonight his many injuries would not have been visible."

"You think that was deliberate? That someone has been beating this man for some time, but carefully, so as to keep his abuse hidden?"

"More than one person, I believe," Holmes replied. He held up the man's right hand. "Notice that although the skin is tough, as befits one who does manual work aboard a ship, the nails are not recently broken nor are there any cuts or other marks on their backs. Sailors are no shrinking violets, Watson, as I am sure you are aware. It seems exceedingly unlikely that our victim would not at least attempt to fight back against a single assailant, given time and repeated attacks."

"A gang, then?"

"I would say so. Two men at least to hold him, while another administered the blows." He considered the scene again. "More like a punishment than an assault."

"An official punishment?" I asked, doubtfully.

"To this degree? Of course not!"

He shook his head briskly, but his face was puzzled as he re-examined the man's wounds. "We are looking at the problem from the wrong end, Watson. It matters not, for the moment, how he gained these old bruises, but how he came to receive the new. How and why did regular beatings turn to murder?"

"Could he have defended himself, on this last occasion? Fought back and so provoked his attackers that they made an end of him? Three men you said, Holmes! What if there were only two at the outset, allowing their victim to defend himself for once. It remains two against one, of course, so he still takes a beating, but perhaps he holds his own for long enough to worry his assailants that they will be discovered. Long enough, even, for a third man to make an appearance, coming up behind this poor man and cutting his throat!"

I admit I was pleased with my theory; it fitted all the facts admirably. It was clear from the look on his face, however, that Holmes did not share my enthusiasm.

"I hardly know–" he began, only to be interrupted by a shout from the deck. A head appeared over the side of the lifeboat, as Agnew returned with further news. The dead man's bunkmate had been accused of the crime and was being held in his cabin until Sherlock Holmes could question him.

Holmes, however, did not move. Instead, he pulled out the magnifying glass he always carried and held it close to the wound on the victim's neck.

"Holmes?" I said, as the officer cleared his throat loudly. "I think we are wanted elsewhere."

For a moment I thought he had not heard me, then he whipped his head round and, with no attempt to conceal his irritation, snapped, "Nonsense. If they already have the murderer, then a delay of a few minutes while I ensure that I have all that I need will make no difference, and if the killer is *not* he, then this examination is certainly a better use of my time than an unnecessary interview. Now, do you have pencil and paper about you?"

Used as I was to Holmes and his often eccentric behaviour, I had made sure to bring both items with me from my cabin. I handed them to him and watched as he drew two horizontal lines, one long with a very slight upturn at one end, the other shorter but straighter, the two lines just barely touching at their tips.

"That should suffice," he said and, without warning, jumped to his feet and gestured impatiently for Agnew to get out of his way. Within moments he was back on the deck. I followed him more sedately, feeling my old Afghan wound begin to flare up as I manoeuvred my way down the ladder to the deck.

"If you will just follow me, gentlemen, I will take you to Fireman Bellamy's cabin," began our guide, but Holmes cut him off with a raised hand.

The Counterfeit Detective

"Never mind that for now," he said. "Answer me this one question instead. Is the dead man's cabin mate clean-shaven?"

No doubt I looked as perplexed as Agnew at that moment, but the sailor quickly rallied. "Not clean-shaven, no, but neither does he have a full beard, Mr Holmes. Many of the crew below decks only shave occasionally. Bob Peters is such a one."

Holmes brushed some dirt from his sleeve before he replied. "In which case, I do not need to speak to Mr Peters. What I do need to know is exactly where Bellamy worked. *That* is where I need to go."

Agnew was clearly torn between a desire to help the famous Sherlock Holmes and a need to satisfy the orders of his captain. In the end, obedience to authority won out, and he shook his head. "I'm afraid I can't take you down to the engine room, Mr Holmes. Not only is the area forbidden to passengers, but it is dirty and dangerous – and besides, Bellamy's bunkmate has as good as admitted doing the deed!"

"Really?" I said, then, hoping to find some compromise, "Do you hear that, Holmes? The fellow's admitted it." Though I remained keen to see Holmes alleviate his ennui by investigating a case, I preferred to do so in a comfortable cabin rather than amidst the filth and noise of a ship's engines.

It was a disappointment, therefore, when Holmes pedantically corrected me. "*As good as* admitted it, I believe. Which is not quite the same thing as an actual confession." He turned his attention to the officer, who was by now barely hiding his impatience. "How – exactly – has this helpful soul confessed to the murder of this man?"

"The razor Dr Watson discovered is his, and he cannot account for its whereabouts, or his own, earlier this evening!" announced Agnew triumphantly, then, with every sign that he considered this entirely conclusive, added, "And the two were seen arguing violently this morning. In fact, Andrew Harper, Bellamy's foreman in the engine room, overheard Peters threaten to kill him just a few hours ago and warned the two of them to sort out their differences before their next shift." He swallowed heavily and I was struck by his extreme youth. "I doubt that he had this in mind, though," he finished quietly.

"No, I think not," Holmes replied solemnly, but with Agnew continuing to press, he did at least agree to go to speak to Peters and see what he had to say for himself. We left the corpse to the crew, and followed the young officer back inside the body of the ship.

Chapter Two

It was approaching eleven by the time we made our way along the deck and through a heavy door marked "CREW ONLY". The sensation of stepping into another world was distinct. Where outside on the deck all was quiet and still, with only a very occasional passenger taking the night air or stopping for one final cigarette in the moonlight, inside was all hustle and bustle, even at this late hour. As we followed our guide through a labyrinth of almost identical, wholly functional corridors, crewmen of all sorts pushed past us, appearing from and disappearing into one hatchway or another, like rabbits traversing their warren. Beyond one door I spied chefs in loose white jackets and waiting staff in unbuttoned waistcoats, playing cards around a low table, while another room appeared to contain only a teetering tower of freshly laundered white towels. Finally, we were directed towards one particular room, outside which stood a seaman holding a heavy, wooden paddle of some kind. Stooping to enter, we found ourselves in the cramped quarters that had, until today, been shared by the victim and the man accused of his murder.

That same man sat on the lower level of a set of bunk beds that took up almost half of the available space, smoking a cigarette, which shook in his hand as he brought it up to his mouth. He had not heard us enter, it seemed, and so I was able to take a good look at him before we spoke. I placed his height at around five foot eight and weight about eleven stone, though not a pound of that was fat. He was dressed in heavy blue working overalls and a collarless shirt, with a dirty white linen scarf tied round his neck.

Agnew chose that moment to step into the cabin, however, and any chance of further, covert observation was ended as he ordered Peters to his feet.

The prisoner – for there was no doubt that that was what he was – came to his feet carefully. He raised what was left of his cigarette to his lips, only to have it dashed away by Agnew.

"Put that down, man! Have you no conception of the trouble you're in?" Agnew barked, though his calm face drew much of the sting from his words. A more than capable young man, I thought approvingly, ensuring Peters knew the gravity of the situation but not allowing him to be overwhelmed. The accused, for his part, obviously respected Agnew well enough, for he made no protest and mumbled an apology to me and Holmes.

As expected, Holmes gave no indication he had heard either Agnew or Peters speak. Instead he walked slowly round the little room, circumnavigating Peters as though he were a globe.

Finally he stopped in front of Agnew. "As I said earlier," he began, "this is not the murderer, and the time we have spent on this pointless exercise would have been better utilised in confronting the real killer." He shook his head. "Quite why this unfortunate soul was suspected at all is beyond me entirely. Mr Peters," he said, with a smile that was obviously intended to reassure, "do you shave often?"

"Coupla times a week," Peters mumbled in response without raising his head. "Less in winter."

"And as evidenced by your hirsute chin, you are currently on your winter schedule, is that correct?"

Peters looked at Agnew in confusion, but that stalwart officer was unable to shed any light on matters. Holmes, again, appeared not to notice and carried on as though Peters had answered in full.

"So you have not had cause to lay hands on your razor today? And more likely not for a day before that, more than enough time in which someone might have slipped into your cabin and stolen it." Holmes glanced round the cramped space. "There are not, I would suggest, many places where you might store the blade. It would be a matter of a minute at most to make off with it."

"Are you saying that you believe Peters to be innocent on the basis of his toilet habits?" Agnew interrupted. "You think someone else is trying to implicate him?"

Holmes nodded sharply. "Of course. Could anything be more obvious?"

I might have warned Agnew to be silent then, but with that combination of bravado and foolishness that marks every young officer, he had clearly decided already that perhaps the reputation of Baker Street's finest was somewhat exaggerated. "How can you say that with such conviction, Mr Holmes, when Peters's razor was found underneath the body?" He half-turned towards the accused man. "I am sorry, Peters, but it is hard to see beyond the weight of evidence against you, especially when all Mr Holmes can offer in your defence is the beginnings of a beard."

Peters shrugged, and I wondered if he entirely followed what was happening. There was something about his eyes that troubled me. If anything, his confusion seemed to be growing. Holmes could have that effect on the brightest and most thoughtful of men, I knew, but there was something distracting Peters, I felt sure.

Before I could remark on this, however, Holmes had resumed his education of Sub-Lieutenant Agnew. "Hardly 'all that I can offer', Agnew. Consider the most obvious defence of all. What sort of murderer must Peters here be if, having slit the throat of his victim, he decides to leave the murder weapon – even though it has his initials on it and is known to be his – at the scene of the crime?"

"Stranger things have happened, Mr Holmes," Agnew replied with a grim smile. "If murderers were never careless, I suspect your own profession might prove considerably more difficult."

Holmes acknowledged the truth of this with a slight nod. "Perhaps there is merit in your claim, but in this case we have additional concerns that, placed one by one, will build a sturdy defence around Mr Peters." Suddenly he addressed the accused man directly. "Will you be so kind as to lift up your shirt, Mr Peters?"

It was immediately apparent that Peters was not keen to do as Holmes had asked. He glanced at Agnew, but that sturdy officer simply indicated that he should do as he was bidden and, when Peters continued to delay, finally informed him that if he would not lift his shirt voluntarily, then he would be obliged to do so by force. Reluctantly, Peters unbuckled the top half of his overalls and, with a shrug, pulled the shirt over his head.

The reason for his hesitation was at once clear to see. Stretching in a muddy river of muted purples, blues and browns from collarbone to hips were a series of bruises, very similar to those we had examined on the corpse of Thomas Bellamy.

Agnew, to his credit, made no effort to conceal his shock. "Who did this, Peters? Come on, man, tell us."

"You will note," said Holmes placidly, "that while some of these contusions are fresh, many of them are older and already healing, just as we saw on the unfortunate Mr Bellamy." He held a hand out. "If I might ask you to show Dr Watson your hand, Mr Peters? The left one, if you please."

I was unsure exactly what to expect, but I knew Holmes had spotted something. I turned the hand over but, other than the expected calluses of the manual worker, could see nothing exceptional. "What am I looking for, Holmes?" I was finally forced to ask in exasperation.

Holmes's voice was sharp in response. "Really, Watson, I expected better!" He took Peters's hand in one of his, then gestured for the other, which he flipped over so that the two palms were displayed alongside one another. "You see now?" he said impatiently.

The right palm was far smoother and less marked than the left, indicating that Peters was left-handed, but I failed to see why that was significant and said as much to Holmes. There were times when his preference for the dramatic revelation could become tiresome, to be frank.

"It is the only thing that is significant, Watson. Can you not see that?" Holmes, never the most patient of men when dealing with others less gifted than himself, would not have made a truly great teacher, I think it fair to say. Brusquely, he dropped Peters's hands and pulled from his pocket the paper and pencil that I had given him earlier.

"Hold this, if you will, and take a seat," he said to Agnew, passing the folded sheet to him, before speaking to Peters again. "And if you could take a step forward, Mr Peters, and stand with your back to me. Thank you."

The sailors did as they were asked. As soon as everyone was in place, Holmes whispered something in Peters's ear as he took up a position directly behind him, the pencil held in his left hand. Then, with a swift, unstoppable movement, he drew the pencil across Peters's throat like a knife, slashing from right to left in a single deadly motion.

The implication was clear, but I was surprised that Holmes had missed a very obvious objection. Perhaps he was slipping. "That is how a left-handed killer might surprise and murder his victim, yes," I said hesitantly, with no wish to make my friend look less capable, "but Holmes, that exactly matches the wound on Bellamy's neck. That too traverses the throat from right to left. Whoever killed Bellamy was a left-handed man!"

Peters looked stricken, as well he might, and Agnew began to rise from his seat, but Holmes was not at all flustered by my words.

"Not so," he said, without force but with utter conviction. He turned to Agnew. "At the risk of sounding like some sideshow conjurer, I would be obliged if you would open the paper I gave you earlier and show it to Watson. It will, I am confident, fully prove Mr Peters's innocence."

Agnew did as he was asked, carefully unfolding the paper and smoothing it out on his knee. Even before he handed it to me, however, I could see that all it showed was a thin line drawn across the centre of the sheet. I was puzzled as to what it could possibly mean, far less prove.

Viewed close up, I was able to delineate two distinct lines rather than a single unbroken one, yet the meaning remained entirely unclear. I glanced at Holmes querulously until he deigned to explain the mystery.

"It's simple enough, Watson. We have established that if Bellamy was killed by a single man then the attack must have been swift and had the element of surprise, hence the lack of defensive markings on his hands. The best – almost the only – way in which to cut a man's throat by surprise is to come up behind him and dispatch him with one quick cut, across the width of the throat, bisecting the carotid artery. A sufficiently deep cut, that is, one that cuts straight through the artery–"

"–will cause a jet of blood to pulse from the wound for around thirty seconds," I interrupted, irritated by Holmes's high-handed attitude and willingness to lecture me on medical matters. "But if you are about to point out that there was little blood in the lifeboat, you will recall that I made that very point at the time, and suggested that the actual killing had been done elsewhere and the body merely hidden in the boat."

Holmes seemed mildly chastened by my outburst. "All quite correct, Watson," he said, "and my apologies for forgetting that you would be far more able than I to explain the issue at hand to Lieutenant Agnew and Mr Peters. However, I was not speaking about the missing blood – though that is a matter of great importance, as it happens – but of the manner in which a fatal cut might be administered." He indicated Peters's neck, on which the necklace-like mark of the pencil indentation was gradually fading. "In order to achieve the required firm pressure, the cut must be made in one quick movement, leaving a solitary wound, such as can be seen on Mr Peters. This is true whether the assailant is left or right handed." He paused for a moment to allow me to speak, then, when I failed to do so, continued, "You would agree, Watson?"

I was intrigued to know what Holmes had in mind. Though I was entirely in accord with his analysis, the conclusions he had evidently drawn eluded me completely. "Agreed, Holmes," I said, "but how does that help us? Whether left or right handed, the cut to the throat would be identical."

"You disappoint me, Watson. Will you never learn to *observe*, rather than merely *look*? Even in a common case of throat-cutting it is typically possible to differentiate between a left to right cut and the converse, using the depth of the wound as a gauge. In our present case, however, it is simpler still." He held out a hand. "If you would pass me the sheet of paper Agnew gave you?" he asked.

The difference in Holmes when he was involved in a case was, as ever, remarkable. No longer did he seem distracted and melancholy. Now he flourished the paper with its unremarkable pencil line as though it were his personal banner, his eyes bright with pleasure and his cheeks faintly flushed with the excitement of the puzzle before him. He ran a long finger along the line, stopping where it bifurcated.

"Observe this break, Watson," he instructed. "Mr Agnew, too, you see it? It marks the point at which the real killer was forced by biology to stop cutting and reposition himself, the better to conclude his grisly business."

"But why would he do that, Mr Holmes?" Agnew asked, casting a suspicious look at Peters, who twisted his hands together uneasily. "Why would he need to change position, when you said all it takes is a quick cut to kill?"

But I had finally grasped Holmes's point. "Because the cut was made from the front, not the rear!" I gasped. I realised, too, that I had seen similar sights in Afghanistan, though never on a man. I had, however, seen goats hung by their feet before having their throats sliced open. The initial laceration could only extend so far before the knifeman's knuckles intervened and it was necessary to complete the cut from the other side, with the two incisions meeting in the middle – just as Holmes's pencil sketch of Bellamy's wound showed.

"Quite, Watson. Mr Bellamy was not attacked from behind, though I fear that the killer was keen for us to believe otherwise. Furthermore, the depth of the cut clearly demonstrates that whoever made the cut – I do not say the killer, as this was certainly not the deadly injury – was right-handed."

I flushed with embarrassment at Holmes's words. I have always prided myself that I am a more than competent medical practitioner, and if my practice was not nowadays as busy as heretofore, that was no excuse for my erroneous insistence that a cut throat had been the cause of Bellamy's death. I was not so concerned by my own mistake, however, that I failed to notice Peters give a sob of relief and bury his head in his hands. He, at least, viewed Holmes's words as exoneration, even if Agnew still looked a little doubtful. I ventured to put both men's minds at rest. "So, Mr Peters cannot have been the man who wielded the blade?" I asked.

Holmes shook his head decisively. "Have I not just said as much, Watson? Really, you must pay more attention. No, Peters cannot have cut his colleague's throat. The throat cutting is of little interest, in any case. It was obviously done at a later point, to implicate Peters, here, and remove any threat of suspicion from the real killer."

"Then how did he die?" Agnew asked, the confusion plain on his face.

Holmes nodded his approval. "A far more useful question. You remember the cut by the late Mr Bellamy's eye? That, you will find on closer inspection, is the blow that ended that poor man's life. From my own cursory examination, I have no doubt that a heavy blow crushed his temple, causing his immediate demise."

"A sufficiently forceful blow to the temple can bring about a fatal epidural haemorrhage," I confirmed. "In simple terms, blood builds up between the brain and the skull, causing a compression of the brain. Death can take several hours in some cases, but can also occur almost instantaneously."

If anything, Agnew looked more perplexed now than he had before my explanation, but Peters unconsciously nodded to himself as I concluded. He remained ashen-faced, but I noticed he stood more erectly as Holmes turned to him.

"Now, Mr Peters," he said, "perhaps you can aid me by telling me how long you have been receiving beatings from Andrew Harper, and what you know of Mr Bellamy's last hours?"

"Andrew Harper?" The doubt in Agnew's voice was unmistakable. "You think Andrew Harper is involved in this, Mr Holmes? Why, Harper is as experienced an engineer as can be found outside the Royal Navy. I have never heard a man under his command say a bad word about him, and many of them have worked with him for years, moving from one ship to another as a single group. The *Oceanic* was lucky to get him and his team, I can tell you." He looked round the small cabin, as though seeking inspiration with which to convince us. "No," he said after a moment of thought. "I cannot believe Andrew Harper had any part in Bellamy's murder."

In the silence that followed Agnew's speech, Peters's voice was soft but unhesitating. "About a year, sir," he said quietly. "It's been at least that long since me and Tom Bellamy signed up with Harper's crew."

"He has been abusing you all that time?" Holmes asked.

"It was all right for the first few weeks. Everyone knows as how Harper and his boys get all the best jobs and the most money. And we did. Me and Tom couldn't believe our luck."

"But then...?"

"Then, once we'd been with Harper for a month or so, he comes up one night, with a crowd of his cronies, and tells us that we need to give him half our pay from then on. Well, we thinks he's joking and Tom laughs right loud, but there's something in Harper's face stops me joining in – not that it made any difference in the end. Once we realised he wasn't having us on, we tells him that we ain't no African slave boys to be working and getting no push at the end of the day. And he gives a signal to his boys, and before you know it, there's a couple on each of us, holding our arms behind our backs. We can't move, can we, so Harper takes his time, marking us where it can't be seen. Just his fists that first time, but when me and Tom try to complain the next day, well nobody's likely to listen to us are they, and the next time it's a wooden stave he uses. Didn't take too long before we decided to give Harper what he wanted."

"Why didn't you leave, man?" I could not help but interject.

Peters's look was gently contemptuous. "On board a ship?" he asked. "Where would we go?"

I took his point. "When next you docked, then?"

"Harper told us what would happen if we tried to run. Like the lieutenant said, he's got a name in the trade, and a lot of men owe him a favour or two. He said he'd put it round that we'd been caught stealing from another hand, and that'd be us finished."

I was sympathetic, and even Holmes seemed somewhat chastened by the man's predicament. "And what was different this time? What did Mr Bellamy do that led to his death?"

"Nothing! He did nothing!" Peters paused. "Well, maybe he talked back to Harper or something, I don't know, I wasn't there, was I? But whatever he might have done, he didn't deserve to die for it, did he? Harper shouldn't have killed him, should he?"

At this, Agnew spoke up. "Let's not jump to conclusions here. There's no evidence yet that Harper is guilty of anything."

"Would you say not?" Holmes allowed a note of surprise to enter his voice. "The man who Peters says abused both him and Bellamy happens also to be the sole witness to the supposed fight between Bellamy and Peters? A man, to boot, with sufficient support behind him to put together the gang required to hold two strong men while they are mercilessly beaten? A man, moreover, whom I have personally witnessed shouting the most foul and disgusting things at those who work beneath him – I should tell you, Agnew, that I have spent the last few interminable days exploring this ship from top to bottom, and had already marked Mr Harper down as someone who would bear watching. It does not surprise me in the slightest that such a man as I have observed should be involved in murder, or that he would then attempt to place the blame on an innocent.

"But there is a simple enough way to test my theory. Take yourself to Harper's cabin and search thoroughly. I am confident that, should you do so, you will find a quantity of money far beyond that which an engineer – even one in the engine room of a vessel as prestigious as the *Oceanic* – could possibly have saved from his own pay."

Eager to be of assistance, I suggested that Agnew also check Harper's knuckles. The kind of beating that had been evident on Bellamy's face must have left its mark on the perpetrator's hands.

"An excellent suggestion, Doctor," Holmes agreed and held the door open for Agnew. "You would, I think, be best served by going to make your checks at once, Mr Agnew, before word gets round that Peters here has not been thrown in the brig. Dr Watson and I shall take ourselves to the library in the meantime. Perhaps you could arrange for some helpful porter to bring us refreshments? I confess, I am suddenly filled with an unexpected energy and fear I will not sleep tonight." With a nod to the ashen-faced Peters, he followed the young officer out and I trailed behind him, the belated and babbled thanks of the reprieved man ringing in our ears.

As might have been expected, Holmes's conjecture proved to be correct in every detail. Agnew, surprising Harper carousing with some cronies, discovered a cache of money hidden in a locker for which the thuggish engineer was unable to account. Taken individually to speak to the captain, it was not long before one man after another crumbled and informed on Harper as quickly as they could. Harper himself remained silent until Agnew hinted that a full confession was his only hope of avoiding the noose, given the weight of evidence against him. At that, we were told later, he broke like an oak tree in a storm and admitted everything, begging for mercy and sobbing in a less than manly fashion. I was gratified to discover that the knuckles on his right hand were cut and scraped, just as I had suggested.

The remainder of the voyage was uneventful. Holmes and I spent the next forty-eight hours reading and taking the sea air, with regular stops for food and drink. In consequence, we reached New York harbour – marvelling all the while at the magnificent Lady of Liberty statue which rose from the bay as both a welcome and a warning – fully rested and eager to proceed with our mission.

Chapter Three

It was not yet eight in the morning when we took our first steps on American soil. In some ways, the dockside reminded me of London as we were pushed and buffeted by crowds of industrious dock workers, lounging roughnecks and disembarking passengers laden with bulky cases. The combined smells of freshly landed fish and spilled machine oil were as overpowering here as at any similar spot in London.

Small things stood out, however, which marked this to be almost as foreign a location as an Afghani marketplace or Arab souk. Street cleaners in white trousers and jackets, topped with white helmets, moved here and there along the streets, and the accents of the youngsters selling newspapers on each corner were thick and at times difficult to comprehend. I stopped to purchase a 'paper and took the opportunity to ask the seller for directions to Spring Street and the offices of Holmes's doppelganger, which we had obtained from Gregson prior to our departure. To Holmes's delight, the address was within walking distance, and so, having arranged for our luggage to be taken to our hotel, my friend and I set off into New York.

During our sea voyage I had taken the opportunity to familiarise myself, at least a little, with the geography of the city, and had admired the manner in which much of it was made up of long, straight streets, intersecting and crossing one another in a grid-like pattern. Even so, I must admit my surprise at the general air of cleanliness and prosperity as Holmes and I made our way out of the port area and into the city itself. Glancing from one side to the other in the bright sunlight as we walked, I could easily have believed myself to be in one of the newer parts of London, and said as much to Holmes.

"Do you say so, Watson?" he replied, with a smile. "Well, perhaps you are right. Certainly, there is something about the air that invigorates the senses. After my recent travails on behalf of Mycroft, this trip, regardless of its unfortunate cause, may be exactly what I need."

He smiled again as though to demonstrate his sincerity. This was the first time Holmes had mentioned his secret work since we had left England and I hoped he might unburden himself further, but he said nothing more and so we continued in companionable silence along the street.

Half an hour's brisk walking brought us to the celebrated Cancer Hospital. From there it was but five minutes further to the prosaically named 106th Street, along which our quarry had his offices. I noticed that Holmes's pace quickened as we neared the stairs leading to the door of the building occupied by his supposed namesake. Built of a brown stone, it rose three floors, with wide steps leading up to a slightly inset main door and large bay windows on either side.

"Wait a moment, Holmes," I said. "I know that I have mentioned this several times on our voyage over, but I will say it again. Would it not be prudent to speak to the American authorities before we beard this imposter in his den?"

"Perhaps," replied my friend. "But it is probable that the man is on friendly terms with the police force, and I would prefer not to risk a warning being sent to him."

"Have you any reason to suppose that to be likely?"

"I would like to think, were our respective positions reversed and this was London not New York, that the occasional assistance I have been able to provide to Scotland Yard would be enough to warrant such a warning. Why should this colonial facsimile be any less favoured?"

The point was a reasonable one. I nodded my agreement and held out an arm before me, indicating the half dozen steps that led to the door of the rooms of Sherlock Holmes, imposter. "After you."

He brushed past me and, taking the steps two at a time, was soon knocking on the door. There was no reply. He knocked again, then a third time, but the office remained silent.

"Clearly there is no one at home," I remarked, aware even as I spoke that Holmes would not thank me for stating the obvious.

Holmes nodded distractedly. His attention was focused on the large window to the left of the door. Slatted wooden blinds obscured the interior, but a faint glow indicated that a light burned somewhere within. Holmes leaned across the metal rail that lined the stairs and tugged, without effect, at the window frame, attempting to open the lower half. When that failed, he knelt down in front of the door and pushed open the letterbox. I began to protest, but had no time to do so before the door flew open to reveal the imposing figure of a frowning New York matron, who glared down at the top of Holmes's head.

I took a step backwards and prepared to make such excuses as I could quickly bring to mind, but before I could say a word, Holmes rose to his feet in a single, fluid movement and bade the lady a hearty good morning.

"And may I say that it is gratifying to see a Russell & Erwin kept in such pristine condition," he continued, as though recommencing an interrupted conversation. He turned and invited me to examine the doorknob, of all things. "You will agree, John, that this is a particularly delightful example of the ironworkers' craft. Circa 1860, if I'm not mistaken, from their Connecticut factory."

He pulled a handkerchief from his pocket and used it to polish the knob, which, to me, looked entirely commonplace and unworthy of such attention. It would not have done to say so, of course, so I contented myself with a short – and, I hoped, non-committal – nod and a barely audible grunt of agreement. I had no idea who or what Russell & Erwin might be, and clearly neither did the lady, who continued to bar the doorway suspiciously. A few more moments of praise for the splendour of her door ornamentation, however, and she began to visibly thaw in the face of Holmes's English charms (of which he had more than enough, when the mood took him) and enquired, in a voice that, if it did not simper, did at least seem friendly, how she might be of service.

While Holmes explained that we were English colleagues of Mr Sherlock Holmes, come to visit, I took the opportunity to examine the lady in more detail, continuing to exercise my observational powers. Of medium height, and stocky in build, she appeared to be in the later middle years of her life, and – given that she was dressed entirely in black – in all likelihood a widow. A wisp of brown hair had escaped from her tight bun, somewhat softening her otherwise rather harsh features, as did the slight smile she allowed to cross her lips as Holmes continued to work his charms. I knew the type – a landlady to the bone, I had no doubt, of similar stripe to our own treasured Mrs Hudson. No sooner had the comparison occurred to me than she invited us inside, with the promise of refreshment while we waited for our friend who, it seemed, was not at home.

"Follow me, gentlemen," our hostess said as she led the way into the interior of the house, past several closed doors, arrayed evenly along each side of a broad hallway. I glanced at each door as I passed, and was surprised to see that every one had its own letterbox, and above that a small brass plaque with the name of a business engraved upon it. The first to the left as we entered read, in ornate calligraphic script,

Mr Sherlock Holmes – Consulting Detective.

Before I could draw Holmes's attention to this, however, we passed through a curtained archway and into the section of the house evidently reserved as the lady's private quarters.

"Make yourselves comfortable, gentlemen," she said, taking her own seat in the rather stuffy and overcrowded room in which we found ourselves. "And do tell me all about your strange fascination with my doorknob!"

She smiled as she spoke, in order, I thought, to take any potential sting from her words. The impression grew on me that she was a lonely soul, quick both to take offence and to forgive, for whom our appearance was a welcome break in an otherwise solitary existence. That impression was all but confirmed as she proceeded to listen, with every sign of interest, while Holmes expatiated for several uninterrupted and tedious minutes on the subject of decorative ironmongery in the United States and our own alleged mania for the topic. The breadth of his knowledge on all manner of subjects had long since ceased to surprise me, but even so I made a mental note to ask him about this particularly arcane example later, for all that my interest in his current lecture was minimal.

My attention must indeed have wandered for I can recall nothing of the specifics of Holmes's descriptions of door knockers and boot scrapers, only rays of morning sunlight catching motes of dust suspended in the air and the heavy, sweet fragrance of the lady's scent, and then the sharp, insistent sound of a bell ringing.

I quickly refocused my attention on Holmes and our hostess who, I now saw, was ringing a small hand bell in order, I assumed, to summon a servant. A moment later a young maid entered and took instruction from her mistress, before bustling away to prepare refreshments.

Conversation had evidently moved on during my spell of inattention. "Yes, I've lived here my entire adult life," the lady continued in answer to a question I had missed, as Holmes made indistinct sounds of encouragement and interest. "I did consider packing up and heading back to Pennsylvania – that's where I hail from – when my husband, Mr van Raalte, passed away. But I have roots here now, and it seemed more sensible to rent out rooms to select gentlemen and ladies of good character rather than leave my friends. And between you and me," she confided, "it was not a good time, then, at which to sell such a large property. New York is like that, you will discover: changeable and not always to be relied on. Like a woman, Mr van Raalte used to say!"

Her laugh was fond and quickly smothered, and her eyes welled up as she recalled her late husband. Holmes smiled thinly, uncomfortable with such a show of emotion, but also took the opportunity of this break in her narrative to introduce me to the lady.

"Mrs van Raalte, I have been terribly remiss in failing properly to introduce my dear friend, John Murray. Please do forgive me. My only excuse is that, in my delight in your company, the matter completely slipped my mind." He twisted in his chair until he was side-on to us both. "Mrs van Raalte, may I introduce Mr John Murray? Like myself, Mr Murray is an aficionado of domestic ironmongery and, also like myself, I am sure he would agree that it is a most happy accident that a visit to our colleague Holmes should expose us, not only to your excellent mid-period doorknob, but also to your gracious self."

I feared that he was laying it on too thickly, but the lady seemed pleased with the attention.

"You are a long way from home, Mr Lestrade," she observed, and I must admit that it was fortunate that we had not yet been served tea, as I fear I would have struggled to drink it while stifling a chuckle at Holmes's choice of alias.

"Indeed we are, madam," Holmes replied smoothly. "Mr Murray and I have travelled across the ocean in search of opportunity, leaving the fog-shrouded streets of London behind us." He gestured towards the nearest window, through which sunlight warmed the room. "Far behind us, in fact," he concluded, as a knock at the door was followed by the little maid carrying a tea tray into the room.

As she busied herself pouring tea, Mrs van Raalte resumed her train of thought. To my alarm, however, she addressed her next remarks to me. "Mr Lestrade said that you are colleagues of Mr Holmes, come from England to pay him a visit?"

I flatter myself that I have learned a few things during my time with Holmes, though it is true that I have had some facility with play-acting since my university days. Whatever the cause, I was not long wrong-footed by the question.

"Yes indeed, Mrs van Raalte. We were able to assist Mr Holmes with a case in London some years ago, in a minor manner. Knowing that we would be in New York for a few days, we thought to surprise our old friend with a visit." I smiled, ruefully. "Given his absence, it might after all have been wiser to send word of our arrival."

While I spoke, Mrs van Raalte looked from myself to Holmes and back again, a question, which she held back for only as long as I was speaking, obviously on the tip of her tongue. As expected, as soon as I stopped, she enquired of me, "Are you also famous detectives then?" then clapped her hands together with pleasure as she continued, "Should I have heard of you both? Are you as famous as Mr Holmes?"

"Good Lord, no, not at all," Holmes broke in before I could reply. "We were simply fortunate enough to provide very minor assistance to that great and talented man. There is nobody," he concluded with a smile, "to compare to Mr Holmes. He is one of a kind."

"There's no denying his unique nature, certainly," I could not help but add, with a slightly malicious smile of my own.

Fortunately, our hostess showed no sign of recognising either Holmes's barely disguised braggadocio or my own jest. Instead, she fiercely nodded her agreement with Holmes's assessment of his own character. It was clear she was proud to have a famous detective under her roof, and I briefly wondered if Mrs Hudson felt the same. The thought prompted another, which I quickly put to Mrs van Raalte.

"Does Sherlock have rooms here, or does he rent only office space from you?" I asked.

"Mr Holmes rents only a single unfurnished room, which he uses as an office, Mr Murray. I do not rent accommodation to single men, even those with the reputation of Mr Holmes." She sniffed, and I was aware that I had committed a social faux pas, but before I could apologise, she continued, "Though Mr Holmes has been with me for a year at least, and in the time has never been anything other than gentleman-like, and would make a fine husband for any woman, should he so choose!" At this, she positively giggled and rolled her eyes, and I was uncomfortably reminded of love-struck youngsters half her age.

The conversation was, I feared, about to take an awkward turn. It came as a great relief, therefore, when Holmes took pity on me and chose that moment to interrupt.

"Sadly, we are short of time this morning, having only recently arrived in your fair city. We should really make our way to our hotel to refresh ourselves and return later to meet up with Holmes."

He rose to leave, then stopped suddenly as if a thought had freshly occurred to him. "I wonder, would it be possible to leave a note for Sherlock?" he asked. "I could put it on his desk, even, so that he would be sure to see it."

I could not be certain, but it seemed to me that Mrs van Raalte's voice was colder as she replied. "I would be happy to oblige you, Mr Lestrade, but there is only one key to each room, and Mr Holmes keeps his on his person at all times. He is a very private man, you see."

"Perhaps I could drop a note through the letterbox I saw on Holmes's office door on my way inside?"

Mrs van Raalte smiled, though there was little warmth in it. "I'm afraid that that letterbox is too stiff for my old fingers," she admitted. "There's not been a letter through it in a decade or more."

"How, then, does Sherlock receive his mail?"

Mrs van Raalte shook her head at the question. "Oh, I send any mail on to a friend to keep for him if he's not present in person when it arrives. He does travel a great deal, you know."

"And does that happen often? That he is not available when the mail arrives?"

Our hostess hesitated before replying, and even then her words were tentative and uncertain. "Sometimes. Quite often. I can't say exactly. He *is* a busy man, you know," she rallied, evidently considering Holmes's question to be an attack of sorts on her tenant.

Holmes's face was a mask of confusion. "How can any man carry on the business of a consulting detective if he does not consult? Surely a swift response to letters and telegrams is the bare minimum required to carry out such an undertaking?"

Mrs van Raalte again shook her head, and this time I was sure that her look was less friendly. "I couldn't really say, Mr Lestrade. I consider his business to be his own and have never questioned him about it."

"Of course," Holmes quickly responded. "I meant no impertinence, but was simply concerned for an old friend." He picked up his hat and gloves from the table at his side and indicated with a nod that it was time that we left. Mrs van Raalte bustled around as I followed Holmes out of the room and back down the hallway towards the entrance.

As we passed the imposter's office, however, Holmes darted to the side and knelt in front of the door, ignoring Mrs van Raalte's gasp of surprise.

"My apologies, madam," he called over his shoulder as he worked the tip of his fingers into a gap in the letterbox. "I could not in all conscience leave such a decorative piece of ironwork in so unfortunate a condition without making some effort to fix it." He pushed harder and gave a small grunt of exertion. "No, no, do not thank me, Mrs van Raalte," he said (though the lady showed no sign of doing any such thing), "it is only a little stiff from lack of use. I'll soon have it free."

With a loud creak and a sharp cracking retort, the flap sprang open and Holmes immediately leaned in and fastened his eyes on the office hidden behind it. Only for a few seconds though, lest our hostess become suspicious.

Indeed, the lady was about to say something, I felt sure, only to reconsider when Holmes leaped back to his feet and gave her a small, if theatrical, bow. "All fixed!" he announced gleefully. "And now we must be away, my dear lady." He grinned conspiratorially at Mrs van Raalte then stage-whispered, "We will be back tomorrow though. Unless–" Holmes stopped in his tracks, as if an idea had suddenly struck him. "Unless we could obtain his address – that to which you send on his mail – and surprise him at home, as it were?"

Mrs van Raalte's reply was emphatic. "No, Mr Lestrade, I couldn't do that for any reason. Mr Holmes appreciates his privacy, and I couldn't dream of handing out his personal details to strangers."

I thought that Holmes would protest, but instead he bowed his head in acquiescence. "Of course. Quite commendable of you, Mrs van Raalte. Well, if you should see Sherlock before then, I beg you do not tell him you have seen us. We would very much like to surprise our old friend when we visit tomorrow!"

The invitation to act as co-conspirator was enough to restore a little of Mrs van Raalte's good humour. "Why, of course, Mr Lestrade!" she exclaimed. "Though I don't suppose I shall see Mr Holmes today."

"And in case we should, by chance, see him in the street and wish to preserve the surprise, can you tell me – does Sherlock still sport that ridiculous beard and side whiskers?"

Mrs van Raalte frowned in fresh suspicion. "Why no, Mr Lestrade. Mr Holmes is clean-shaven and his hair styled much like your own." She shook her head. "You know, I don't believe I have ever seen him with so much as a hint of whiskers."

Holmes's smile was unmistakably rueful. "You hear that, Murray? Sherlock has changed his appearance again." He turned back to Mrs van Raalte. "It is a consequence of his profession, my dear lady, that Holmes need constantly disguise himself, the better to stay a step ahead of those of a criminal mind who would wish him harm. Clearly, he has done so since last we three met."

The lady was wide-eyed as she signalled her understanding. "Well, you'd never guess he was anything but a smartly dressed young man to look at him, Mr Lestrade."

"That is, of course, his intention," Holmes replied.

"Yes, I see that." The romance of the notion clearly appealed to Mrs van Raalte, for a small smile played about her mouth as she considered "Mr Holmes's" need for secrecy.

She was still smiling as the door closed behind us and Holmes and I found ourselves on the pavement once more.

"Tell me, then – what did you see inside?" I asked as we began walking in the direction of our hotel.

"In truth, not a great deal, Watson. There is a short hallway leading from the door into the main body of the office, which, sadly, is largely hidden from sight of anyone in the position in which I found myself. The little I could see, however, was much as one might expect. A desk upon which are piled documents and trays, a small table lamp, a wooden cabinet against the back wall. All entirely unexceptional."

We walked along in silence for a minute, considering and digesting the small amount we had learned so far. We might have done so until we found a cab, had I not recalled something that had temporarily slipped my mind.

"Mr Lestrade?" I asked mischievously, making no attempt to stifle the note of amusement in my voice.

"I found myself unexpectedly in need of a pseudonym, and the inspector's was the first name which came to mind."

"So it seems," I replied. "I have one question, however. Will that remain your name of choice for the entirety of our time in the Americas, or should I expect to find strangers addressing you as Athelney Jones or Tobias Gregson in the near future?"

The laughter I had been suppressing since leaving Mrs van Raalte could be contained no longer as Holmes threw a scowl in my direction. Fortunately, for all his devotion to logic and reason, my friend is not without a sense of humour, and before we had walked a dozen yards he had joined in my laughter, appreciating the irony of beginning his quest to uncover an imposter by himself borrowing the name of another.

We were still chuckling as we hailed a passing hansom cab and gave the driver directions to our hotel.

Chapter Four

The hotel in which we had arranged to stay sat partway along the long, wide road known as Broadway, a street which stretched the length of the central section of Manhattan, and which was lined with opulent hotels and theatres standing cheek by jowl with ornate churches and other places of worship. Crowds of people moved purposefully about their business as our hansom pulled up, and we made our way inside.

The interior of the hotel was marble-floored and dotted with slender marble columns. Delicate carvings and paintings adorned the walls, and large plate glass windows allowed the sunlight to illuminate the hanging artwork. I admit I found myself comparing it to the great hotels of London and finding that this hotel did not fall far short even of our greatest.

We had an appointment with Gregson's erstwhile colleague, Bullock, in the afternoon, but, it being as yet a little before eleven, we took the opportunity to refresh ourselves and change clothes before going to meet with him.

While Holmes shaved, I remembered the newspaper I had bought earlier and glanced through it in hopes of uncovering a mention of our mysterious quarry. There was, however, little of immediate note to be found amongst the typical American melodrama that dominated its pages. Lurid reporting of a socialite allegedly murdered by her fiancé – a man now on the run from the authorities – took up much of the front page, while the interior contained reports on the likelihood of the invention of a flying machine within a decade, and on the growth of organised criminal gangs in the city. The only mention of "Holmes" was a report that the "popular English detective" had not been seen around town for a few days and was believed to be involved in a new case in the north of the state.

I mentioned this last detail to Holmes when he returned from his ablutions.

"It is of little consequence, Watson. It may, in fact, work in our favour. A day or two in which we might make a fuller investigation into the activities of this imposter can only help us in the long run."

"And if he does not return? What if he has moved on?"

"Why should he? He has no reason to leave his present, comfortable existence behind."

"Perhaps he has had wind of our arrival?"

"Again, Watson, why should he have? Do you suppose he haunts the docks of New York, examining passenger lists daily, in fear of his unmasking?" Holmes laughed. "No, our man will resurface in due course. But in the meantime we should find out all we can about his activities in New York. A conversation with Inspector Bullock should make the ideal start, and may even provide us with the information we need to deal with this scoundrel."

Holmes's reasoning was impeccable. I left for my own room

to change, keen to begin our investigations and hopeful of a swift conclusion.

Simeon Bullock was a tall, spare man with thinning grey hair and a neat, grey moustache, who exuded an air of quiet competence. He wore a suit cut in the American style, fastened only by the top button, but when he greeted us, gripping each of our hands in both of his, his accent had lost little of its Yorkshire roots. He invited us to take a seat in his spacious office, lit a small cigar and asked us to explain once again what he could do to help us.

"You understand, gentlemen, that I'm more than happy to do what I can for friends of Tobias, but I'm not entirely clear what it is you believe I *can* do." He picked up the letter from Gregson again and ran his eye down the few lines of text. "If I have the right of this, you claim that the gentleman known as Sherlock Holmes, a detective whose success has monopolised the front pages of our newspapers for some time now, is, in fact, no such thing and that you, not he, are the real Sherlock Holmes. Is that correct?"

"It is," Holmes agreed.

"And you further allege that this New York Holmes is trading upon your good name in order to generate business for himself?"

"Exactly so, Inspector."

"And you can prove that you are the genuine Sherlock Holmes, of international repute, and that this other gent is not?"

"Prove?" Where another man might have found offence in Bullock's words, Holmes was unruffled. "I have a copy of an extract from the Birth Register as bona fides for my own identity. And 'Sherlock Holmes' is sufficiently uncommon a name that I would confidently wager that that is not this scoundrel's true moniker."

Bullock considered this for a moment, then nodded his agreement. "That appears satisfactory, though the fact that Tobias Gregson vouches for you is all the proof that I personally require. Now, how much do you know of your alter ego?"

We owned that our knowledge of the man was scant and consisted almost entirely of a handful of newspaper clippings describing his appearance on the New York scene, and his office address – which had, of course, been supplied by Bullock himself. Of more interest to the inspector was our recent conversation with Mrs van Raalte, which Holmes recounted to him without delay. He listened quietly, interrupting only twice, the first time to ask Holmes to spell the name of the imposter's landlady, and the second to clarify that no mail was delivered to the office.

"He has another address in the city and an accomplice, then," he remarked thoughtfully. "That's interesting, is that."

"How so?" I asked.

"Well, you must understand, gentlemen, that, like as not, this fellow, imposter though he may be, has committed no crime that I can make out."

I began to protest, but Bullock continued to speak, explaining his reasoning.

"No, Dr Watson, there's no call for protestation. You and Mr Holmes say that this chap has stolen both a name and a reputation and has used them to line his own pockets. All well and good, and I believe you to be speaking the truth, but so far as I know there's no crime in calling yourself anything you like, nor in opening a – what was it? – consulting detective business. Nobody has filed a complaint against the man claiming his work is lacking, nor that his morals are lax, and, by the by and not that it has any bearing on criminal matters, he's got friends up high in New York society."

He sat back in his seat, blowing cheroot smoke towards the ceiling. "You see my problem, Mr Holmes? There's no crime here for me to investigate, and that's the truth of it. But an office that receives no correspondence? Well, that's no crime either, but it is out of the ordinary, and out of the ordinary is often a good place to start looking, I find."

Throughout this speech, Holmes had sat quietly. Now, as Bullock fell silent in his turn, my friend spoke up. "I take your point, Inspector. Of course, a man may call himself Charles Harrod if it pleases him, and he would have my good wishes if he did so, but if that same man then opens a grocery shop, questions might be asked. I suggest that the same principle applies here."

"That's too fine a distinction for me, Mr Holmes," the inspector replied after a moment's thought. "And where this second Harrods would, presumably, take business from the first, this imposter Sherlock Holmes is having no effect on your own business back in London, is he?"

"Not as such, no, but even so…!" Holmes was by nature a calm man and rarely allowed his temper to show, but I, who had known him for so long, could tell by the slight flush on his cheek that Inspector Bullock's words had proved irksome to him.

Bullock too must have had some inkling, for he held up his hands as though in surrender. "Forgive me, Mr Holmes, but I am merely playing the part of the magistrate, for he will say all of these things, should I apprehend the false Holmes and you press charges. Don't forget what I said. He has friends of influence, and they are as likely to believe that he is the real Sherlock and you the imposter. I don't say they will, mind, but the odds are stacked against you, and if you wish to put a stop to this fellow's activities, you would do well to remember that. There must be proof of wrong-doing before I can act in an official capacity."

I had heard enough. I appreciated that the inspector was playing the realist and knew this city better than Holmes or I, but the case seemed so clear-cut that I could not help but protest. "But it is fraud, at least, surely, Inspector? And that remains a crime, even in the United States!"

"It does indeed, Doctor," replied the inspector patiently. "And if we can prove that someone engaged the fake Holmes in the belief that he was the famous English detective – and if that person can be persuaded to press charges, which seems unlikely given that the fake has yet to fail with a case, so far as I know – if all that happens, then perhaps something might be done. But until then, my hands are tied. For Tobias's sake, I'll do what I can, but that's likely to be a mite less than you'd hoped for."

I could tell that Holmes was displeased with Bullock's words, but I understood the inspector's caution. For all his desire to help, he was a busy man with many demands on his time, and if the imposter had broken no laws, then there seemed little he – or we – could easily or swiftly achieve. If he could only advise, then it might be that we would have to be content with that. I feared, however, that Holmes – never over-imbued with respect for the police force – would not see it that way.

Fortunately, Bullock had a greater degree of assistance in mind than I had given him credit for.

"What I can do is take you back to this office and have a look inside. The tale you've told me is enough for that, I should think."

Holmes brightened visibly at these words and was at once anxious to be away. "Capital, Inspector!" he exclaimed. "We could not have asked for a better place to begin."

He pushed back his chair and rose to his feet, already reaching for his hat and gloves. Bullock followed suit, striding to the door to shout for some unseen subordinate to arrange transport. Finding myself the only one still seated, I hurriedly buttoned my jacket and followed the two men out of Bullock's office.

Mrs van Raalte was surprised to see us again so soon, and with that surprise came a return of her earlier suspicion of us.

"Mr Lestrade and Mr Murray! This is unexpected. I'm afraid Mr Holmes hasn't returned yet, and I don't know when he shall, as I told you."

She stood hesitantly in the doorway, obviously unsure as to our purpose and wondering who the third member of our party might be.

Bullock, playing the part Holmes had sketched out for him on the journey over, tipped his hat and introduced himself as an inspector in New York's police force. "We were wondering if we might have a look inside your Mr Holmes's office," he said as the lady invited us inside, any trepidation she might have felt partially ameliorated by the sight of Bullock's identification card. "These gentlemen are intimately acquainted with Mr Holmes and are concerned that some harm may have befallen him."

Mrs van Raalte raised a hand to her mouth and gave a small cry of shock. "Harm?" she asked.

"It may be nothing, ma'am, but if you could allow us a quick glance within, it would be enough to put their minds at rest, likely enough."

The warring desires to aid the police and to protect the privacy of her tenant were plain on her face. She looked from one of us to the next, gnawing unconsciously at her lower lip, until, her mind made up, she asked us to wait. "I need to fetch something," she explained, and bustled off to her own living quarters, leaving us standing in the hallway outside the imposter's office door.

We had no time to discuss her disappearance before she returned, holding a heavy bunch of keys. "I wasn't too sure of you before, you see," she explained. "A mite too charming for your own good, I reckoned. So I wasn't letting on I had a key to Mr Holmes's office until I spoke to him, made sure you were who you said." She stepped around us and unlocked the office door. "But seeing as you have the police with you, I think it'll be all right. In you go then," she concluded, waving us impatiently inside.

The office was as Holmes had described, with a short hallway that opened out into a small, square room. Directly opposite us as we stood in the entrance was a cheap wooden desk, piled high on one side with papers, blotters and other common instruments of business. Moving into the room, I was surprised to note how bare everything seemed. An empty coat rack stood in the far corner, but other than a chair behind the desk and another in front of it and a scuffed wooden cabinet against the rear wall, the room was devoid of furnishings. Holmes immediately darted to the cabinet and pulled at one of the drawers after another, but uttered a cry of annoyance as every one proved to be locked. Bullock meanwhile had crossed to the desk, where he examined the sheaf of papers in a tray marked "OUT".

"That's peculiar," he said after a moment's perusal. "Every one of these is blank." He pulled open a desk drawer. "Drawer's empty too."

He handed me the papers and called to Holmes. "Anything in the cabinet?"

"Unfortunately, the drawers are locked, Inspector," I heard Holmes say as I dropped the blank sheets on the desk. Bullock replied that that would be no hindrance, pulled a small cloth wrap from his jacket pocket and extracted a long, thin piece of metal from inside it. "I took these from a Scotch cracksman a year or so back, and they've proven useful with more than one lock since then."

He bent over the first cabinet drawer and slipped the metal sliver into the lock, ignoring Holmes's unexpected declaration that it was entirely unnecessary. Twisting his wrist, he turned the metal in one direction then, more carefully, brought it back slightly and pressed inwards. With a final flourish he took hold of the drawer handle and pulled it open, just as Holmes murmured, "It will also be empty."

I knew he would be right even before Bullock said, "How did you know?" I had heard that same tone in Holmes's voice many times before and rarely known him to be wrong.

In reply, Holmes invited us to follow him back down the hallway. Standing with his back to the closed door, he crouched down on his heels and indicated that we should do the same. Feeling more than a little foolish, I did so, squatting uncomfortably between Holmes and Bullock.

"Now, Inspector," said Holmes, "tell me what you see."

Bullock's voice betrayed his scepticism, but he answered Holmes's question seriously. "The office. One part of the desk, some papers on it and the back wall with a cabinet against it. Why?" he asked. "What do you see that I don't?"

Holmes's voice was silken. "Nothing," he said. "I see nothing else. Because there *is* nothing else. There is only a half-covered desk, a cabinet and some blank sheets of paper. And all visible to anyone enterprising enough to wrench open the letterbox and look. But nothing more. Our man is careful, I'll give him that much."

Bullock looked none the wiser for Holmes's explanation, but I believed I had grasped his point. "The office is as fake as its occupant!" I exclaimed. "Designed only to be viewed from afar and from a specific vantage point, proscribed by the area visible from the letterbox."

"Bravo, Watson! You have it exactly. This office is a decoy prepared by our quarry, and nothing more. A stalking horse, perhaps, designed to draw in those too interested in his activities, or a convenient address at which he might meet his associates. I cannot say for certain. But one thing is clear. Whoever this 'Mr Holmes' might be, he is not a detective."

"Not a detective such as yourself, you mean, Mr Holmes," interrupted Bullock. "There are other ways to conduct such a business than your own."

"It was never in doubt that this man is not a detective such as I, Inspector," Holmes snapped with some acerbity. "But there is no reason to set up a fake business if a genuine one exists, you would agree? And if there is no genuine business, then what is there? How does my namesake make his living? How does he attract the standard of client that you tell me he does?"

He left the question hanging in the air for a second, then rose to his feet. "Come, gentlemen," he said. "It is time we were away and allowed the good Mrs van Raalte some peace and quiet. It has been a busy day for us all, and I for one am in need of dinner. Perhaps Inspector Bullock could recommend a restaurant, and join us?"

Bullock nodded distractedly, Holmes's questions obviously still playing on his mind. "Of course, Mr Holmes," he muttered. "I'd be happy to."

* * *

Dinner proved to be a pleasant surprise. I had not, of course, expected the type of primitive, frontier fayre so beloved of the so-called dime novelists, but still, the food was a good deal better than I could have hoped. The restaurant itself occupied a small, well-hidden building down a side street and, from the outside, seemed as unprepossessing as anything from the adventures of Buffalo Bill Cody. A dusty window barely served as a means by which to view the interior, and it struck me, glancing at the chipped paint and grubby, handwritten menu pinned outside, that this was perhaps deliberate.

Inside, however, everything was clean if plain, and the food was exceptional. I joined Holmes in a dish of mussels before trying a famous New York steak. Both were delicious, and it was only after we had each completed our repast that we settled down to discuss the business at hand.

"I'll tell you what I can of the man, Mr Holmes," Bullock began. His attitude to Holmes, which had admittedly been friendly since we arrived, now held an additional layer of respect. It was plain that the revelations Holmes had been able to glean from a single minute in the imposter's office had made a deep impression, and Bullock was now more eager than ever to provide what help he could. "He was first seen in New York around a year ago and is reputed to solve every case he takes on. Complete discretion is his watchword, it's said – to the point that I can't tell you why he has been called in on any case, nor even what sort of crime has been committed, never mind actual details."

"And his appearance?" Holmes asked eagerly.

"Much as yourself, I'm afraid, sir. Tall and slim, with dark hair in a similar style to your own. And with an English accent, of course."

"You have seen him personally?"

"No, never. But I have heard him described."

"By Americans?"

"Well, yes, Mr Holmes. There are a fair few of them in the area."

Holmes smiled thinly. "I do not mean to give offence or to suggest any inferiority in our colonial cousins, Inspector, but an American is far less likely to be able to differentiate between specific English regional accents than an Englishman might. You would admit that your own English accent and that of Dr Watson are quite distinct? Or mine and that of a gentleman from the north?"

"Ah, I take your meaning," the inspector responded. "Unfortunately, however, I know of no English native who has spoken to the man, so cannot narrow his accent any further than 'English', I'm afraid."

"No matter. It is a relatively minor point, in light of our current location. There cannot be many English detectives of any sort in New York, so the question of whether our quarry hails from Surrey or Northumbria can wait a while. Now, is there anything else you can tell us?"

"I can think of nothing further, I'm afraid, Mr Holmes. What I can do, though, is introduce you to the other Mr Holmes's most recent client, or at least the most recent that I know about."

"Really? That is excellent news! And the lady's name? I assume it is a lady, or you would surely have been less cautious about revealing her existence."

"Mrs Elizabeth Lockhart. She's a bit of a battle-axe and would sooner protect her family's honour than breathe, so she'll likely prove uncooperative, but she's all I can provide for the minute."

This was more than I expected, and I could tell that Holmes too had been wrong-footed by this offer of a potential source of fresh information. Bullock could obviously sense our surprise, for he rushed to explain that the lady in question had sufficient influence in New York to end the career of a mere police inspector.

"At first, Tobias's letter notwithstanding, I wasn't sure about either of you, truth be told. Two London toffs come to make my life difficult for no good reason, I thought. But that trick you played at Holmes's – the other Holmes, that is – office? Well, I reckon that showed there's more to this than meets the eye, that maybe this fake is up to more than just imitating Sherlock Holmes so as to pick up a customer or two." He tapped one of his cheroots on the back of his hand, but left it unlit. "And that's probably worth me taking a risk with the likes of Mrs Lockhart."

Holmes nodded. "I thank you for that, Inspector, and appreciate both the risk you are taking and the confidence you have shared with us. I too am beginning to wonder if there is not more to this matter than simple impersonation and, in this foreign country, Watson and I are grateful for all the help we can get."

I struck a match and leaned forward as Holmes concluded this little speech. Bullock accepted the light and, after I had lit my own cigarette, we three sat and smoked companionably for some time.

Chapter Five

Elizabeth Lockhart was a *grande dame* of the old school, who would not have looked out of place at Henley Regatta or a Chelsea tea party. She sat in a high-backed wing chair, her spine as straight as any guardsman's, and observed us disapprovingly through her pince-nez. Holmes had taken an immediate dislike to her, and she to him.

"Come now, Mrs Lockhart," he said, barely concealing the impatience in his voice, "you must be able to tell us something about the work this man carried out on your behalf. I do not ask for intimate details, merely a very general idea of the scope of the task he was set."

When Mrs Lockhart continued to stare at him as though he were an incompetent kitchen maid, pursing her lips and saying nothing, Holmes pressed on, the last vestiges of courtesy beginning to fray at the edges.

"Was it a theft, madam? An assault? Did you perhaps discover that your illustrious family is descended from Black Country leather-workers or Scandinavian herring fishermen?"

In his defence, Mrs Lockhart had been nothing but obstructive since we had arrived, and Holmes had spent the last ten minutes attempting to cajole the slightest useful morsel of information from our unresponsive host. Still, discourtesy was unlikely to aid our cause, and so I did my best to pour oil on these particular troubled waters.

"I think my friend is trying to say that, while we fully understand that – quite rightly – you have no desire for your private business to be discussed with strangers, if you could see your way to providing a general – a *very* general – idea why you called in a detective, it would be most helpful to us."

Mrs Lockhart turned her attention to me. "And you say that you are policemen?" she said after a long, thoughtful pause.

"We are assisting the police, yes," I confirmed, and consoled myself that I had not exactly lied, though it would have been more accurate to say that a single policeman was assisting us, and that quite unofficially.

"Assisting, yes…" Her voice faded; then, as though coming to a decision, she addressed herself to me again, ignoring Holmes entirely.

"I will tell you one thing, and after that I would be obliged if you would leave me and my house in peace, and take your unpleasant companion with you. His eyes are too close together. He has the look about him of a Bohemian or an anarchist."

I felt Holmes bridle beside me, but I laid a hand on his arm in warning.

"Any information that you could supply would be extremely helpful and much appreciated."

"If you absolutely must know, and if that is the only way in which I shall be rid of you both, I engaged Mr Holmes to investigate a spate of petty thefts."

"Domestic thefts?" Holmes interjected. "Did these thefts occur here, in the family home?"

"I am aware of the definition, thank you," Mrs Lockhart replied acidly. "And yes, the dishonesty in question was of a domestic nature."

"And Holmes was able to help?"

Mrs Lockhart's glare could have frozen water solid. "I believe I have told you all that you asked. Suffice it to say that Mr Holmes was thoroughly professional and that the whole matter was cleared up satisfactorily."

"How, though, did you know that the man you spoke to actually *was* Sherlock Holmes?"

I thought for a moment that I saw a momentary flash of something fearful behind the old lady's eyes, but if I did, it was quickly replaced by a scornful glare. "Other than the successful conclusion of our business, you mean? I have also viewed several sketches of him, and Mr Holmes was as like his image as any man I have seen." She rang a small bell that sat on a table to one side of her chair. "Now if you will excuse me, I am expecting visitors. *Invited* visitors."

I rose and prepared to bid the lady good day, but Holmes would not be silenced.

"One last question, if I may, Mrs Lockhart," he began. "When did you last see Mr Holmes?"

"About six weeks ago. I paid him in full in cash, and he left at once. I hope never to see him – or you! – again."

The door behind us opened, and the butler who had shown us in indicated that we should now follow him out. Any further questions Holmes might have had would have to wait. The lady opened a slim volume that had lain in her lap and, ignoring our farewells, read until we had left the room.

Or rather, almost until we had left the room, for as the door swung closed behind us, Holmes turned smartly on his heel and pushed his head back into Mrs Lockhart's drawing room.

"One more thing, if you don't mind, Mrs Lockhart," I heard him say. "Did Dr Watson accompany Mr Holmes when he called upon you?"

I could not make out the muffled reply, but I heard Holmes say, "He did? Excellent. Then I will trouble you no more, madam," as he finally closed the door and joined the butler and me in the hall.

"Shall we be on our way, do you think, Watson?" he asked, with every appearance of satisfaction. He strode past the butler, taking his hat and gloves from the man as he did so. I followed, my mind oddly troubled by the thought of a fake John Watson joining the fake Sherlock Holmes.

As was often the case when deep in thought, Holmes preferred not to speak in the cab we took back to the hotel. Instead we sat in silence and I took the opportunity to examine the streets as we passed through them.

Even more than in London, splendour and poverty existed in close proximity to one another here, and as we progressed towards Broadway, I was conscious that many of the side streets and alleys I glimpsed as the hansom sped along were dark, dirty places, redolent of the worst slums at home. Growing weary of the silence, I remarked as much to Holmes, but he gave no sign that he had heard me. If his interest was not to be piqued by a comparison of the two cities, I thought perhaps an appeal to his vanity might prove more successful.

"Tell me, Holmes," I enquired, "how did you know to ask whether the fake Holmes has an equally false Watson?"

Holmes's eyes at once lit up. "I did not know, I confess," he said with a small smile. "But I was reasonably certain – certain enough in any case to test the theory."

"You guessed, then?"

"Never!" Holmes was insistent, as I knew he would be. I now had his full attention. "As you know, I do not guess. Guessing is a waste of both my time and my intellect, each of which is precious and not to be frittered away by idle conjecture. No," he continued, "I had a theory, that is all."

"A theory?"

"Exactly so. One created whole from the available facts, and then tested by direct interrogation."

"What facts, Holmes? I have seen and heard nothing to suggest an accomplice."

"Are you forgetting the friend who holds the imposter's correspondence when he is out of town?"

I could not hide my surprise. I confess I *had* forgotten, but even if I had not, it seemed a small base on which to build a theory. I said as much to Holmes, but that only heightened his evident satisfaction.

"Not just that, Watson! You are overlooking the coat rack," he exclaimed, rubbing his hands together with pleasure. "Did it not occur to you to wonder why there was a coat rack in the imposter's office? It surely did not come with the room, for Mrs van Raalte said the room was rented unfurnished, nor can it be seen from the doorway, so it was not part of the dressing of the office. No, our man took the time and effort to purchase a coat rack and place it there."

"Perhaps he wished for somewhere to hang his coat?"

"In an office that was not an office, and hence contained no clients? Why should he? On the rare occasions he was there alone, he could leave his hat and overcoat on the spare chair. Far more likely that he had a regular visitor and so felt the need of a rack. And the most likely such visitor is, of course, a close acquaintance – or an accomplice, as you put it. Having established that, what else would such a man be called but John Watson?" Satisfied with his own reasoning, Holmes chuckled at the look on my face, then broke off as a new thought occurred to him. "Why," he cried suddenly, "I'm sure that Mrs van Raalte could settle the matter and tell us if 'Holmes' had a regular visitor of any sort."

He knocked on the roof of the cab and when it pulled to a stop shouted up that he wished to be taken to Mrs van Raalte's address.

"Shall I come with you?" I asked.

"Not this time, Watson. I will not be long, and besides we are supposed to be meeting Inspector Bullock at the hotel." He leaned out of the cab window and looked down the street. "It cannot be more than half a mile – a mile at most – to the hotel from here. The walk will do you the world of good, I'm sure."

Before I had time to protest, I found myself on the pavement, watching Holmes's cab disappear into the distance. The hotel was nowhere in sight, and I recognised none of the buildings around me, but I knew the direction at least.

As I made certain that I had my bearings, I had the unsettling feeling that I was being watched. Making every attempt at subtlety, I shaded my eyes against the low sun and took surreptitious stock of my surroundings. The street was busy but not overly so, and it was not hard to pick out the one man in the vicinity who was staring in my direction. A dark figure stood just inside an alleyway across the street from me, his face, where it was not already hidden by the shadows, shaded by a wide-brimmed bowler hat, worn tipped forward at an angle so that the brim almost touched his nose.

I had barely wondered whether I should confront the man or simply return to the hotel, when the decision was made for me. The figure stepped backwards into the gloom and was gone, and by the time I arrived at the spot he had vacated, there was nobody to be seen. I took a few steps down the alley, but was acutely aware of the filth under my feet and the looming tenements that seemed to lean towards me the further I progressed down the path. Behind me on Broadway, the sun was shining and industrious people buzzed around like bees, pushing this fledgling country forward by sheer willpower and hard work. Here, though, mere yards from the main thoroughfare, a different world emerged to greet me, one spawned in poverty and nurtured in filth and violence. Even the light seemed dimmer, as the tenements crowded together at their peaks, leaning in like drunkards and blocking the light.

I confess I stood on the spot for several minutes, so shocked was I by the sudden change. Of course, I had been in the slums of London on many occasions, but though Limehouse, Holborn and the rest were as hideous as anything New York had to offer, they stood relatively distinct in their deprivation, separated from the better areas of town by more than just a dozen feet of paving stone.

In any case, it appeared that whoever had been watching me was gone. The only person in sight was a pale-faced child of indeterminate age (somewhere between twelve and seventeen, I would hazard) – a girl, with large grey eyes and short-cut, greasy hair which visibly crawled with vermin.

"Excuse me, young lady. Did anyone pass you in the last few minutes?" I asked her, for the position in which she stood, in the only doorway in sight, facing out into the alley and commanding a view of both the archway through which I had just come and the corner ahead of me, was an ideal one for observation.

She must have heard my words, for her head turned slowly in my direction. She blinked heavily several times but said nothing in reply, though her mouth opened and closed again as if there was something she wished to say. I repeated my question, but this time she turned away, suddenly uninterested in me.

The new focus of her interest was swiftly made clear. A group of grimy toughs rounded the corner in front of me and stood directly in my path. The girl shuffled inside the doorway, pulling the door shut behind her as the men walked towards me, but I could see her face indistinctly at the nearest window. The gang came to a halt a few feet in front of me, and the man foremost – the leader, I assumed – reached inside his jacket and slowly removed a wicked-looking razor, which he opened and allowed to rest casually in his hand. Recognising that I was not welcome in the alley, I made discretion my byword and beat a retreat back into the light of the main street.

Nobody followed me and so, with a sigh, I began to walk towards the hotel, occasionally casting a glance behind me. After a hundred yards, and with no sign of pursuit, I was able to relax and consider what had just happened. I was certain that the man standing in the entranceway had been watching Holmes and me, but for what reason? Though we had made no attempt to hide our identities, neither had we advertised them, and we had only been in the country for a day and a half. In fact, the only people we had spoken to at any length had been Bullock, and the two ladies, Mrs van Raalte and Mrs Lockhart. The latter could be ruled out, I thought, on the grounds that we had only just left her, and she could hardly have arranged for a confederate to have us under observation so quickly, even if she knew our intended destination. Which was all very well, but I could not envisage the other two potential suspects being involved either. Bullock was on our side, I was sure, and I did not imagine that a boarding house landlady had the resources to have us followed. The question must perforce wait for Holmes's input.

With this thought in mind, I doubled my speed, keener than ever to speak to my old friend.

To my annoyance, the hotel turned out to be a good deal further away than Holmes had claimed, and it took me over an hour to walk there. My mood was not improved by a steady, if light, drizzle that set in some ten minutes after I began walking and which clung to my trousers and jacket and left me sodden, nor by the discovery that Holmes had found Mrs van Raalte absent and so had taken the cab straight back to the hotel. As I arrived wetly at the entrance, I could see both him and Bullock in front of a roaring fire in the lobby, enjoying a glass of whisky and a pipe apiece.

I wasted no time in interrupting them. "Well, I am glad to see you so comfortable, Holmes!" I began, but I was allowed to go no further in my outburst before he leapt to his feet and ushered me into his seat in front of the fire. Before I could say a word he had called over a waiter, ordered a fresh set of drinks and offered me a cigarette from his case. In light of his solicitude, it would have been churlish to continue to lambast him for his thoughtlessness, so I contented myself with lighting the cigarette and basking in the heat of the fire while he explained himself.

"There was, sadly, no sign of the good lady. I waited ten minutes or more, in the event that Mrs van Raalte might return from whatever errand had taken her away, but when she continued to be absent, I saw no purpose in remaining and ordered the cab to bring me back here. The inspector was already ensconced where you see him now, awaiting our joint arrival."

"I was wondering how you'd manage with Mrs Lockhart, if truth be told. But Mr Holmes has already brought me up to date. I'm only sorry that she wasn't of more help."

Holmes rushed to demur. "Not at all, Inspector. Mrs Lockhart was exceedingly helpful in her own way."

Bullock cocked a quizzical eyebrow in Holmes's direction at this, nor could I hide my own confusion. It had seemed to me that the meeting with Mrs Lockhart had been a disappointment, seeing as we had garnered only the bare fact that Holmes had a companion. I said so to Holmes, and asked – with some vigour I admit, for I was not entirely placated for my long walk in the rain – what vital clue had I missed?

"Not a clue as such, Watson. More an unwillingness to speak, which in itself spoke volumes on the lady's behalf." He knocked the ashes from his pipe and placed it on the table at his side before continuing; Holmes, I suspect, enjoyed these moments of anticipation almost as much as the revelation itself. "No? You do not see it? You did not remark on the lady's almost violent desire not to speak of the case undertaken by the imposter on her behalf?"

"I considered it no more than a natural embarrassment at having her dirty laundry aired in public. I don't doubt that most women would have reacted in a similar manner."

"To a simple matter of a dishonest servant? Come now, Watson, did the lady strike you as so shrinking a violet?"

I could not deny that Mrs Lockhart had appeared a woman

of strong personality. "Perhaps not. But even so, what does her reticence tell you?"

"That the matter was not one of petty theft, for one thing. And that whatever service this faker provided for Mrs Lockhart, it was one that filled her with shame, not gratitude. You heard her say that she hoped to see neither myself nor the other Holmes ever again?"

Now that I thought on it, I had indeed heard her say those very words, but until that point it had entirely slipped my mind. It was certainly an unexpected thing to hear about someone who had done the lady a service.

"She is unlikely to do so." Inspector Bullock was emphatic in his interruption. "As far as I can tell, no client has ever engaged the man's services a second time."

Holmes's eyes lit up at this information. "Do you say so? Not a single client? That is a fact particularly worthy of thought."

He fell silent and stared pensively into the fire for several minutes, absent-mindedly tapping his fingers on his knee as he did so. "A possibility suggests itself, but we must speak to his other clientele, I think, before we can be certain."

I recalled what Bullock had said previously regarding the unofficial status of our investigation, fearing that his further assistance would prove impossible, but I need not have worried. Clearly, the mystery had piqued his interest and, in consequence, he was more than happy to remain involved.

"I will put together a list of all the imposter's known cases and have it ready for you first thing in the morning," he offered immediately.

"All known?"

"I'm afraid I can be no more accurate than that, Mr Holmes. The truth is that nobody knows for sure how the other Mr Holmes comes by his cases, since he does not advertise and – unlike your good self – is neither affiliated with, nor keen to help, the police."

"Nobody makes use of the man's talents within the police force?"

"Not that I know of, Mr Holmes, no."

"And he has never approached your department and offered his services?"

"Again, I'm not aware of it if he has."

"And would you be?" I interjected. "Aware of it, I mean."

"I'm senior officer at present, Doctor, so yes, I would be informed if a civilian was involved in any of our cases."

"Don't you consider that odd, Inspector?" asked Holmes. "In my experience, while police officers are prone to a lack of thought, a paucity of foresight and an absence of deductive powers, they are always keen to take what help they can from a gifted amateur."

"The credit too," I added with a smile.

"There is that," Holmes agreed. "Perhaps one of your number has availed himself of the imposter's services but kept that fact to himself, the better to impress his superiors? After all, whatever other failings he might have, the man appears to have pleased all his clients and may, therefore, be a formidable investigator." He sniffed pointedly. "Though it pains me to admit as much."

I had felt Bullock tense beside me as Holmes rather thoughtlessly denigrated his profession, and now he rushed to its defence. "No, no, Mr Holmes, I refuse to believe that. No man in the New York Police Department would ever filch credit for another man's work. Nor would he employ the services of – forgive me, Mr Holmes – an untrained amateur detective."

Holmes's thin smile spoke volumes to one who knew him well, but for all his perceived prickly nature, no one could accuse Holmes of allowing personal feelings to impinge upon his work, and he did not rise to the bait. Instead, he was at pains to placate the inspector.

"He has been doing rather well for an untrained amateur, has he not, Inspector? But I take your point. Personally, I have spent a lifetime studying crime and criminals, but I believe it no great self-flattery on my part to state that no other detective has done the same. An experienced police officer would find little assistance from such an untutored fellow, I'm sure."

Mollified by Holmes's words, Bullock relaxed and, as is often the case when a painful disagreement has been narrowly averted, was, if anything, even more well-disposed to us than previously.

"Give me until tomorrow morning and I'll drop a list in with the concierge," he declared, adding, "It may not help, however. One wealthy New York socialite is much like the next, I'm afraid."

"Even so, we could not hope for more, Inspector," I replied gratefully. "It is good of you to give so much of your time to two visitors to your city."

"No matter, Dr Watson. I would fain help a countryman, and a friend of Tobias Gregson more than most. Now," he said, rising to his feet and beckoning for his overcoat, "I must be away. Eager as I may be to assist you, I must also look to those other, more official cases I have currently in hand. My captain is a good man, but a stickler for the rules, and he would not look kindly on any unauthorised activities on my part."

"He shall hear nothing but praise from us, should the opportunity ever arise," Holmes assured him, while I shook his hand in farewell. "Your assistance has been invaluable already, and should you be able to provide the names of further of the imposter's clients, we will be in your debt."

We stood and watched as Bullock disappeared into the street, then resumed our seats by the fire.

"Could he have left the city, do you think?" I asked, the question having played on my mind for some time. "The fake Holmes," I clarified. "Could he have moved on altogether, assumed a new name and shifted his base of operations elsewhere?"

Holmes shook his head decisively. "Why should he have? He had no expectation that we would ever discover his duplicity, far less that we should make our way across the Atlantic to confront him. And with no reason to run, he has even less cause to change his name. No, he remains in New York, I am sure of it. Besides," he concluded, "if we assume he has gone and so leave ourselves, what is to prevent the blackguard from returning the very next day and re-establishing himself as 'Sherlock Holmes'?"

"Bullock would be looking out for him," I protested. "Far more difficult for him to work his tricks with a police inspector watching over his shoulder."

Holmes tutted impatiently. "Bullock himself said that the police do not have so much as a complete listing of the imposter's cases, suggesting that he has never been of interest to them in any meaningful sense. And while you are quite correct that the inspector would take more of an interest in any future sighting of the man, he has in all likelihood committed no crime – leaving the police impotent to act and, in a busy city such as this, unlikely to spare a thought for a fake detective who, it seems, makes their lives a little easier by solving every case presented to him. No, Watson, I cannot look to anyone else to safeguard my interests. I must find this man myself." Before I could protest, he corrected himself with a smile. "Rather, we must find this man ourselves."

That decided, we called a waiter over and ordered dinner. There was nothing else to be done until morning.

Chapter Six

Bullock proved as good as his word. When we made our way downstairs at nine o'clock the following morning, the concierge approached and handed me a note giving the details of six people. I showed the note to Holmes as we breakfasted, but, like me, he confessed to recognising none of the names.

"Wealthy enough – the addresses are in good areas of the city – but not famous, and with no hint of celebrity about them. Solid citizens, I imagine, who would wish no breath of scandal to taint their reputations."

"Just the sort to engage the services of a private detective."

"Perhaps."

"Only perhaps?" I was puzzled by Holmes's apparent lack of certainty, given that he had made the initial statement that discretion would be a byword for such people, but he would be drawn no further and turned his attention to the kippers and excellent coffee that a waiter had placed in front of him.

While he ate I smoked a cigarette and once more marvelled

at the tide of humanity on the streets outside. Lace curtains covered the bottom three-quarters of the dining room windows, so all I could make out were the tops of heads and the upper portions of hats, but even with the view so curtailed, I was struck once more by the impression of vitality that the bustling passers-by created. London, busy though it was, somehow failed to conjure up quite such an impression of constant motion, much as a middle-aged gentleman might have many interests, yet never appear as energetic nor as dynamic as a younger man. I was musing on the differences between the populations of the two cities when, to my surprise, Inspector Bullock hurried across my line of sight and, having entered, made directly for our table.

It was plain before he spoke that he was the bearer of bad news. It did not require Sherlock Holmes to notice the flush in his face or the beads of sweat on his forehead, indicating he had rushed to the hotel, nor his hang-dog expression.

His first words confirmed my somewhat amorphous fears, though they were not at all what I had expected. "The landlady from yesterday, Mrs van Raalte? Her body's been found in a stale beer shop in Bayard. Luckily, an officer chased a dipper – a pickpocket – into the building and literally stumbled over the body, or we might never have found her."

Though Holmes was not the unemotional man that the poorer sort of newspaper occasionally claimed, neither was he one unthinkingly to pander to conventions. Consequently, he wasted no time in expressing his horror at the crime, nor his sorrow at the death of Mrs van Raalte. "Have you discovered anything of note yet? It would be useful to send someone to look around her home as well as the hostelry in which the body was found. She did not strike me as a woman likely to have many enemies, but you've obviously considered the possibility that this killing is linked to the man posing as myself?"

"Indeed, Mr Holmes, the thought had crossed my mind."

"Where was she found?"

"Bayard Street is part of a larger area known as the Five Points," Bullock explained. "During the day the street itself isn't so terrible, just a wide, dirty road between tenement-houses six and seven storeys high, and filled with carts and tables and stalls along its length, selling all sorts of rubbish.

"At night though… then it's a different matter. In the dark, the tenements are like high walls, trapping the unwary between them and forcing those who know no better to brave their interiors or cut through one of the alleyways that separate them one from the other. Either way, any innocent caught in so desperate a situation would swiftly find himself in trouble. Hundreds of souls crowd each tenement, all of them dirt poor and desperate, and many of them not so fussed what they need do to survive. Rare's the morning in the Points when there's not half a dozen corpses to be moved to a pauper's grave."

The description was vivid and relayed with unexpected emotion. Clearly the Five Points was a problem close to Bullock's heart, but I had remembered something else the inspector had mentioned upon which he had not elaborated. "And a stale beer shop?" I asked. "What does that involve?"

"Not so much *what*, Doctor, as *who*. There's no lower level to which a New Yorker can sink than the stale beer shops. The opium dens of the Chinaman are palaces compared to the average stale beer joint, and once a man ends up drinking in one, his fate is sealed. There's no way back."

"Not a location in which one would expect to encounter a respectable landlady."

The inspector was emphatic. "No, not at all."

Holmes had been silent throughout this exchange, but now he spoke up. "And she had definitely been murdered, in your opinion?"

"Undoubtedly," the inspector agreed. He pulled out his notebook and read from it. "Marks of strangulation round the neck, covered by a scarf that may or may not have been the murder weapon. Victim found sitting up against a wall, no other signs of violence."

"Was any money or jewellery found on her person?"

"None, but fall asleep in a place like that, even for five minutes, and you'd be lucky to wake up still in your clothes, never mind in possession of your wallet."

"No way of knowing if robbery was the motive then."

"The very fact that the lady was in such a place, Holmes," I protested. "Surely that militates against the possibility of opportune robbery?"

"A good point, Watson. You are most definitely improving – finally. But perhaps the lady was lured there under false pretences and then robbed? Or robbed and killed elsewhere, then her body dumped where it would not be noticed for some time? Unlikely, given the attempt to disguise her injuries, and more trouble, I suspect, than it would be worth, but not impossible. Still," he paused and marshalled his thoughts for a moment, "best to concentrate on the likely for now and leave the unlikely for more desperate times. Inspector," he asked suddenly, "*was* the lady killed where she was found?"

"Difficult to tell, Mr Holmes," Bullock replied. "The rooms from which such shops are run are filthy at the best of times. Puddles of blood – and worse – are commonplace. Add in the lack of illumination and the chances of locating usable evidence are slight, at best."

"Still, I should like to see for myself, if I may?"

I was unsurprised by Holmes's request; the look that crossed Bullock's face did, however, surprise me a little. He completely failed to suppress a smile as he gave a sharp nod of assent and agreed to lead us to the beer shop, almost as if he looked forward to the task. While, as I say, Holmes had a reputation for cold-bloodedness, nothing he had ever done or said had struck me as quite so lacking in human feeling as that smile on the inspector's face.

I was still troubled by the inspector's reaction on the short cab ride to the Five Points, while Bullock explained how a stale beer shop operated. It seemed that 'stale beer' was a drink composed largely of the unwholesome dregs taken from almost empty barrels of beer left outside local hostelries. Mixed together, and with narcotics or even paraffin oil added, it was a drink for the truly lost, the nameless tramps and hopeless dipsomaniacs who, Bullock informed us, made their home in the Points.

"Not that the place is as bad as it used to be," he went on, more cheerfully. "Why, when I landed in New York, Mulberry Bend still stood and the last few Dead Rabbits still ruled the roost round about. It's been knocked flat now, turned into a park would you believe, and the Points a sight safer for it. Still, though," he concluded contemplatively, "it's no place to go if you've no need and no place for any lady at any time."

He sighed and knocked on the roof of the cab, telling the driver to stop, and then we stepped into the infamous Five Points district for the first time.

In truth, while obviously not overly prosperous, there was little to mark out Bayard Street from any other street we had seen thus far in New York. True, the plethora of stalls on each side of the road spilled onto the pavement at regular intervals, blocking our progress, and the area as a whole was malodorous, but the people buying and selling bore little resemblance to the alcohol-sodden vagrants I had expected. A buzz of industry surrounded us, and I wondered if perhaps too many years in the United States had caused Inspector Bullock to forget what real poverty looked like. A green park, glimpsed through the gap between two tenements, simply added to my feeling that New York's worst streets were not as bad as all that.

"This way, gentlemen," Bullock called over his shoulder as he strode towards a building positioned on a corner where Bayard and another unnamed street crossed one another. "The body was found only hours since, so I had the room cleared and set an officer to keep watch until you arrived."

As he led us into the building and directly to an interior door which, I assumed, belonged to the beer shop, he ordered the policeman who stood guard to allow us access. The door was pushed open and we stepped inside, exchanging the crisp air of the street for the stale stench of tobacco, alcohol and death.

The room was about ten feet square, uncarpeted, with patches of brown paint peeling from the walls and a ceiling turned black by decades of smoke. A window, devoid of glass but patched with pieces of card, looked out onto the crossroads, letting in the muted murmur of people moving about outside, and giving enough light to make out the contents of the room. Puddles of spilled beer and who knew what else pooled on the uneven floor and assaulted our noses with their stench. What little furniture there was consisted of two barrels in one corner and half a dozen rickety chairs arrayed in a semi-circle around them, but other than that the room was empty, except for a pile of filthy rags and scraps of newspaper heaped in its centre. A second policeman stood directly in front of this heap of refuse, facing the door through which we had just come, but stepped to one side as we approached.

Bullock hurried to explain himself. "Tobias Gregson mentioned more in his letters than just the fact you were on your way, Mr Holmes. He also told me that you were meticulous in your methods and made quite a song and dance about the need to keep the location of a crime untouched. I have tried to follow his instructions as closely as possible."

Now the cause of the inspector's good humour became clear. Bullock had taken Gregson's words to heart and had ensured that the scene of this particular crime was as undisturbed as could be managed. I was on the verge of saying that all we were missing was the unfortunate victim herself when Holmes fell to his knees on the filthy floor with a cry of satisfaction and placed his palms flat against the top of the pile of rancid rubbish.

"Oh well done, Inspector, well done indeed," he said without looking up. "This is where the body lay?" Without waiting for Bullock's reply in the affirmative, he continued carefully to pull scraps of rag from the pile and discard them, until he had exactly what he wanted in front of him. Whatever it was, he scooped it up in his hand, then spent the next ten minutes criss-crossing the room on his haunches, occasionally darting down to examine something which had caught his interest, each time to be followed by a *tsk* of irritation as the object proved a disappointment. Bullock and his subordinate watched this performance in bemused silence, though I believe I saw the flicker of an occasional smile on the inspector's face.

Finally, Holmes came to a halt behind the two barrels and, with a groan of exertion, pushed himself back to his feet. "You were quite correct, Inspector," he began, without further preamble. "This room is so polluted that it is well-nigh impossible to differentiate the genuine clue from the discarded detritus of the drinkers who routinely pass their time here." He opened his palm, exposing the small object he had discovered beside Mrs van Raalte's last resting place. "But this may prove of interest, I think."

At first I was unclear what it was that he was showing us. The poor light didn't help, but even in the broadest sunlight I might have struggled to ascertain any especial significance in the small, mud-encrusted lump that Holmes held. I said as much, but Holmes simply tipped the object into my hand and invited me to examine it more closely.

It was a quarter of an inch in diameter, coated in dirt that Holmes had scraped off at one corner, exposing the golden shine of brass beneath.

"Get the rest of the mud off with your handkerchief, there's a good fellow," Holmes instructed as Bullock crossed the room to join us. "I fancy there's something of interest under there."

I did as I was bidden, but it proved unnecessary to ruin a perfectly good handkerchief, for the dirt slid off easily as I held it out for Bullock to see. The metal exposed beneath was indeed brass; it was a small button which had once been inscribed around its circumference, but which age and use had smoothed to an indecipherable flatness. I turned it over in my hand but, other than the eye through which the button must once have been fastened to its parent, there was nothing to see on the reverse. I passed it to Bullock but, though he took it over to the doorway and examined it in better light, I had little expectation of his spotting anything significant on so small an object. So it proved. He returned to us after a minute's examination and handed the button back to Holmes.

"There's not much to be gleaned from this, Mr Holmes," he announced. "It's just a brass button. I'll bet there's similar lost every day in the Five Points."

Holmes nodded, though it was impossible to tell if he were agreeing with Bullock or not. "Perhaps," he said eventually. "But this is a button that has been polished often, both in the past and more recently. It is obviously of a high quality manufacture and a distinguished vintage – you will have noticed that there was at one time an inscription – and has not lain here long, hence the ease with which dirt may be cleaned from it. An unusual thing to discover near a body in a drinking den of this sort, would you not agree?"

"But does it bring us nearer the murderer?" Bullock's priorities were clear, and little wonder. He had provided us with informal assistance as a favour for an old friend, but what had begun as a minor case of impersonation had blossomed into a murder, and he must now fear the reaction of his superiors.

"Immediately?" Holmes shook his head. "No, not immediately. But later, when we have a suspect to hand? A missing coat button, and a match between this stray and those remaining, might prove very useful indeed."

Bullock conceded Holmes's point with a grunt of approval. "Very true, Mr Holmes, but first we need–"

Whatever the inspector might have been about to say was lost as a rock crashed through the flimsy cardboard that stood in place of window glass and smashed itself against the rear wall, missing us by a matter of feet. Bullock at once ordered his subordinate to look out of the window, but before he could do so, the young officer who had been guarding the door stepped through it and reported that a large crowd had gathered outside and were calling for the police inside to leave.

"How many?" Bullock asked.

"More'n fifty, sir. Some of them's armed, sir." The officer was more youthful than I had thought, nineteen or twenty at most, and his voice trembled for a moment as he spoke, before he quickly regained control of his nerves. "What d'you want we should do, sir?"

Bullock was utterly calm. "Any other officers nearby?"

"No, sir. Just you, me an' Jackson, sir, plus the two gentlemen."

"I have my revolver, Inspector," I reminded Bullock. "I'm happy to put it to whatever use you judge best."

"Oh, there's no need for that, Doctor. Maybury here is letting his imagination get the better of him, that's all. The people round here remember the bad old days, when the New York police were not the gentlest, nor the most honest, and not above breaking a few heads for no reason at all. But that was fifty years ago, and though they still don't like strangers on their patch, the folk round here know that harming a policeman is the quickest way to earn themselves an early grave. They make plenty of noise and throw the occasional brick, but nothing more terrible than that."

"All sound and fury, signifying nothing, eh?"

"Exactly, Doctor. Very well put. Now," he said briskly, evidently keen to settle the business at hand, "if you're finished here, Mr Holmes, there seems no point in causing further unrest with our presence."

Holmes agreed that there was nothing else he needed to see and so, with Bullock to the fore, we left the room and, after a brief pause at the tenement entrance, emerged onto the street.

Traffic had been forced to a halt by the crowd that greeted us, and which had spilled out into the road itself. I would have estimated there were close to one hundred men and women before us, with a similar number of grubby children interspersed amongst them, their shrill voices added to the indignant cries of their elders. It was impossible in the hubbub to make out individual protests, and in fact they were clearly recent immigrants for I could hear no English being spoken, but the general mood was clear; the police – and those with them – were not welcome in the Five Points. I saw one or two in the front rows with rocks already in their hands and, further back, others holding iron bars, staves of wood and, in one case, a pickaxe, ready for action. The temptation to pull my revolver from my pocket was immense, but I had faced far greater threat in the army and I knew that even reaching for my pocket might be enough to turn this from a discontented crowd into a murderous mob. Consequently, I stood back as Bullock raised his hands for silence and, in the relative quiet that descended, declared that we would be leaving now and that the crowd should peacefully disperse. There were one or two loud grumbles at that, but as we stepped forward, the crowd parted before us and we were able to walk unmolested through them and out the other side. A few minutes' walk and we were back at our cab, which had patiently awaited our return.

As it pulled away and began down the road, I looked back, but the crowd had already dispersed and the streets behind us looked exactly as they had when we arrived, with no sign we had ever been there.

* * *

Bullock had the cab drop us at our hotel, while he returned to his office. Holmes spent the journey back in contemplation, resting his chin on his palm and closing his eyes the better to concentrate. Only when we were settled once more in front of the fire in the hotel lounge did he describe the situation as he saw it.

"It strains too far the bounds of possibility for the murder of Mrs van Raalte so soon after we visited her not to be connected to my missing doppelganger. Clearly, the mere occasion of our visit, or something arising from it, was sufficient to require her death, and quickly, for you will recall that the lady was not at home when I visited her yesterday. The task for us – or rather, for you, my dear fellow – is to ascertain exactly what it was that brought this tragedy about. I spoke to the inspector as we left that blighted tenement, and he has given us permission to enter the van Raalte residence and examine the contents, though we may take nothing away. In spite of the unlikelihood of such a coincidence, the inspector is concerned that murderer and doppelganger may not be the same man or even connected, and naturally feels that his murder takes precedence over our own investigation into a mere fraudster."

"As it should, of course," I said.

"Only if the two cases are not intimately connected, which I strongly believe they are. But ignore that for now. Take a cab to the van Raalte residence and see what you can find. I would go with you myself," he explained, "but I have another appointment. One of the people on Bullock's list, a Pastor Hoffmann, was visited by the imposter within a day or two of the latter's arrival in the city, and I now have his address. I intend to present myself as working in collaboration with the police – for are we not, strictly speaking, doing so? – and see if I cannot winkle a useful fact or two from the man."

"Pastor, you said? The imposter's first client is a man of the cloth?" I said, in surprise. Many ministers had come through the doors of Baker Street in the past, of course, but they tended to a certain timidity and were always keen on absolute discretion. Holmes had a hard-won reputation for probity, which guaranteed this last requirement, but I was at a loss to understand how a detective newly arrived in town could possibly be viewed as equally trustworthy. Perhaps it was this that had prompted him to purloin the name "Sherlock Holmes" for his own use.

Holmes, however, was already far ahead of me. "Exactly so," he confirmed, then continued, "I do wonder who the pastor thought he was engaging, however – an untried investigator freshly arrived and with his train ticket still in his hand, or Sherlock Holmes, the renowned consulting detective of London, England." He slipped his fingers into his waistcoat pocket and fidgeted with the brass button that I knew he had placed within. "But let us put that to one side for now. We have a greater conundrum to consider, do we not? The imposter would, of necessity, have needed to advertise his services somewhere for the pastor to have knowledge of him at all – and the inspector has already told us that he did not do so."

He trailed off and fell into a brown study, observing the flickering of the flames for several minutes, his fingers tapping a steady beat on the arm of his chair. Finally, just as I was beginning to wonder if my friend intended to remain thus for the entire day, he jumped to his feet and stood before me, rubbing his hands together. "Lunch first though, I think, Watson. This morning's events have supplied mental nourishment, but my body is now in need of more tangible sustenance."

Chapter Seven

After lunch, I left Holmes to finish one of the American cigarillos he had taken to smoking since our arrival, and hailed a cab in the street outside the hotel.

An early afternoon shower had slicked the pavement outside Mrs van Raalte's house, and an expanse of grey clouds overhead promised more to come in the very near future. I hurried up the steps to the front door, made myself known to the policeman standing there, and let myself in just as the first few heavy drops began to fall, glad to have avoided a drenching, but less than happy at the thought of poking through a dead woman's possessions. Holmes would have pointed out that by doing so I might improve our chances of identifying the murderer, but I found no consolation in the thought and made my way along the deserted corridor reluctantly.

The sitting room was unchanged since our visit, suggesting that Mrs van Raalte had not been killed at home. It was cooler than before, undoubtedly due to the inclement weather outside and the lack of people within, but there remained a heaviness to the air, and I had the unsettling sensation that the late Mrs van Raalte had merely stepped outside and could return at any moment. As though to lend weight to my morbid flight of fancy, I noticed a teacup, still containing dregs of tea, on a small table by one of the chairs. I hesitantly pushed it to one side, still uncomfortable with my role as examiner of the deceased's effects, but there was nothing underneath it.

This would never do, I knew. Holmes was relying on me to search these rooms thoroughly, and I could hardly do so while in such a melancholy mood. I gave myself a mental shake, and set to.

Half an hour later, I had discovered nothing of special interest. Mrs van Raalte had lived as I expect many women of her age and status live; quietly, carefully and without ostentation. Far from uncovering a clue as to her killer, in fact, I had merely accumulated a small pile of the most mundane items imaginable. A programme for an evening of cultural events, dated more than a decade previously; a modest collection of letters, tied with a ribbon and written in a foreign language that I took to be Dutch; and a card with an image of a large waterfall on it – these were the highlights of my trove, leaving me painfully aware that I had thus far been wasting my time. I dropped the papers onto the nearest table and, in my haste and lack of attention, contrived to knock the teacup to the floor, where it smashed into several pieces. The sound of breaking china echoed through the empty house, far louder than I would have expected.

There was a small utility room off the sitting room, containing, I felt certain, a brush and shovel with which I could clean up the mess. Sure enough, exactly what I needed stood just inside the door. I was reaching over a low dresser that was in the way and had just pulled the brush towards me when I heard a creaking sound and a cough, coming from somewhere outside the sitting room door.

The combination of the stuffy atmosphere, the long period of silence and my general unease had left me unsure of myself and ready to believe the worst. I cursed the fact that I had not thought to bring my revolver with me, and I cast my eyes quickly round the utility room in search of a potential weapon. To my delight, a slightly bent iron poker lay immediately to hand. I grabbed it with a sigh of relief. The very feel of the heavy metal in my hand restored much of my equanimity, and it was with a confidence that had hitherto eluded me that I slowly crept towards the closed sitting room door.

I stood as close to the door as I dared and, holding my breath, listened for further evidence of an intruder. The thought that the police officer outside might simply have come in out of the rain occurred to me, but was as swiftly discarded. Certainly, he would have called out my name as soon as he entered the house, and not crept around like a petty burglar.

Just then, I heard a heavy breath immediately on the other side of the door and so, raising the poker above my head, I pushed it quickly open and rushed through, determined to confront the intruder, whoever he might be.

"Good afternoon, my dear sir!"

The gentleman who stood before me was barely five feet tall, portly to an unhealthy degree and smelled strongly of whisky. As I burst through the door he was mopping his brow with a voluminous handkerchief, which had the fortunate effect of blocking his vision and so allowing me to hide the poker behind my back, out of sight. Whoever he might be, I very much doubted he posed a physical threat.

"Good afternoon," I replied in kind, then, "My name is Dr John Watson. Forgive me, but may I ask your name, and what you are doing in Mrs van Raalte's apartments?"

"Algernon Hinton at your service, though all my friends call me Algy." He held out a hand and I, after transferring the poker to my left, shook it in greeting before inviting him to join me in the sitting room.

I quickly discovered both that Algy Hinton was a talkative man and that he had a fondness for strong liquor. Within a few minutes, he had told me his life story, recounting his upbringing in the interior of the country, his desire as a young man to better himself, his move to the city twenty years previously and his current role as a writer of romantic fiction for several of the smaller New York publishing firms. He rented, he concluded, a small room in the house in which he wrote his romances.

In turn, I explained that a colleague and I were helping the police in the matter of Mrs van Raalte.

"The matter of… why, what is wrong with that dear, precious lady? I have been asleep all morning with a painful head and have seen no one."

Either Hinton was telling the truth and knew nothing of his landlady's untimely demise, or he was the finest actor I had ever encountered. As I elaborated, his face, until that point a faint purple in colour, blanched as much as it possibly could and tears sprang to his eyes. I feared for a second that he would weep, but thankfully he chose instead to push himself to his feet and cross to a cupboard that sat under the window of Mrs van Raalte's sitting room. He took out a bottle of brandy and two glasses, then poured us each a substantial measure. It was rather too early in the day for me to be drinking spirits, but I sipped at my drink while he gulped his down and poured himself another.

"I'm sure she shouldn't mind our partaking of a drop of her medicinal brandy," he said once he was settled again in his chair. He sighed sadly and drained his glass before refilling it for a second time. "Not that we can ask her, even if we wanted to," he added with a slow shake of his head.

"Had you known Mrs van Raalte for long, Mr Hinton?" I asked, keen to move the conversation along before Hinton became completely intoxicated, which he showed every sign of doing in the very near future. "How did you come to be her tenant?"

"Algy, please. Call me Algy." He smiled brightly and stirred his drink with a finger. "Let me see, it must be five years I've known that most wonderful of landladies. Yes, five years. I'm sure of it. Her husband had recently died and she had decided that changed finances meant a change in her life. Not lodgers though. Oh no, not lodgers. She told me herself when I answered her little notice – 'I will not have lodgers, Mr Hinton,' she said. 'No man will sleep under the same roof as me except Mr van Raalte,' and then she wept like a baby. Little did she know the relentless way some swine would pursue her."

His face fell as he considered his late landlady and, in the manner of drunken men from Kandahar to Coventry, quickly moved from cheerful good humour to maudlin self-pity. "And now we shall never speak again, she and I. And I will be forced to move offices! If I can even find suitable new premises at a decent price…" He fell silent and blinked at me glassily several times. "Who did you say you were? The police?" He attempted to stand but he had imbibed enough brandy to make that a fool's errand and he fell back, spilling his latest drink down his shirt front.

"Show me some identification then!" His words were slurred but the belligerence in his voice was unmistakable. It was plain that I would obtain no further information from him.

I left him where he sat with an empty bottle in his hand and walked back round towards the front of the house, passing what I assumed was his office on the way. The door stood ajar and, though I paused on the threshold for a minute or more, I knew Holmes would expect me to investigate while I had the opportunity.

Listening carefully for footsteps above the drumming sound of the rain outside, I pushed the door open and slipped inside. The room within was physically a duplicate of the imposter's office, with a corridor opening out to the right into a square area, but where the fake Holmes had placed a desk within sight of the door, Hinton had pushed his up against the wall, hidden from the view of casual visitors.

The reason was obvious. An empty bottle of whisky lay on its side under a chair, a mirror of its equally empty twin on the desk. An overflowing ashtray and a selection of alcohol-stained manuscript pages completed the clichéd image of the dissolute artist at work, but when I examined some of the papers more closely, I wondered just how much of an artist Algy Hinton actually was. No single page had more than a line or two on it, primarily the worst sort of doggerel – limericks, "humorous" stories that led nowhere and poor quality puns predominated – with, here and there, a few lines of what might have been autobiography or rough entries for a diary. The writing was sufficiently scrawled that I struggled to read much of it, and so I pulled open the desk drawers in search of more useful details.

The first drawer was empty, but the second contained a folder, inside which nestled a sheaf of closely spaced, typewritten pages.

A cursory inspection suggested that these pages constituted a clean copy of the diary notes I had already discarded, with references to Hinton's arrival in the city and a period spent living as a tramp on the streets. I doubted Holmes would have much interest in tales of Hinton sleeping on a park bench, so I flipped forward a dozen pages and was rewarded by the sight of Mrs van Raalte's name in the very first paragraph.

Mrs van Raalte – Edith, as she had been so kind as to invite me to address her – has proven a true friend, an angel in earthly form, a veritable savior! More like a wife than my own ever was, I find myself daily admiring her further. Not, I should add, simply because she has rescued me from the perilous existence I had heretofore led. No, not because of that at all, in fact! I admire and respect her because, in this modern, immoral world, she has remained true to the memory of her beloved late husband and has turned down offers of matrimony that a lesser, weaker woman would have embraced wholeheartedly.

She told me so herself, on our very first meeting, in fact. We sipped a glass of wine in her sitting room, while she recounted such tales as would make an honest man's hair turn white overnight! How, like vultures, confidence tricksters and criminals swooped down on her while Mr van Raalte was barely cold in the ground, asking for her hand in marriage – and the money that went with it!

And it did not stop there! Only this morning as I woke from a pleasant nap at my desk, I heard that black-hearted fiend Sherlock Holmes bother the dear lady once again, whispering his vile flatteries to her just yards from my own office door, even though she is a decade his senior, at least! And she will weaken in the end, I know it, for she has told me before that Holmes would do anything to make her his wife, and she is only a woman after all, alone in the world with nobody to protect her!

I wished to strengthen her weakening resolve, so I pushed my larger dictionary to the floor in order to startle him, which thankfully it did, but still – the morals of the man are no better than those of a weasel!

I believe that I shall be forced to speak to Holmes if he does not take his unwanted offers and leave this otherwise contented house in peace. I must be careful though – if I am to confront the blackguard, it must be when his voiceless ape, Watson, is not around. That silent horror is enough to make even the bravest of souls quiver in his boots! But I would have my path devoid of thorns!

The page ended there, and by the next Hinton had changed topic altogether, but there was a date at the top, exactly a month ago. I scrabbled in a drawer for a pencil and piece of paper and copied the entire entry down, snorting to myself at the description of the "ape Watson", and considering – as a fellow scribe – Hinton's rather frantic writing style.

An extended coughing fit and the sound of a chair scraping against the floor in Mrs van Raalte's quarters jerked me back to the present, however. I stuffed the sheet of paper into my jacket pocket and, after a last quick look around the room, made my way to the front door and out into the wet street. I asked the policeman still standing outside in the rain to check on Hinton and make sure he did himself no harm in his inebriated condition, then hailed a passing cab before the continuing downpour soaked me completely.

I had been gone only an hour and a half but, to my surprise, Holmes had beaten me back to the hotel once more. He beckoned me over to his table and, before I could even begin to recount my adventures, insisted that I light my pipe while he told me of his own.

"The pastor lives at the other end of the island," Holmes began as I made myself comfortable, "but such is the splendidly logical nature of the roads here that it took hardly any time to travel there by hansom cab. The house itself is equally impressive, on three floors, plus a below-stairs area, and reminded me of the sort of townhouse that might be found in one of the better areas of London. The front door is approached via half a dozen stone steps, with a servants' entrance to the right of the main entrance, down a flight of iron stairs. I knocked on the former and, having given my name as Inspector Lestrade once again, was shown into a large public room by a servant, describing myself, as I said I would, as a colleague of Inspector Bullock. The pastor was already present, standing with his back to a large, open fire, and asked me to take a seat in a high-backed silver chair that sat nearby."

Holmes gave a sudden bark of laughter and glanced at me with a mocking gleam in his eye. "I hope you appreciate the pains I have taken to remember the furnishings and the like, Watson. I know your audience delight in your gift for describing the most mundane elements in excruciating detail and I would hate for them to be disappointed by our American adventure."

I waved these words away impatiently, keen to hear more of Pastor Hoffmann. "Very humorous, Holmes," I countered, "but my audience far prefers to hear of the events that took place, rather than the place itself."

Holmes was contrite. "My sincere apologies, Watson. That was mischievous of me, I admit." He stubbed out his cigarillo and lit another before continuing his narrative. "As I say, the pastor stood by the fire and I sat in front of him. He evidently thought that a clever thing to do, placing me in an inferior position from the beginning, but I imagined myself the schoolmaster and he the errant pupil and was swiftly in control of the conversation. Or so I thought!"

"You mean Hoffmann was obstructive?"

"In a manner of speaking, yes. We began with the usual social pleasantries, Hoffmann asking how long I had known Bullock, how I found New York and so on, and I, without lying directly, allowing him to think I had been called over from Scotland Yard in order to track down a dangerous criminal, recently fled to the United States from England. It was obvious at once that the pastor was not an amiable man, nor one given to levity, and he seemed from the off to be disinclined to help if it were likely to prove inconvenient to himself. But he called down to the kitchens – he used a speaking tube situated by the fireplace, you might like to know – for tea and was willing to answer a few questions, so long as it did not take up too much of his time."

"Kind of him."

"Indeed. In any case, once the tea had been served, the pastor hooked his fingers in his waistcoat like some riverboat gambler and told me to 'go ahead and state my case'. As you can imagine, Watson, I was loath to tell such a man that someone who might well have been carrying out a confidential and personally embarrassing task for him was an imposter. Instead, I implied that Bullock had asked me to put together a file on all known private detectives working in New York, with a view to enlisting their help in catching my mysterious master criminal.

"The effect of my words was as surprising as it was instantaneous. Where before the pastor had been polite, if not welcoming, now his attitude was one of pure rage. He railed at me directly, asking why he thought I could help him in such an endeavour, what business it was of mine how private individuals chose to spend their money, and who had given me his name. He then rang for his servants and, with two of the burlier in close attendance, had me shown to the door."

"My word, Holmes!" I exclaimed. "So you were threatened and expelled for no good reason? You found nothing out while you were there?"

"Not quite, Watson, not quite. You see, having discovered that the pastor had an ungovernable temper, I contrived to make him as angry as I could, by taunting him that I knew all about his secrets and that in England we had a better class of religious leader than he."

"You said that even though he had two thugs ready to silence you? I'm not sure whether to call you brave or idiotic, Holmes."

"Neither, I hope. No, it was a calculated risk, that is all. I thought it unlikely that a minister of the church, no matter how ill-tempered, would risk the adverse publicity concomitant with such an action, and I doubted the two large gentlemen who escorted me from the building would care to assault someone they believed to be a police officer."

"Still a risk, Holmes."

"It may have been, I suppose, but even if it were, the result more than justified the risk."

"The result?"

"As we traded insults, Hoffmann became more and more intemperate in his rage until, just as the door was slammed on me, he screamed one final thing in my direction."

Holmes straightened the crease in his trousers and waited for me to ask about this occurrence. There was little point in pretending that I would not eventually do so, and so I put the question to him.

"He screamed this, Watson. 'You'd already be speaking to Donaldson, if you were as smart as you think, Lestrade!'" Satisfied with his trouser crease, Holmes smoothed his hair back and reached for his pipe. "We have a new name, Watson, and one that promises much progress in our search for the imposter. I have already sent a telegram to Inspector Bullock, asking him to search police files for any mention of Donaldson. But I forget myself – how did you get on at Mrs van Raalte's home?"

In comparison to Holmes's tale, my own desultory search through the van Raalte residence and brief meeting with a dipsomaniacal romance author felt distinctly anti-climactic. Still, I recounted events to Holmes and showed him the diary entry I had copied from Hinton's desk, taking pains to highlight the section that mentioned "Sherlock Holmes" and "Watson". To my surprise, however, Holmes was less interested in this than he was in Hinton's description of his relationship with Mrs van Raalte.

"She drank wine with him and told him that many men had made her offers of marriage," he said, tapping the paper with a long finger. "That is not impossible of course. A widow, still relatively young, with a fine house as dowry. She would indeed make a good catch for an ambitious New Yorker."

"Your double certainly seemed to think so," I exclaimed. "He would do anything to win her hand, apparently."

Holmes scowled. "Not quite, Watson. As is so often the case, the exact wording is of vital import. Holmes *would do anything to make her his wife.* Is that an accurate recollection? If so, we might profitably consider whether those were the words she herself used to Mr Hinton. To a woman reconciled to a life alone, the experience of being pursued by an eligible young man such as Holmes would be flattering, even intoxicating. And if he then sought her hand in marriage, why should she not enjoy the attention while, for form's sake at least, playing hard to get and refusing a proposal or two?"

Holmes's point eluded me. "What if it did, Holmes? I fail to see how, even if all of what you have said is the truth, the exact words used are of any importance."

"Because, my dear fellow, those may have been the words Holmes himself used. *I would do anything to make you my wife.* And although a love-struck widow might put the best possible interpretation on such a phrase, my more cynical mind wonders, and reflects that a wife may not give evidence against her husband."

"But why?"

"I am no mind reader, Watson, and cannot answer that question as yet. But given time, I may."

"Something related to his imposture, presumably." I cursed the misfortune that had led us to leave Mrs van Raalte's without obtaining all the information we could from her, then felt a chill of shock as I realised that the fake Holmes had probably killed the poor woman to prevent that very information – whatever it was – from falling into our hands. I would never have thought that a mere case of impersonation could have led to such violence.

Holmes had obviously been thinking along similar lines. "I do not believe so. It is, naturally, entirely possible for a man to kill with far less cause, but it is my experience that fraudsters are rarely men of violence. Indeed, with the exception of our investigation into the so-called Real Pretender in Inverness last year, I cannot recall a single dedicated fraudster who has ever killed in cold blood. And what, really, had the imposter to fear from exposure? His investigations have been successful, after all. He no longer has any need of the name Sherlock Holmes, when all's said and done. Besides, did the lady strike you as capable of the level of dissembling to such a degree? Her reactions appeared genuine to me; she showed no sign of believing that my counterpart was anything other than the consulting detective he claimed to be. Why then should he kill her?"

Laid out thus, I could see no flaw in Holmes's argument. There was one obvious suspect other than the imposter, however. "What about Algernon Hinton? He clearly loved Mrs van Raalte, and drunken men are capable of acts of great cruelty and violence."

"No, Watson, he is not our man." Holmes's tone was certain. "Even if the short, overweight man you described were capable of overpowering and strangling Mrs van Raalte, how on earth could he contrive to transport her body to the Five Points, seek out a hovel in which he might safely leave her body, then make his escape unnoticed, only to engage you in conversation about the lady the following day, as though nothing had occurred?"

"What about the other Watson, then? Hinton described him as an ape."

"There I cannot be so certain," Holmes admitted. "In the absence of concrete evidence it is possible that your namesake is the killer. As plausibly, he is simply hired muscle, present only to intimidate. There is a great deal in all this to consider…" His voice trailed off as he reached for his pipe and, pulling his tobacco pouch from his pocket, began to fill it. "I think this will require more than a single bowl," he said distractedly to me, and I, knowing I would get no conversation out of him for some time, left him alone, deep in thought.

Chapter Eight

For the next hour I amused myself in conversation with an émigré from Birmingham by the name of Smith, then ate a solitary dinner while Holmes smoked and considered recent events, befouling the air around him to such an extent that he was eventually asked if he would mind retiring to his room.

I discovered these facts later, when I followed in his footsteps, having been unable to locate him downstairs. Not that he exhibited any sign of irritation at the inconvenience, or embarrassment at the request. Far from it – in fact, as soon as I saw him, I knew that he had had some form of breakthrough. His eyes gleamed with triumph and the very way he held himself had subtly changed, as though his physical form had been transformed by intellectual success. The first words from his mouth confirmed my suspicions, even if they did not immediately aid my understanding.

"Nobody spoke English, Watson! Thus he would have been too visible if he had!"

"You will need to be less obscure than that if you wish me to understand, Holmes," I complained half-heartedly, knowing that this was simply how he preferred to unveil his revelations. "Who would have been too visible, and where?"

"At the moment, I am unable to answer your first question, but as to the second, why the Five Points, of course. English is not a common tongue there, if this morning is any gauge."

"Agreed, but even so, I fail to see why that is so important?"

"Because immigrant communities are tight-knit and closed to outsiders. Think of the Chinese in London, Watson, only in far greater numbers and with the addition of large conglomerations of other nationalities not often seen in England. Remember what I suggested earlier regarding your acquaintance, Mr Hinton," he continued insistently. "He would never have been able to move a body to that slop house. And nor would anyone not already known there. A man who speaks the language and knows the customs both of the streets of New York and the foreign society left behind."

I began to see what Holmes had in mind. "So, if we identify the language that predominates around the stale beer shop we visited, we will have an idea of the nationality of the killer?"

"Not quite, Watson. There is no reason to believe that the killer is necessarily a native of one country or another, only that he speaks the language. English is spoken in Canada, Australia, India and Gibraltar, as well as England. Why, even the Scots manage to speak a form of it. Would you describe inhabitants of each of these countries as English? No, of course you would not. But an English-speaking Canadian would find it a good deal easier to settle in London than another man of the same age and experience, but with no English at all."

"True," I conceded, "but I fail to see the great benefit we would accrue from such knowledge. We can hardly go around the Five

Points asking after a man who may be known there, based entirely on one language he might possibly speak."

"I think your heavy dinner has dulled your wits, Watson," Holmes replied impatiently. "But let the details lie for the moment. Let us first discover the predominant immigrant tongue used in the area in which the body was found. If you will excuse me for a few minutes…"

With that he hurried from his room, leaving me alone. It was growing dark outside, with rain thudding off the window and running in streaks down the panes. I lit a cigarette and was still smoking it when Holmes returned.

"A Bohemian area, according to the boy at the desk. German speakers in the main, with a smattering of Dutch, Flemish and Hungarian, of all things."

"Very well," I replied, without enthusiasm. I could not keep a note of annoyance out of my voice and, in truth, made little attempt to do so. Holmes was behaving unusually high-handedly, even by his standards, and I was losing patience with his guessing games. I believe he sensed my mood, for all at once he began to explain exactly what he had heretofore merely been hinting at.

"To return to your earlier question, Watson, I think it plausible that not only is the murderer of Mrs van Raalte known in the neighbourhood of the stale beer shop, but that he lives there too, or certainly close by."

"Why is your assumption that the killer lives somewhere close by? Surely he could as easily have dropped Mrs van Raalte there because it was convenient, or because he knew nobody in those warrens would quickly report anything to the police?"

"It is hardly convenient, Watson. The shop in question is some distance from Mrs van Raalte's home, and she was not a slender woman to be gaily thrown over a shoulder and carried some miles across town. And while you are of course correct that the police have few friends in such places, I suspect that Inspector Bullock will confirm that the police take a keen interest in the area and are often in the vicinity. No, the reason that the unfortunate Mrs van Raalte ended her days there is a simple one. This is the one place in New York in which our killer feels secure that he will not be challenged. The contention that strangers are unwelcome in these tenements is undeniable, as we have recently seen ourselves. Conversely, known faces are allowed a degree of scope that they would receive nowhere else. And did Inspector Bullock not say that there are several murders a week amongst these people?"

"He did," I confirmed. "Life is worth little, hereabouts, he said."

"Where better, then, to dump a body? In the darkened, reeking corner of some squalid slum a corpse might not be noticed for days, and even then might well go unreported. Fortunate it was that one of the inspector's officers happened across the poor lady in the course of his pursuit, or we might never have found her."

"Even so, Holmes, how can we hope to find one man in such a warren?"

"We have no need to seek him out. You recall Mrs van Raalte telling us that she forwarded on all of the imposter's post? All we need do is ascertain the post office that she used, then make enquiries as to the address in the Five Points to which she most commonly sent correspondence."

Holmes checked his watch and tutted in annoyance. "Far too late to hope to find any post office still open. We will have to leave further investigation until the morning. Though that may work in our favour too, as we can take Bullock with us, in case the postmaster should prove obstructive."

* * *

The next morning brought a break in the weather, with the incessant rain replaced by the warm sunshine we had experienced on our arrival. Holmes had telegraphed Bullock, asking him to meet us at the hotel at nine a.m., and sure enough, he pulled up in a police wagon a few minutes before the hour and joined us in the dining room, where we were finishing our breakfast coffee, there being nothing available that I would dignify with the name "tea".

He wasted no time in idle chatter. "So, Mr Holmes, what is this great breakthrough you spoke of, and what can I do to help you with it?"

Holmes was equally businesslike as he quickly explained his thoughts of the previous evening. "...and we intend, therefore, to visit the nearest post office and enquire within as to forwarded mail from Mrs van Raalte to the Five Points or its close environs," he concluded as the waiter arrived to clear away our coffee cups.

"And you would like me to provide official weight, if needs be?"

"Exactly so, Inspector. While I have some facility for disguise, and Watson is the very archetype of probity and trust, two foreigners asking after a local man in a rough area is likely to prove a fruitless exercise. But invite a representative of officialdom along and, if the American working man is anything like the English, tongues will undoubtedly be loosened."

"Very well, then. Now this is a murder investigation I've far more leeway to lend a hand to you and Dr Watson, and you do seem to be making more progress than I, though it's early days yet. I'll just let my office know where I am, then we can be off."

With that, he stood and headed towards the front desk, leaving Holmes to comment that Bullock was a surprisingly sound investigator, for a policeman. I smiled inwardly at this, recalling the times when my friend had lambasted Lestrade, Gregson, Jones and the other Scotland Yard detectives. Bullock had evidently made a positive impression on Holmes. We collected our coats, hats and gloves and, with Bullock leading the way, took seats in the wagon as it turned in the direction of 106th Street.

The journey was not a long one, for the roads were quieter in the morning, and we were soon standing outside a small, neat shop, with a sign alongside its door reading "General Store and Post Office". A bell tinkled above our heads as we pushed the heavy door open and made our way into the musty, overcrowded interior. Immediately inside, the shop broadened enough for the owner to have fitted a pair of glass counters, facing one another but separated by a narrow corridor that ran between them and then opened up to create a square storage area to the rear. A soft-faced young woman stood, partially obscured behind the left-hand counter, surrounded by the type of offerings one might find in a greengrocer's in England. She stepped forward into the light, which illuminated her face and allowed me to make out her large brown eyes. Though it was difficult to be sure, I estimated her age at around twenty-five.

I raised my hat in greeting. "Good day, I wonder if my colleagues and I might ask you a few questions?" I said with a tiny bow. I felt, rather than saw, Holmes arch an amused eyebrow at my side, but Bullock had already pulled identification from his jacket pocket and slid it across the counter. The woman, ignoring my query – and myself – entirely, picked it up and held it close to her face, squinting attractively to bring the details into focus.

"This says youse is police, do it?" she said eventually, in an accent so thick that I struggled to make sense of it. "What about they two? Is they police too?"

"These gentlemen are assisting the police," Bullock said, allowing his lack of clarity to reassure the girl. "And, hopefully, so will you in a moment. Now, what's your name?"

The girl looked uncertain, her eyes flicking nervously over the three of us before she answered. "Jessie Harries," she said in the end. "This is my da's store. He's out a message, but he'll be back, soon as anything."

She crossed her arms in front of her and glared at Bullock. Now that I could see her better, I could tell that she was younger than I'd first believed, closer to twenty than twenty-five. Her nervousness was plain, for all that she had put up a barrier of defiance, and Bullock was experienced enough to spot that and attempt to take advantage of it.

"I'm sure he will, Jessie," he said slowly. "But there's no need to trouble him, now is there? All we're after is one address, and we'll be on our way."

"What address? Who lives there?" Jessie's voice remained strident and defensive, but I had the sense that curiosity warred with suspicion. I doubted that working in this little shop was an exciting life for a young woman, and our presence was perhaps the most unexpected and thrilling event to take place there for many a month.

"Thing is, Jessie, we don't know who lives there yet." Bullock was no fool, and appealed to her vanity. "We need your help to find that out. There's nobody else can help us but you."

Still I felt she hesitated. "Why should I help youse?"

Bullock, feeling he was not getting through to the girl, tried a different tack. "Think of it as your public duty, Jessie," he said firmly and, when Jessie remained unconvinced, added a stick to the carrot. "What would your da say if I told him you'd been causing trouble for the police?"

I could tell at once that he had said the wrong thing. Jessie's face hardened immediately, as she pressed her thin lips together in anger. I doubted if she would talk willingly now.

"Do you remember Edith van Raalte?" Holmes suddenly interjected. Until now his attention had been focused on a box of spare buttons on the counter, but now he turned the full force of his gaze on Jessie Harries. "Mrs van Raalte, who owned the boarding house round the corner? A kind woman, was she not? Friendly and always happy to talk. You know that she is dead? Murdered and her body discarded as though she were worthless, of no value. You know how that feels, don't you, Jessie? You know what it feels like to be ignored, to be worked half to death and receive no thanks, to be handed only neglect in return for all your labour. For some people, life is a place of little hope and no escape, except in suffering and death, isn't that so, Jessie?"

He reached forward with a soft "May I?" and gently raised the arm of her blouse a few inches. The bruise this exposed was ugly, shaded blue, brown and purple.

"You know I'm not lying, don't you, Jessie?" he said quietly.

I thought at first the girl would flee, for she had stiffened with shock as Holmes lifted her sleeve, then took a step backwards as he released it, as if preparing to run. Instead, she looked up at Holmes with an unexpected shyness and whispered something too quietly for me to hear.

Holmes, however, evidently had sharper ears than I, for he replied, "I thought so. Do not worry. We have only a few questions and no harm will come to you. Not now, or in the future," he concluded, casting a glance at Bullock, who nodded his understanding. Someone from the police would be having a quiet word with Jessie's father before the day was out.

Holmes explained our mission to the girl. "We have reason to believe that Mrs van Raalte often used to forward on post that had arrived for one of her tenants. We do not know the name or address of the recipient, but we have a rough idea of the area and are in desperate need of any information you can supply. Can you help us, Jessie?"

In response, the girl crossed to the other counter, and pulled a ledger from a drawer concealed somewhere out of our line of sight. She laid the heavy volume flat on the counter and began slowly to flick through its pages. She had not gone far when she came to the page she sought and, with a nervous smile aimed at Holmes, turned the book around so that we could see it. As I expected, the page was one of many identical lined sheets, with information arranged in three columns, headed FROM, TO and COST. Halfway down the FROM column was the notation "Mrs v R" and in the TO column, a selection of addresses.

"The missus was on account, see, so Da writ down where her stuff went, so's she can't complain later and not pay."

"Do you have many customers on account, Jessie?" asked Holmes.

"No sir. That's how I knows where she is in the book, 'cos there ain't many in there."

Holmes smiled in return and assured the girl she had been a great help already, but that his colleague (by which he meant me) would just copy down the details, if that was acceptable?

I had already pulled a notebook and pencil from my pocket

and, while Jessie gazed with unconcealed adoration at Holmes, I quickly ran my eye down the various addresses. Each of them was unknown to me, but a single part of one address I did recognise.

"Five Points. It says Five Points." I wrote down the full address, apparently that of a shopkeeper by the name of de Groot. Of more immediate import, however, was the other name, that of the party to whom the correspondence should eventually be delivered: "FAO SHERLOCK HOLMES".

Chapter Nine

I have had cause to remark before now that my friend Sherlock Holmes was possessed of an almost supernatural excess of energy when in the midst of an interesting case. When bored he was capable of the most foolishly self-destructive acts, preferring to render his brain useless during periods of enforced indolence, rather than suffer tedium for a moment longer than necessary. When in hot pursuit, however, he was unstoppable, and the only possible action to be taken by one such as I, caught up in his wake, was to try to hold on.

So it proved in this case. No sooner had I announced the name of the shop to which Mrs van Raalte forwarded the imposter's mail than Holmes was pushing past me and out the door, a bellowed "Come on then, Watson!" the only indication he had even remembered my presence. Bullock too rushed from the post office, and it was left to me to thank Jessie for her help, and to promise that the inspector would ensure that no harm befell her because of it. I made a mental note to be sure to remind him of that fact very soon.

I hurried after my two colleagues. I had seen that look on Holmes's face many times before; he was wholly concentrated on the case, and would forget even to eat if I did not remind him. The mood might last an hour or a week, but at that very moment all that mattered to him was that he should speak to the recipient of Mrs van Raalte's mail.

The driver of the police wagon must have sensed Holmes's impatience, for he drove his horse hard through the streets to Five Points, though there was no particular need for haste. As a result of his endeavours, however, we soon found ourselves standing outside the filthy window of a dirty shop not two hundred yards from the tenement in which Mrs van Raalte's body had been discovered. There was no sign in the window, nor above the door, but Bullock informed us that it was known locally as Bill's Place, a combination of grocer, wine supplier, hardware retailer and post office, serving several of the especially impoverished sections of the Points.

"Criminals use it a lot," Bullock confided in us, laying a hand on Holmes's arm to prevent him going inside before he had said his piece. "We know that Bill himself is a fence, and probably worse, but we can't prove it and, though I shouldn't say it, he's a handy man to have in plain sight, if you know what I mean."

As we delayed on the pavement outside, the truth of Bullock's words was made clear. Several shifty, unkempt men approached the shop, then, seeing Bullock waiting by the door, turned on their heels and disappeared again into the warren of back alleys from which they had moments ago emerged. I found myself wondering just how much legitimate trade was ever carried out within its walls. Bullock apparently decided that we were drawing undue attention, and led us inside.

"I'll leave the talking to you, Mr Holmes," he murmured as we entered, "but I'm known here and I know Bill, and I'll step in if I think I have to."

"Understood," replied Holmes with the smallest of nods. I closed the door behind us and took a moment to look around the interior.

In comparison to the shop we had just left, which was clean and airy, if over-stocked and cramped, Bill's Place was a hovel. The window proved to be so engrained with dirt that it might as well have been coated in paint or covered with thick brown paper, for it permitted no light whatsoever to enter. All illumination, therefore, was provided by half a dozen misshapen candles, which sputtered and spat and added black smoke to the already polluted atmosphere. The stock, such as it was, consisted of a variety of alcoholic liquors, and an unappetising selection of cheap cuts of meat displayed on old newspaper. A box of pencils and another of matches completed the entire visible inventory of the shop, and I wondered afresh about the owner's less legal activities.

A small, hard-faced man whom I took to be the owner sat on a stool behind the sole counter, which dominated the rear of the room. Completely bald, he sported an unkempt black moustache, just beginning to turn to grey, which curled from his upper lip to his ears and disappeared behind them. As we entered, he looked up from a chunk of wood he was idly whittling.

"Inspector Bullock, this is a pleasure," he said, "and a surprise, also." His accent was Teutonic, I thought, and if his grasp of the English tongue was occasionally idiosyncratic, it was perfectly comprehensible; besides, it was a good deal better than my own German.

"Bill," the inspector replied cautiously, with a nod. I was aware of an undercurrent, both in Bill's greeting and Bullock's response:

two professionals about their business, exchanging courtesies.

"I am thinking that you are needing some information, Inspector? This is correct, yes?"

Holmes chose that moment to assert his presence. He had been standing to one side of Bullock, but now he stepped in front of him and, without preamble or salutation, asked if Bill knew anyone named Sherlock Holmes.

The German cocked his head to one side, for all the world like a small bird, and considered Holmes's question. Finally, he rose from his seat and leaned across the counter, until his face was close to my friend's. "Who is this one, Inspector?" he asked, never taking his eyes from Holmes.

Bullock's reply was slow and clear, allowing for no misunderstandings. "This gent is a friend, Bill. Think of him as like a brother to me." He too leaned forward over the counter. "Just like Benjamin is your brother. And young Benji would still be locked away if it weren't for me. Remember that."

"I remember." Bill was obviously unhappy at the reminder, but equally he was aware that whatever debt Bullock referred to still needed to be repaid. "I do not know any Sherlock Holmes, but I know the man who collects his packages."

"It is not Holmes himself?" Holmes interrupted, but the little man continued to ignore him and addressed his reply to Bullock.

"Did I not just say this? No, I do not know Sherlock Holmes. But I know the man who comes to my store to collect packages with Sherlock Holmes's name on them, even if he says nothing to me." He pulled a tobacco pouch from under the counter and began to roll a cigarette. "What is it you want to know about this man?"

"His name and where he lives, to start with. We believe that Holmes and another man receive their mail here, forwarded on from a Mrs van Raalte on 106th Street."

The German looked from Holmes to Bullock and back again, then shook his head. "No letters for no other man. Only Holmes gets letters. Big ones also, every few days. Only Hans collects them. No other man."

Holmes turned to Bullock and me, his voice low: "Large envelopes. Doubtless, Mrs van Raalte was in the habit of putting several items of mail into one large envelope and sending it that way, thus saving on extra postage." To Bill he said, "Do you have any of these envelopes just now?"

Bill shook his head again. "Nothing here now. Hans comes yesterday, takes his letter. And no more letters today."

It was plain from the way that he shuffled from foot to foot that Bill was keen for us to leave, but Holmes was not finished.

"Do you know where Hans lives? Also, his surname, if you know it."

"Piennar is his name. Hans Piennar. It says this on the card he shows me on the first day he makes collection."

"His card?" I exclaimed in surprise. "He gave you his card? Do you still have it?"

"I do not. He takes it back once I have read it. Why should I keep it, when only he has a use for it?"

I admit I was confused by this, but Holmes clearly was not. "Why did only he have use for the card?" he asked eagerly.

"It has his name on it! Have I not just said this? Without it, how else does anyone know his name? How else can he tell anyone?"

"Because he cannot say his name!" Holmes clapped his hands together with pleasure. "Hans Piennar is a mute, Watson. That is the truth of it, is it not, Bill? This man cannot speak!"

The little man shrugged, as though uninterested in Hans

Piennar or those who were looking for him. "I have said. He does not speak. He lives near. Two blocks down. The door, it has been smashed. In splinters. He is on the third floor. That is all I know."

Holmes glanced at Bullock, who gave the smallest of nods. We had discovered all we would from the shopkeeper.

"Thank you for your assistance, Bill. The city of New York thanks you, and I thank you. Mind, we'll speak again should this information turn out to be less than one hundred per cent correct."

"It is one hundred correct, Inspector. One hundred!" He glared at the policeman for a second, then his shoulders sagged and he sat back down on his stool. "This means that the help of my brother is repaid?"

He looked up at Bullock, who gave no indication he had even heard. "Let's go," he said, and led the way out of the shop and back into the street.

Outside, I noticed several passers-by glance at us suspiciously as Bullock ordered Holmes and me to wait while he quickly checked the tenement identified by the shopkeeper. He returned within a minute or two.

"It's as Bill said, gentlemen. The door's been smashed in, though not recently. It's not unusual in these parts," he assured us, "but it's not exactly a good sign. We'd be well advised to get ourselves out of the Points for the moment, and come back first thing in the morning with a few lads as backup."

"Is there a reason we cannot investigate further today?" Holmes asked, quite reasonably, given that it was not yet noon.

In reply, Bullock removed his hat and, under cover of doing so, quickly flicked a finger in the direction of two young men – little more than boys, really – ostensibly lounging against a wall nearby, smoking tiny rolled-up cigarettes that threatened to burn their fingers at any moment. "Behind us too," Bullock muttered so quietly I almost missed it. "Those ones are better hidden, but you can bet your last dollar that they're there. No, sir, the time to go into the tenements with an arrest in mind is dawn, when the man you're after – and his friends – are all still asleep."

Holmes considered this for a second. "What about the middle of the night? Would that not be even better, while the miscreants are asleep?"

"Far too dangerous, Mr Holmes. Get caught inside a room in one of those tenements and you might never get out again. You recall the mob yesterday? Now picture the same mob, except place yourself with your back to a filthy wall, in a room as black as the devil's heart, and no means to escape except directly through the very mob baying for your blood."

The inspector painted a vivid picture and I, for one, was pleased that we would not be attempting any heroics until the morrow. I could tell that Holmes felt otherwise, and I thought that he was about to protest, but there was nothing we could do without Bullock's assistance and so, with reasonably good grace, he acquiesced to the policeman's suggestion and agreed that we should be dropped off at the hotel while Bullock returned to work.

In the end, we spent a pleasant afternoon walking in the vicinity of our hotel and then, as the early autumn night drew in, we dined in the hotel once more, before Holmes roundly defeated me at chess, in spite of a two-pawn handicap. After several days of hectic business, it was exactly what we needed, I felt sure.

The only minor thorn during our perambulation was a small group of young men who seemed to be following us at one point as we walked. I mentioned them to Holmes and contrived to point them out at the earliest possible moment, but he dismissed my concerns and noted that we were walking along a busy and well-used thoroughfare, rendering it unsurprising that we should happen to see the same individuals now and again. I was unconvinced, but a few minutes later I looked around and they were gone.

Later, sitting in front of a roaring fire with a glass of brandy in one hand and a more than decent cigar in the other, I reflected that the life of the consulting detective (and his faithful chronicler) was not always an unpleasant or a hazardous one, and that perhaps I should be more accepting of that fact. I bade Holmes a good night and made my way upstairs, fuzzily content with my lot.

Chapter Ten

The following morning, Holmes had disappeared.

The previous few days had been busy and I slept soundly until eight thirty, when I washed and dressed and strolled along the corridor to Holmes's room. I was surprised to receive no response to my initial knock, as Holmes tended to sleep little and rise early when in the midst of a case, but when he failed to respond to further, increasingly loud knocks, my mind turned to the gang that had observed us the day before. Bullock had been confident that no harm would come to us, but although his words had seemed sensible at the time, now I worried that I had been too quick to accept his reassurance.

I tried the door handle on the off chance but the room was locked, and with Holmes conspicuous in his silence, I had no choice but to run downstairs and explain the situation to the hotel manager. To his credit he wasted no time questioning me, but accompanied me back upstairs, along with one of the porters, and opened Holmes's room with a master key.

Inside, there was no sign that anyone had been staying there at all. The bed was neatly made, the room entirely free of the sort of clutter with which Holmes surrounded himself at home. A monogrammed tiepin carelessly dropped in the top drawer of a bedside cabinet was the only indication that Holmes had ever occupied the room. More worryingly, the wardrobe contained Holmes's coat, gloves and scarf. The nights were not as yet freezing, but even Holmes would have taken his jacket at least, had he gone on an evening – or even a very early morning – stroll.

The manager was solicitous but unconcerned. "Your friend, is he the sort to wander off, Dr Watson?"

"Well…" I hesitated, painfully aware that my friend was exactly the sort to wander off, should he feel it necessary to do so. But there had been the gang of thugs, and Holmes had mentioned nothing of an evening out when we had parted the previous night. Combine that with his recent inconsistent mood, his frequent distraction and his exertions of the past few months, and I could not say with any certainty *what* Holmes was likely to do. Even so…

"No," I said after a brief pause. "He would have informed me if he intended to stay out last night."

"Perhaps a lady…" His voice faltered, the unspoken question an insinuation that I was quick to quash.

"I hardly think that likely! Mr Holmes and I parted at about ten o'clock last night, each to our own room. He said nothing regarding leaving the hotel, has taken neither coat nor scarf, and is most certainly not in the habit of chasing ladies around strange cities, as you seem to be suggesting!"

I could hear the growing concern in my own voice and knew that barking at the hotel staff would not bring Holmes safely back. What was needed was Bullock. He had the authority that we would require if we were to catch the gang – who I now firmly believed had snatched Holmes from his bed. "I must contact Inspector Simeon Bullock of the New York Police–" I began, but the manager interrupted me.

"That will not be necessary, sir. The inspector is currently in the Guests' Lounge. I am informed that he is waiting for you, in fact, Dr Watson."

With barely a word of thanks to the man, I bustled past him and leapt down the stairs two at a time, all but sprinting to the Guests' Lounge in my hurry to tell Bullock what had happened. I saw him before he saw me. He was sitting with his hands on his knees, like a sailor at attention, a frown contorting his face. The thought occurred that he had come to deliver the worst of news, but I dismissed it as unworthy and foolish; after all, he would hardly sit in the lounge waiting for me in such a circumstance.

"Inspector!" I called across the room as I threaded my way through an obstacle course of tables and chairs. He looked up and, seeing me approach, rose to his feet, the frown not leaving his face.

"Mr Holmes–" he said, dolefully, and had I not been standing by a tall chair against which I was able to lean, I think that my legs would have given way underneath me.

"What has happened to him?" I cried loudly, heedless of the other customers who turned to investigate the source of the disturbance.

"What? To Mr Holmes? Nothing much, though that's precious little thanks to his self." Bullock's Yorkshire brogue became more pronounced when he was angry, I noticed, and at that moment it held an entirely English tone. "Left to his own devices, however, he might have come to a great deal of harm, and we'd be having a different conversation just now."

In my state of heightened emotion, it took me some time to

process the inspector's words. Had Holmes come to harm, as he seemed to be suggesting? No, not that – but something untoward had taken place and Holmes had, at some point in the recent past, found himself in some type of trouble.

Bullock obviously saw the confusion on my face and took pity on me.

"Sherlock Holmes might be the greatest detective the world has ever seen, Doctor. He may in fact be the brightest and the best that England has to offer. He certainly seems to think so. I cannot say either way, if I'm honest. But what I do know is that he is amongst the most stubborn and the most idiotic men I have ever had the misfortune to rescue from a drinking den full of thieves and killers!"

At last I guessed what had transpired. Clearly, in spite of Bullock's warnings and my own trepidation, Holmes had decided to visit Hans Piennar in his tenement last night, and had evidently walked directly into trouble.

"He returned to Five Points last night?" I asked, already knowing the answer, and beginning to feel a degree of anger of my own. "Of all the foolish, inconsiderate—" I broke off as it occurred to me that Holmes remained conspicuous by his absence. "But where is he?" I asked the inspector, who responded with a satisfied smile.

"We have him in our cells at present, Dr Watson. Best and safest place for him at the moment, in my opinion, and he'll remain there until I can release him into your care."

I could well imagine Holmes's reaction to that. "Thank you, Inspector, I'm sure Holmes appreciates your concern. But what exactly happened last night?"

Bullock waved for a waiter and ordered coffee. He resumed his seat and I joined him as he recounted his – and Holmes's – activities the previous night.

"I don't know if you noticed, but Mr Holmes baulked at my refusal to take action against the man Hans Piennar yesterday afternoon. He said nothing, of course, but I've spent enough time around guilty men to recognise when a man is suppressing something he wishes to say. Still – and I blame myself for this – I thought little enough of it. Of course, he would wish to rush to justice and, were he back home in London, perhaps he would have been able to do so.

"But New York is a more lawless city than London. Murder, even of respectable citizens, is not rare here. Perhaps you've seen the case which currently fills the front pages of the more sensational rags? A young girl of good family gunned down by her fiancé, of all things. And that is not a unique case, by any means."

He shook his head sorrowfully. "But Mr Holmes obviously thinks he knows best. Luckily for him, I came here with information for him late last night and found him missing from his room. Guessing that he intended to return to the Points on his own, I dirtied myself up and followed, thinking to grab him before he even got as far as Hans Piennar's lodgings. He must have left almost as soon as you retired to bed, though, for there was no sign of him in the street outside the tenement. I can tell you, Dr Watson, I nearly left him to his fate, but I remembered I had promised Tobias Gregson to keep an eye on you both, so in I went.

"In his defence, it took me some time to find him, he was so well disguised. I stepped over him twice, in fact, taking little notice of a barely conscious tramp slumped against a wall as I kept a weather eye out for an English detective and anyone who might recognise me as police. Eventually, though, as I came back through the same corridor, I caught a glimpse under his collar as he took a swig from his bottle. No genuine down-and-out has skin so clean. I grabbed him by the scruff of the neck and pulled him out of there before he could utter a word of protest."

"Did Holmes say anything afterwards?"

"Oh yes. He said plenty. Mainly about the interference of busybody policemen and the hindrance that caused to his investigations in London – and now in New York as well. I considered bringing him back here, but worried that he might go out again. So he's in the cells and there he'll stay for the minute."

There was nothing I could say. I had had cause many times before to curse Holmes's impetuous streak, and consequently was unable to criticise the inspector's actions. Indeed, I was grateful to him for extricating Holmes from a situation that could well have proved deadly. That thought prompted another, which I put to Bullock as a question.

"Did you find Piennar while you were looking for Holmes?"

"Not at the time, no. Well, not since either, if truth be told." He ran a hand across his face, the tiredness in his eyes unmistakable. "I was concentrating on finding Mr Holmes when I first went in, and so saw nothing of our quarry, but after I dropped him off at the station, I returned to check on the room Bill identified for us. Piennar was nowhere to be seen, and the family who had taken up residency in his absence said he'd not been around for a few days, and might not be back at all."

"Not back at all? Why not? Does he know that we are looking for him, do you think?"

"No, I don't believe it's down to our enquiries. According to the father of the family, the rumour is that our man Piennar is working for the police, and as a result it's not safe for him to be seen around the Points. The irony is that it can only be the fake Holmes that's being referred to. A detective, not a policeman."

He gave a tired laugh. "And now, if you've no objection, Doctor, I'll escort you to the station, where you can take Holmes away with you, and I can go home and get some much-needed sleep."

"Give me two minutes to collect my coat and hat from my room, and I'll be with you, Inspector," I said, rising to my feet, while Bullock settled his bill. Now that I knew that Holmes was not hurt, and that we had made some progress in the case, I was less inclined to be angry with him for his reckless behaviour, and keener to hear what he made of Piennar's disappearance.

Chapter Eleven

Over the years, I have met, and worked with, policemen on three continents, and on every occasion the men involved have been of similar type: dogged and reliable, intelligent but occasionally lacking in imagination, and with an unflinching determination to catch their prey. At the station, Bullock proved himself to be of similar stripe.

I had expected him simply to pass me on to a subordinate, but instead he arranged for Holmes to be brought to his office, where he and I waited and discussed less weighty matters than usual – primarily points of interest to a traveller in New York, for I had a notion to stay on for a week or so after the case was closed, in order to see the sights. Bullock was just describing a particularly pleasant walk along the coast when the door opened and Holmes was shown in.

I had brought Holmes a change of clothing, so that he at least resembled a gentleman, but there was no hiding the stench of cheap alcohol, tobacco smoke and dirt that surrounded him. His face and hands too retained the grime of his erstwhile disguise, and I fancied I spied a small twig entangled in his hair.

In spite of this, he seemed quite cheerful, and he strode into the room with a grin on his face and his hand outstretched in greeting. Soon he was sitting in a chair beside me, opposite the inspector, a cigarette lit and a look of intense interest on his face.

"So, Inspector," he began without preamble, "you said last night that you had some information for me? In connection with the man Donaldson, regarding whom Pastor Hoffmann was so helpfully vocal."

I felt sure that Bullock would take this opportunity to lecture Holmes on his actions of the previous evening, but either he had already done so, or he knew Holmes well enough by that point to understand that such a speech would have no effect on his future activities. For whatever reason, he simply opened the file that sat in front of him and began to read.

"James Donaldson. New York-born businessman, primarily dealing in precious gems, with a side interest in expensive artwork. Took his own life, at home, on February last: a single bullet to the temple. No suicide note was found, and it says here that his business was doing well, he was in good health and had no family issues that the officer investigating could discover. His sister claimed there had been no warning signs; he had been in good spirits in recent months and they had even been discussing a forthcoming trip to Europe."

"Last February!" The date was, I felt, the key fact in Bullock's recital. How could the imposter be linked to a death that occurred some months before he even arrived in the city? "You said that the fake Holmes first came to your attention a year ago, Inspector. And Mrs van Raalte said he had been renting from her for the same length of time. So how can he have anything to do with Donaldson?"

"That remains to be seen, for the present," Holmes replied, leaning forward to turn the file towards him, with Bullock's nodded permission. "But Pastor Hoffmann would not have shouted his name in my face had there not been some connection."

"I admit I can see none," Bullock interposed with a yawn that he tried unsuccessfully to stifle. He chuckled in self-deprecation. "Though I may be less than at my best this morning, I grant you."

"At the moment, I too fail to spy a connection," Holmes admitted, "but there is no obvious reason why a successful man such as Donaldson should suddenly kill himself. No, to be driven to such a step would require the insertion of some new and disturbing factor into his life. In light of the pastor's admonition, it is a reasonable inference that the imposter was responsible for introducing this new element."

Perhaps it was the night in the cells, or perhaps Holmes had imbibed more cheap alcohol than he had intended, but he seemed to me to be in danger of building his case on rather unsteady foundations.

"An unexpected diagnosis of terminal illness has caused men to take similarly drastic steps in the past, Holmes," I warned.

"A burly, well-built man, in good health," Holmes replied, stabbing a finger at the file in front of him.

"Perhaps his business was about to fail…"

"Thriving then and still thriving now," Holmes responded. "A nephew took it over when he died, according to the report."

"And he was unmarried, in case you were about to suggest infidelity," Bullock added, unnecessarily I thought.

"He had some other secret then!" I countered with exasperation.

Holmes had been about to light a cigarillo, but as I spoke his hand froze half to his face. The match burned down as he sat, immobile, until he dropped it in an ashtray then continued to sit with the unlit gasper in his mouth.

"You've thought of something?" I asked after two full minutes had passed and Bullock had begun to make enquiring gestures in my direction.

"Perhaps, Watson…" Holmes was distracted by whatever had sprung to mind, and I knew of old that there was no point interrogating him about it. He would reveal himself when he chose to do so, and not before. My query had been enough to break the spell, however. Holmes shook himself like a dog waking from a deep sleep and stubbed the unlit cigarillo out in the ashtray. "I need to know more about Mr Donaldson before I can advance anything other than a very preliminary and incomplete theory. Do the police have more on the case than these few pages?" he asked, turning to Bullock.

"There are the statements from his friends and the maid who found the body, but nothing else. It was viewed as a straightforward enough case of suicide."

"Did Donaldson have his newspaper delivered?"

Bullock was caught unawares by Holmes's question. "Did–? I confess I've no idea, but I had a constable making further enquiries this morning. I'll check if you'll excuse me for a second."

He rose and left the room but, true to his word, was soon back.

"No, he did not. His usual habit was to leave for work very early, around six a.m., some time before any newsboy delivers in that area."

"Yet it says here that a newspaper was found at his side? And the time of death was…" Holmes flicked over a page and ran his finger down the next, "…in the early hours of the morning, but certainly before eight, when he was discovered by the maid?"

"That's right. He was last seen alive the previous day when he left his office at around eight thirty."

"An industrious man, indeed."

"It would seem so." He held Holmes's gaze with a puzzled expression that I recognised from the faces of Lestrade, Gregson and the other Scotland Yard inspectors Holmes had assisted. "Is any of this important?" he asked, finally.

"That remains to be seen, Inspector. For the moment, it is simple curiosity, no more than that."

At this, the force that had kept Bullock functioning in spite of his lack of rest seemed suddenly to abate, and he sagged a little in his seat.

"In which case I hope you will both excuse me, but I think I'll go home and put my head down for a few hours. There's nothing else I can tell you just now, and last night's jaunt with Mr Holmes has left me in need of sleep."

If Holmes felt any guilt regarding his behaviour the previous night, he gave no sign of it. Instead, he enquired if it would be possible to visit Donaldson's home.

Bullock pinched the bridge of his nose and rubbed his eyes before replying. "I don't see why not. It's stood empty since Donaldson died. People aren't keen on buying property with such a bloody history. I'll have someone write down the address for you and directions to get there. I'd offer you transport, but this enquiry is some distance from that of the death of Mrs van Raalte, and you have, I'm afraid, strayed back into unofficial territory."

Holmes's brow furrowed at this, but I hurried to assure the inspector that we understood entirely. The address and a hansom would suffice, I felt sure.

* * *

James Donaldson's home occupied a central position in a long street of similar three-storey buildings in what was clearly a good area of town. From the front, it presented an imposing façade; a dozen dark stone steps ran up to a black-painted door, with a large, many-paned window to the right-hand side. The curtains were closed, as they were in the smaller windows on the upper floors, and it was impossible to make anything out from the street, which was lined on both sides with tall trees. The aura of patrician wealth was unmistakable.

Closer to, however, Donaldson's house showed signs of neglect commensurate with having been locked up for over a year. The base of the door was scuffed and scratched, as though various people had entered with their hands full, requiring them to push the door open with their feet, and a small golden plaque was so dirty that it was difficult to make out the owner's name. Holmes took a moment to examine it, then opened the door with a key supplied by Bullock, and made his way inside.

The front door opened directly into a short, open hallway, with stairs in front, and two doors to the right-hand side. The second of these, which stood ajar, proved to be a cupboard, empty save for two jackets hanging from pegs and, on the floor, a pair of wellington boots. The first door, however, led to the drawing room where Donaldson had died, a large, square area that took up most of the ground floor. Bullock had warned us that the rest of the house had already been stripped of furniture, so we knew that any clues we might find would have to be discovered within this single space.

The room was dim and musty with disuse and, as Holmes crossed to the window and threw open the curtains, dust billowed in his wake. As soon as the window was propped up to allow fresh air to circulate, it was possible to make out pale green wallpaper decorated with images of parakeets, in the style of William Morris, and a selection of good quality oak furniture, comprising a pair of matching high-backed chairs, a long sofa and several fine sideboards. In the centre of the room a dark red rug covered the polished floorboards between the chairs and sofa.

A landscape painting that even I could recognise was of the highest quality had been hung on the wall facing the fireplace, though currently partially obscured by the open door. The only other decoration was a small photograph of a youngish man, presumably Donaldson himself, on the mantelpiece. In the picture, he was smiling – a blond-haired man of about thirty, wearing a striped blazer and a straw boating hat.

Holmes barely glanced at the photograph, but instead took to his knees and, with his magnifying glass in hand, began to crawl along the floor, examining the skirting boards and the areas underneath the chairs and sofa with particular interest. That process complete, he first crossed to the fireplace where he ran his hand across the wall directly above it, then asked me to help him to lift down the painting opposite.

A large, irregular stain marked the wall behind the painting. I did not need to be a doctor to know that this was blood, nor did I need to be Sherlock Holmes to surmise that the painting had been moved from its more regular position above the fire to its current location in order to hide the most obvious sign of the tragic event that had occurred in this room.

"Someone must have tried to sell the house at some point," Holmes remarked, "though they were apparently unwilling to pay for a proper redecoration."

"Donaldson's nephew, perhaps?" I suggested.

"Perhaps. It is not important. What it gives us is a position from which… aha!" He bounded across the room to one of the chairs and threw himself down in it. Then, placing a finger against his temple, he turned his head to stare directly at the stain on the wall. "Donaldson sat here to carry out the deed. See, small marks, here and here," he said, pointing to several indistinct discolourations of the fabric. "Again, someone has attempted to clean rather than repair or replace." He shifted in the seat and laid a hand on a dusty occasional table to his left. "This must be the table on which he placed his whisky and newspaper."

"Newspaper?" I said, recalling Holmes's question to Bullock earlier.

"Did you not notice? Of course – you did not read the police report, did you? Donaldson was found in a chair in this room, with the remnants of a glass of malt whisky and an unread copy of that morning's newspaper on a table at his side."

"Is the exact position significant?"

"Everything can be significant, Watson. Surely you have grasped that fact by now?"

With that, he slid from the chair and crouched down in front of it, much as he had done at the imposter's office four days before. "I must congratulate you, Watson," he continued, as he slipped his fingers underneath the heavy rug and began to pull it towards him. "I noticed you taking stock of the room when you entered. You are improving, there is no doubt of it. So, having done so, what strikes you about this rug?"

I confess I had paid it little attention before now and could see no reason for his sudden interest. I said as much to Holmes, who shook his head in mock sadness and requested some help in moving it out of the way. I willingly, if not gladly, grabbed one corner and, ignoring the twinges from my old wound at the unwonted effort, helped pull it to one side.

There was nothing to see underneath except floorboards. Holmes, however, thought otherwise, for as soon as the rug had been lifted, he was on his hands and knees, slowly crawling back and forth, his glass held steadily before him.

Minutes passed in this manner before he came to a stop six feet or so from the chair in which he had sat. He stretched himself full-length on the floor and pressed his face almost onto the 'boards, muttering under his breath.

"What is it, Holmes?" I asked when he gave no sign of rising. "Have you found something?"

Whatever it was, it captured my friend's attention, for he did not spare a glance in my direction, but instead reached for his notebook and pencil and, tearing out a page from the former and laying it flat on the floor, proceeded to rub the pencil gently back and forward over it. Only once he had succeeded in obtaining an impression of whatever had so captivated him did he rise and, brushing the begrimed knees of his trousers, favour me with his regard.

"This," was all he would say, pressing the piece of paper into my hand and crossing to the window, where he stood, staring at the street outside.

I held the paper up to the light but all I could see was a triangle of dots, one large and two smaller, standing out starkly against the grey pencilled background. What they were or what they signified, I could not say. I called over to Holmes to explain their significance and he, with a soft groan of irritation, stalked back across the room towards me.

"These three marks are tiny indentations in the floorboards, such as might be made by the placing of a tripod on that spot. The minute scratches around each indentation suggest that the tripod held something heavy, such as a photographic camera, and that the camera was used while in situ, causing a slight movement of the tripod feet."

Holmes's implication was clear. "You think that someone photographed Donaldson on the day he died?"

"I do. The police presumably failed to notice it at first, and once the death was ruled suicide they would have no reason to investigate more thoroughly. I assume that the rug was thrown in place by whoever inherited the house. The red in no way matches the green of the wallpaper, of course. Nobody with the taste to hang that splendid Cozens landscape would place it behind a door or allow the colours in a room to clash so horribly."

I was not convinced. "But why would anyone do such a thing?"

"Let me ask you another question in return," Holmes responded grimly. "Why would a man intending to end his own existence first leave his home in the early hours of the morning to buy a newspaper, and then not even open it, far less read it?"

"The newspaper found by his body was unopened? Obviously, he changed his mind about reading it, Holmes. In view of his state of mind at the time, that is surely not too peculiar a decision?"

Holmes was dismissive of my suggestion. "I think not, Watson. I can think of one other good reason for the presence of a newspaper and a camera with which to photograph it – to establish that an event occurred on a specific date."

"Why should the date matter? I'm sure that news of Donaldson's death was widely reported. The date of his death is not a secret."

Holmes shrugged as he began to pull the rug back into place. "To prove that the killer was with Donaldson on the day of his murder. I think that we can now safely say that the imposter and his fake Watson have more than deception on their consciences. For a reason that temporarily eludes me, they killed James

Donaldson – or forced him to kill himself."

I could not deny the logic of Holmes's words, and I had rarely known him to be wrong when he was so certain that he was right, but there remained a considerable distance between knowledge and proof. Holmes's theory, while plausible, contained no irrefutable evidence with which he might support it, and as yet we not only had neither the imposter nor his assistant in custody, we had never so much as laid eyes on either man!

Holmes, however, was unperturbed by my objections, and in fact seemed barely to register them. "I believe that further investigation into the good Pastor Hoffmann is now appropriate," he muttered. "There is more than murder here, far more…"

He stood for a good while, with his eyes closed in concentration and his long fingers clasped together. I had become used to Holmes's reflective moments over the years, and I spent the time admiring the painting, wondering what had so swiftly changed his mood. Whatever it was, it was evidently to remain a mystery for the moment, for even when Holmes snapped from his daze, it was only to ask me to stop at the police station and let Bullock know what we had discovered.

Without another word, he took one last look around the room, then turned smartly on his heel and left. I heard the front door open before I even realised he had finished with James Donaldson's house or could ask where he was going.

By the time I had made my way to the police station and left a note for the absent Bullock, then taken a cab to our hotel, it was mid-afternoon. Holmes was nowhere to be found, though on this occasion I was not overly concerned. Something had occurred to

Holmes at Donaldson's house, and though I could not imagine what that something was, it took no great genius to guess that he had gone to see Pastor Hoffmann once more.

So it was that, with nothing more pressing to do, I spent the hours before dinner reading and catching up on some notes, resting my increasingly painful leg, and waiting for Holmes's return. So comfortable was I, in fact, that I must have nodded off in my seat before the fire, only to waken as my notebook slipped from my lap and landed on the floor with a heavy thump. Groggily, I struggled to retrieve it, until a Good Samaritan, who happened to be passing by, bent down and picked it up for me. I pushed myself upright in order to thank the man, who was smartly if cheaply dressed, but to my astonishment, rather than moving on, he threw himself down in the seat opposite my own and ordered a brace of whisky and sodas from a passing waiter. The waiter looked at me for confirmation that this unexpected guest was welcome, and I nodded that he was.

It was Holmes, of course. In truth, he had not disguised himself to the extent he often had in the past. In addition to the shiny suit, he had added only glasses and a fair-haired wig. Other than that he was as always.

"Now that was very welcome!" he declared, finishing his drink and waving to the waiter for another. "I have spent the afternoon exchanging morality tales with Pastor Hoffmann's cook! Interminable cups of weak tea, earnest discussion of the cult of youth, and not so much as a single bowl of tobacco to be had! I have suffered in the cause today, Watson, let there be no doubt of that."

The wide smile on his face belied his words, however, and while he sipped at his second whisky, he recounted the tale of his afternoon to me.

"After I left you," he began, "I caught a cab to the pastor's home, intending to infiltrate the back stairs area and discover what I could from the staff about Hoffmann's employment of the pretender. Would you believe that I was actually about to pay the driver when I realised that, not only had I omitted to disguise myself in any way, but that in America I had no way of obtaining the materials needed to effect any of my usual concealments. Fortunately the cab driver was of similar build to myself and respectably dressed and, in exchange for my own trousers and jacket – plus a small financial inducement – was willing to carry out a trade."

"You swapped clothes with a cabman in the street?" I exclaimed.

"Of course not!" Holmes snapped. "I dressed inside the cab."

"And the glasses and wig? Are you about to tell me that you purchased those from an obliging, if short-sighted, bald man who happened to be passing?"

"Do you wish to hear what occurred, or would you prefer to continue your constant sarcasm?" my friend enquired caustically. "If you must know every detail, then know that I usually carry a hairpiece and glasses with me, for just such an eventuality. Often they are all that is required for a reasonable disguise. In this case, they combined with my new suit to create Mr David Taggart, knife sharpener to many of the better New York households.

"The maid who answered the back door showed me through to the kitchen where the cook was more than happy to take a break from her work and chat with a handy gent such as myself. Those were her words, not mine, I assure you, Watson! She poured us each a cup of tea and I, noting the temperance badge on her apron, took the opportunity to ingratiate myself by mentioning my own distaste for strong liquor. Unfortunately, such a gambit, while popular with the lady and successful in its own way, did necessitate the extended period of enervating conversation I mentioned earlier, from which

I struggled to extract a few nuggets of value to our investigation."

He drained his glass and lit a cigarette from my case, which I had placed on the table in front of him.

"You have no idea how good it is to feel tobacco in my lungs again, Watson! I have come up against some of the most vicious criminals England – the world! – has to offer, but I tell you now that three hours spent in the company of an abstemious, judgemental and puritanical colonial cook rivals any torture they might dream up. How the woman could talk, and to what little purpose!"

He shook his head in rueful remembrance, before continuing his tale.

"But discover a nugget or two I did. It seems that the charlatan using my name was a complete stranger to the household until he appeared at the front door one day several months ago, asking to see the master of the house. Clean and tidy, but seemed more used to entering by the back door, according to the cook, with a threadbare suit and polished but elderly shoes. Mr Isherwood, the somewhat sepulchral butler, would have closed the door in his face, in fact, were it not for a large envelope he held, which he said must be shown to the pastor immediately. 'A matter of life and death,' he is alleged to have said.

"Fearing the possibility of harm to his master, no matter how unlikely, Isherwood did as he was bidden and took the letter in to the pastor. What happened next was, in the words of my friend the cook, 'the loudest scream heard in this house,' before the pastor's study door was thrown open and the stranger, who had waited patiently in the hall, was invited to come upstairs at once. The two men remained cloistered together for over an hour, the pastor's voice raised in occasional anger, though what was discussed remains a mystery, for the door was bolted throughout and the good pastor did not call down to the kitchen for refreshments."

"And after they left the study? Did they seem friendly?"

"An excellent question, Watson. However, I cannot respond definitively, for cook was busy preparing dinner when the imposter left and was not present at their parting. Suffice to say, however, that they did not part as sworn enemies, for the man returned to the house three days later."

"Did he indeed!"

"And left not ten minutes afterwards, clutching a heavy carpet bag that he had not brought into the house with him."

"Containing something of value, you think? Payment for services rendered?" I asked.

"Payment of a sort, certainly," my friend replied. "But if a service was rendered, what was it? The man spoke to the pastor twice only, for a total of little over an hour."

A horrible thought had been forming in my head ever since Holmes had revealed the presence of a camera in Donaldson's home and now, as he expressed his puzzlement, I was emboldened to give voice to it. "Could your double be an assassin? A hired killer?"

"Because of the camera?" Holmes asked, with a frown. "You wonder whether he used the photograph of Donaldson on the day he died as proof of the efficacy of his work? That the imposter shot Donaldson, or forced him to shoot himself, and that Pastor Hoffmann then made use of his services in similar vein?"

"Exactly, Holmes!" I agreed enthusiastically. If I was slightly chastened by the fact that Holmes had clearly already considered the matter, that sensation was wholly ameliorated by his agreement with my hypothesis.

Or rather, *apparent* agreement, for no sooner had I spoken than he resumed his initial thought, which entirely clarified his own belief in the matter. "Of course he did not, Watson! If Hoffmann hired himself a killer, why then did the man present himself openly at the front door, rather than surreptitiously, as one might expect from a man engaged in such a profession? Why did Hoffmann not inform his butler that a visitor was expected? Why, for that matter, was Hoffmann heard to rail at the imposter? No, my double is no assassin…"

At that moment, Holmes's brow furrowed slightly and the fingers cradling his cigarette tightened sufficiently to bend it at an angle. His eyes, normally so piercing, became unfocused. "Not an assassin, no," he whispered, so quietly that I wondered if he even remembered I was present. "Something worse than that, in many ways. Less clean, certainly. Less honest. The newspaper in one pocket as he spoke to Donaldson, the revolver in the other. Secrets exposed, dredged up and displayed in the grey light. And the camera, too, with which to commemorate the occasion. In a long bag, perhaps, stored with the tripod." I had to lean close to catch these last few words, while Holmes allowed his cigarette to burn low, leaving a tower of ash behind which trembled and fell to the floor. "A dirty, cold business all round," he declared, and though he still spoke in an undertone, I could sense the fury in his voice. "Bloodless. Reptilian…"

Rarely had I heard Holmes speak in such a manner. In fact, the only other time I could recall was when we had stalked the blackmailer, Charles Augustus Milverton, not six months previously. Holmes's rage against the man he called the worst in London had been as fierce as it had been unexpected, and there was a flavour of that anger in his words now.

"You suspect blackmail?" I asked. I spoke loudly, hoping to snap Holmes from his brown study. The attempt was successful, and my friend blinked heavily and, in a voice rendered dull by dismay, agreed that he feared just such a crime.

"From the moment I heard that Pastor Hoffmann had been surprised by the imposter's arrival, I have suspected exactly that. A consulting detective – even a fake such as the man we seek – is *consulted*. He does not present himself at random doors and offer his services, in the manner of a salesman of mops and brushes! If that was not enough to raise my suspicions, there was also the matter of his entry into the household. Unless butlers are considerably less formidable in the Americas than in England, it is surprising how easily the imposter effected an entrance past Mr Isherwood. A glib tongue and a convincing manner are, you will agree, two of the key hallmarks of the successful blackmailer?"

"Undoubtedly, Holmes," I concurred, "but is that the sole basis for the accusation?"

"Not the sole, but the most telling. As you know, my methods are based in part on the observation of the overlooked, on examining the totality of a scene, with equal emphasis placed on the minutiae as on the glaringly obvious. Consider. The man was smartly but cheaply dressed, suggesting either a fortune on the wane or an attempt to present a respectable appearance. He initially bore bad news, hence Hoffmann's anguished cry on receipt of his envelope, but was swiftly able not only to calm his host, but also – after but one more brief visit – to turn pain into profit."

"You mean the carpetbag?" I asked. I was sure I could see a flaw in Holmes's reasoning, but equally sure that I had missed something self-evident. "But there's nothing to say that that contained a payment of any type and, even if it did, still less to suggest an illicit element to the transaction. For all we know, the pastor may simply have been settling an old debt. That would account for his unexpected arrival, his less than friendly welcome and his second visit – when Hoffmann, having had time to raise the necessary amount, was able to repay the debt in full."

I had known Holmes too long to feel entirely at ease as I settled back in my chair and lit a cigarette. Too often in the past I had been certain of one thing only to have Holmes demonstrate another to be true. This instance was to prove no different.

"Admirably hypothesised, my dear fellow!" Holmes exclaimed. "You have proposed a solution that is both elegant and convincing, and which – in the absence of fresh evidence – I cannot gainsay in any way. That said," he smiled roguishly, "I happen to know that Pastor Hoffmann barely waited until the imposter was in the street before calling for his carriage and following his erstwhile guest for some time."

"You mentioned nothing of this before!" I protested.

"It is a mistake to formulate a theory without all the evidence, Watson," he replied, still smiling. "Had you allowed me to complete the narrative of my visit to Hoffmann's kitchen, you would have heard cook describe to me the abominable mood in which the pastor returned home that day and the inexplicable change in his entire character since then. Below stairs knows nothing else of the affair, but my friendly cook was definitely troubled by the change in her master. 'Like a man lost,' she said. Mark my words, Watson – blackmail lies at the heart of this."

"If you are certain, then we must speak to the pastor again. That this villain was impersonating Sherlock Holmes is one thing, of interest to few people save ourselves, but if he is also using your name in pursuit of an actual crime, and a particularly vile one at that, then we must accelerate our efforts." I spoke with emotion, for, as much as Holmes, I too detested blackmail in all its insidious forms. Only the most repellent murders approached the sheer cruelty of the blackmailer in my opinion (which I knew Holmes shared), and if the imposter was involved in such a scheme, we had more reason than ever to put a stop to his activities. One bright point did occur to me, however: "At least this means that Inspector Bullock will be far more able to assist us. Impersonation may be outside his purview, but blackmail surely is not!"

By now Holmes had entirely shaken off his brief despondency. Still, he tutted to himself at the mention of Bullock's name and waved a hand dismissively in the air. "If Inspector Bullock had left well alone yesterday evening I would have been spared the discomfort of a night in his cells, and I might well have obtained a new avenue of investigation on the heels of Hans Piennar."

He brightened a little as he went on, "But you are quite correct, of course. The inspector is bound to be of more help as we move forward, and we do now have two strong areas of interest that we might profitably pursue. Piennar, for the moment, has eluded us, for I doubt he will reappear at his old lodgings. But there is no reason why we should not pay a more formal return visit to Pastor Hoffmann. Blackmail requires two informed parties, after all. Any information we can obtain directly from the victim cannot help but aid our cause."

I glanced up at the ornate clock that dominated the wall opposite me. It showed the time as a quarter after eight. "A task for tomorrow, Holmes," I said firmly. We had spoken for longer than I'd thought and the realisation of the relatively late hour had reminded me that I had yet to dine. I doubted that Holmes had eaten either, a theory that was swiftly confirmed as Holmes acquiesced to my suggestion. It had been a long day all round, and after I had chivvied him upstairs to change, I hurried across to the dining room to procure a table, before he had a chance to change his mind.

Chapter Twelve

The following day dawned bright and crisp, with a chill in the air that promised a cold winter to come. We had breakfasted early, and then I had gone for a stroll while Holmes surrounded himself with what seemed to be every newspaper in the country. By the time I returned, some forty minutes later, there were discarded sheets of paper scattered across Holmes's room, while the man himself sat in the middle, scissors in hand. A neat pile of articles, freshly cut from the 'papers, was stacked by his crossed legs.

"It is extraordinary just how much vital information slips by us, simply because local news is thought to be of no interest to the international citizen," he declared as soon as I stepped through the door. "*The Times* is not to be bettered for the biggest stories, of course, and our lesser English press do what they can with the more sensational end of the market, but we have nothing to compare with the Americans." As he spoke, he scouted amongst the discarded journals for one particular example, which he now held up. "See here, Watson. A body discovered in a locked bank vault in Des Moines, a train robbed at gunpoint in Arizona and a man convicted of selling Brooklyn Bridge to an Arab prince; all in the space of half a dozen pages of this single San Francisco newspaper!"

Clearly, a decent meal and a good night's sleep had entirely restored Holmes's equilibrium. He had even gone so far as to open one window, so that the smoke of his pipe did not, for once, obscure the entirety of the room. I took a seat and lit my own while he explained what he had in mind for us that day.

"Quite right, Watson – duty before pleasure," he said, reluctantly dropping the newspaper he held to the floor. "This morning we must attend to Pastor Hoffmann. If he is, as I suspect, in the grip of a blackmailer, then he must be made to tell us the name of his persecutor."

Easier said than done, of course, given the finale to Holmes's last meeting with the pastor. "And if he will not?" I asked.

"Then he must be made to!"

"As simple as that, eh, Holmes?" I said, but with a smile which he returned ruefully.

"Perhaps not quite so simple," he admitted, "but the pastor struck me as a man of much noise but little substance. A degree of carefully applied pressure should suffice to unlock his secrets."

A curious incident occurred as we descended from the hansom outside the pastor's residence. A young man, aged about twenty-five I should say, came up to us and tapped Holmes on the shoulder. He turned and the stranger stared at him intently for a few seconds, then swivelled on his heel and strode away. Not a word was said, nor was it possible to make out much of the young man's features, for he wore a low-brimmed hat and a heavy muffler, between which two items the majority of his face was obscured. Fearing a trap of some sort I made to move after the man, but Holmes laid a hand on my arm to hold me back and instead we stood and watched as he strode to the corner, then disappeared around it. When nothing else occurred, Holmes gave my arm a gentle tug and suggested we make our way to Pastor Hoffmann's front door. With no choice but to shrug off the peculiar confrontation, I did as Holmes had asked and gave the door a sharp knock.

Though this was my first visit to the house, there was no mistaking Isherwood, the butler, who stood in the open door before us, pale and thin, with bloodless eyes that protruded slightly from their sockets, the effect of Graves' disease or some other problem of the thyroid, I suspected. As Holmes presented his card, Isherwood gave no sign of recognition, but simply stepped to one side and invited us to wait in the hall while he checked that his master was at home to visitors.

Holmes immediately sat in one of a pair of matching chairs and closed his eyes in thought. With nothing better to do, I examined an over-literal depiction of the death of Lot's wife, done in oils. The small smile on Lot's face was disturbing, I thought, and I would have remarked on the fact to Holmes had Isherwood not chosen that moment to return and ask us to follow him to the pastor's study.

The study was also as Holmes had described it. A large fire, currently unlit but stacked with wood, took up one half of the wall opposite the door. Flanking it were two high-backed chairs covered in silver fabric, beside each of which sat a small wooden occasional table. A formidable desk of polished teak took up a large proportion of the rest of the room, save for the wall to our right as we entered, which was given over entirely to a splendid bookcase, crammed to the rafters with impressively bound volumes of church teachings. A Bible, laid open on a decorative plinth on one corner of the desk, was the only book in actual use that I could see, however.

The owner of the room sat in one of the chairs, staring up at us. My immediate impression was of an ascetic face – piercing eyes, thin lips and an aquiline nose – topped by grey hair. One foot tapped incessantly on the floor, which, combined with the purpling of his face as he viewed Holmes, convinced me that we were not likely to find a welcome here.

The first words he spoke confirmed my fears. "Your nerve astonishes me, Lestrade, truly it does!" he barked at Holmes, without so much as an acknowledgement of my presence. "Was the act of being tossed into the street like a bag of coal not enough to warn you off? Must I have my servants take cudgels to you, sir?"

Holmes was unperturbed, however. "You see," he said, turning to me with a small smile, "how the English and American men of religion differ? I believe I can say, with no fear of contradiction, that I have never heard an English clergyman threaten to have a man cudgelled. Have you?"

"Very rarely," I said, entering into the spirit of the thing. "Even less tossed into the street like a bag of coal." I took a step closer and bent down in order to examine Hoffmann more closely. "Though I'd wager he has problems controlling his blood pressure."

The pastor spluttered in outrage, barely managing to force each word out before it was tripped up by its successor. "How dare... why, I should... what is to stop me..." he spat, seemingly unable to decide which sentence to complete and so failing to finish any at all. It was the small but audible chuckle from Holmes that was enough to push the man over the edge, however. I think, had he been on his feet, he would have struck my friend a serious blow. As he was seated, however, he reached across to a speaking tube pinned to the wall and, after blowing in it, prepared to summon his servants.

Before he could do so, Holmes stepped in front of him and spoke a single sentence that caused Hoffmann to blanch and the tube to fall from his suddenly nerveless fingers.

"We know the secret with which you were blackmailed, Pastor Hoffmann," Holmes said gravely.

The next few moments were spent in silence punctuated by the nervous tapping of Hoffmann's foot on the floor. There could be no doubt now that blackmail lay at the heart of the duplicate's plans. One look at Hoffmann's terror-stricken face had been enough to convince me, and the next words he spoke served to confirm our suspicions in full.

"How did you find out? Did that swine Rawlins tell you?"

Rawlins was a name seemingly conjured from thin air, but Holmes gave no indication that he was at all surprised to hear it.

"Is that how he named himself to you?" he asked, helping himself to a cigarette from a silver case on the desk and taking the chair opposite Hoffmann. I considered taking the chair behind the desk for myself, but it was too far from the others, so I contented myself with leaning against the desk itself while Holmes continued. "He called himself Sherlock Holmes when he spoke to us."

"Do you think me an idiot, sir?" Hoffmann asked, with some spirit. I could see the panic abating in his eyes and was reminded that this was no fool before me. We would have to tread warily, for Hoffmann could prove himself a troublesome enemy if we made him so. "He called himself that when he first arrived at my door, but I knew the name already and almost had him chased from the premises. Sherlock Holmes is a famous detective from London, you see. It was not the worst lie ever, in fairness, for I had heard that the fellow was taking a busman's holiday in New York, but from our first meeting I knew this miscreant was not he. I am an excellent judge of character, you see, sir. As a minister I must be, and I pride myself that I can tell an imposter from the genuine article every time. So tell me, Inspector Lestrade, what exactly did Noah Rawlins – for yes, that is how he then named himself – tell you about me?"

"Only that you had been indiscreet and that he had been able to extract what he would from you in return for his silence."

"You have him in your cells then, Inspector?" A little of Hoffmann's newly recovered confidence ebbed away again as he worried what else Rawlins (how good to have a name for the imposter, at last!) might tell us.

Holmes nodded. "We do. Incidentally, we have not – as yet – pried into the precise nature of your indiscretion. You are a pillar of the community, a moral force for good, and the city police with whom we are engaged would prefer that your name were not sullied in the gutter press. The last thing anyone wants," he concluded with a cold smile, "is to see a headline concerning yourself in the *Examiner*."

I feared for Hoffmann's health as the colour drained once more from his cheeks, and he nodded vigorously in response to Holmes's words. "For which I thank you from the bottom of my heart, Inspector, and so do my poor, sickly wife and my three children. I have been a weak man, I admit it, but I should consider it a great boon if you would allow me to exculpate my sin by providing what assistance I can."

Hoffmann's honeyed words strongly reminded me of those of

a particularly unctuous Home Counties minister I had once heard preaching to a Scottish battalion in Afghanistan. They dripped with insincerity and a false humility that bordered on arrogance. The minister, I recalled with a smile, had been chased from camp by two kilt-wearing Highland privates after he suggested that Edinburgh was the only civilised city in Scotland.

Such a fate seemed unlikely to befall Hoffmann, even though he was currently in some fear for his reputation. "You smile at my predicament, sir?" he asked, with a minor note of bile in his voice that I suspected was closer to his usual character than the role of penitent sinner. "I do not believe we have been introduced."

Holmes, in the guise of Inspector Lestrade, swept between us and made introductions of a sort, describing me as Constable James King of the London constabulary. "King is an invaluable aid to me," he assured our host. "Why, without him I wonder that I could even recall what I was doing last week!"

Hoffmann laughed weakly, desperate to remain in the good graces of "Inspector Lestrade", but Holmes kept him off-balance and more easily controlled by immediately playing the martinet. "You find this funny?" he snapped. "I find such an attitude astonishing, I must say. At home in England, I can assure you that a man in your position, facing professional ruin and personal disgrace, would not be laughing. Far from it. No, he would be begging anyone who might be able to help him to do so, with all possible speed." He stopped suddenly and leaned forward in his chair until he was as close to Hoffmann as he could be. "If you want us to help you, Pastor," he whispered fiercely, "now would be an excellent time for you to tell us everything you know about Mr Rawlins."

The trap was sprung and closed around Hoffmann as though it

were made of Sheffield steel. Holmes had reduced him to a shadow of himself, terrified that his secret, whatever it might be, would come out unless "Lestrade" saved him.

"What can I tell you?" he asked, finally.

Holmes was implacable. "Everything," he said.

Without a word, Hoffmann rose from his seat and crossed to the study door, which he locked. He crossed the room to his desk, where he dropped the key. He then opened a drawer, removed a bottle of whisky and three glasses. He sat heavily in his desk chair, poured the drinks and pushed two in the direction of Holmes and myself.

"This is purely for the shock, Inspector," he said defensively as he drained his glass and quickly poured himself another. Holmes turned his seat around to face the desk, and I did the same with the one recently vacated by Hoffmann. Only once we were all settled did Hoffmann tell his tale.

"If you are to understand the complete story, Inspector, it is necessary for me to begin, not last year, but more than three decades in the past, when I was a young man. I was ambitious, keen to make my mark on the world, as all ambitious young men are. You must understand that at that time I was not a religious man, far less a man of God, and I was prone to idleness, as the ungodly often are. I tell you plainly: I had it in mind to make my fortune with as little effort as possible, and with as little regard for the law as was strictly necessary.

"At that time I was acquainted with a youth named George Appo. Much later, he was a famed pickpocket and green goods man, but then he was just another half-starved orphan willing to do anything for a dime. As for me, I came from a decent family, but I warmed to the life that George led. It seemed to me to be filled with romance and danger, with no man to answer to and no boss but oneself."

He shook his head and topped up his glass, before politely offering us the bottle. When we refused, he shrugged his shoulders and carefully placed it back on the desk before continuing.

"I was a fool, obviously. I see that now. But at the time I believed myself to be the very best and most fortunate of men, lording it in the Five Points with George, drinking and gambling and, now and again, helping him in the less skilful of his crimes. I learned to pick a pocket, though never to George's standard, and how to cut the strap on a purse without the owner even being aware it had gone. I know how to cut a circle of glass from a window and what to place over the glass to prevent any noise being made."

"And it is this you fear may be exposed?" I asked.

"No, Constable, it is not. If a few purloined coins were the sole sin I had to place one day at the feet of my Saviour, I should fear no man, but would admit to my failing and do penance for all such minor transgressions, made thirty years ago as they were." He swallowed, and his eyes fell to the glass in his hand. He whisked the liquid round for a moment, then took a sip before speaking again.

"I took the life of a fellow man, Inspector Lestrade, though I assure you that it was done in self-defence. That's the truth, sir. I swear it on this Bible," he said, reaching across the desk and placing an unsteady hand on the open book, "and if you can do anything to aid me and keep this story from the newspapers, you will have my undying gratitude."

"You killed someone?" Holmes asked. "Who?"

"Another man. A nobody. A filthy, drunken sot." The whisky had not soothed Hoffmann, but roused his less manly emotions, awakening an unattractive self-pity in him. "His face had plagued me for years, but why should it?" he went on, pitifully. "Why should I be punished for the sins of Appo and the others? I didn't want to dip his pocket, but George said I was scared and I couldn't have that, could I? Couldn't look weak in front of them all, not when I was already at a disadvantage, not being from the Points like the rest.

"And he'd been an easy mark. Drunk as a lord, he was, and already fallen once or twice from the look of him. Dirt down the front of his shirt and on the knees of his trousers, and his evening jacket ripped at the elbow. 'But he's got money,' George said. 'Why don't you go and take it off him?' George said. 'He's only going to lose it in any case,' he said. And he would have done, that's the truth of it. Fellow like him staggering through the Points at night, well – he was bound to get turned over. And George was right enough – better we relieve him of his wallet, gentle like, and him on his way none the wiser, than one of the other gangs should come across him and stab him through the heart first, just to be on the safe side."

I could not fail to notice that the pastor's speech had changed over the course of his recital. Even the words he now used spoke of a less well-educated man. He had been drinking, of course, but he was certainly not drunk. Yet I was certain that his accent had coarsened in the last few minutes.

"You can hardly be blamed, then," Holmes said. "Egged on by your friends, and hoping to prevent a greater tragedy in the unfortunate man's near future."

"Exactly, Inspector!" Hoffmann seized on Holmes's words as a drowning man clings to a lifebelt. "Rawlins would not have that, though. He has a black, black heart, that man. He laid all the blame at my feet – and said that others would too. He wasn't wrong there.

I've got enemies, you know, gentlemen. Jealous of the respect due to me on account of my calling, envious of my good name!"

"We understand, Pastor," Holmes interjected smoothly, cutting off Hoffmann before he could expand further on this theme. "But you were talking of your youth, were you not? Of the crime that Rawlins said would ruin you?"

Hoffmann stared at Holmes for a long moment in silence, his lips pressed together. But then – whether from the recollection that only "Lestrade" could save his reputation, or from a genuine desire to unburden himself, I could not say – his face softened a little and he recommenced his narrative.

"Yes, yes, quite right, Inspector. Justice is rarely well served by anger, no matter how justified. But as I said, I would have let the drunken gent pass by unmolested, had George Appo and his cronies not forced me to it."

"You were concealed?" Holmes asked.

"In a dirty side alley, little more than an alcove. The smell of refuse caught my throat and I coughed, and the others laughed because they were more used to breathing in that putrid stench. Appo and I were to the front, the others behind us, but we were all in shadow. The street was empty; I saw nobody when I first popped my head out to rid myself of the worst of the smell. Then I saw this old man making his way towards us. He could barely walk, swaying from side to side, singing something to himself."

"And then?"

"I told George there was someone coming. He winked, like he did, and said we should lift his clip, but I wasn't keen and said so. Said I had a bad feeling about it. And I did. Like a premonition. George might have gone for that, being part-Chinese or something like he was, but the others were laughing, saying I was soft – too soft to hang with them, and maybe I'd be better off back home with Mama, reading my scripture. Doing my needlework, Jimmy Donaldson says, and everyone – even George – laughed loudly at that, so loud I wonder that the drunk didn't hear it.

"Well, I wasn't having that, not from that little weasel, so I stepped out into the street just when the drunk walks up. 'Stop right there, old man,' I said. But he didn't – just kept on walking, like I wasn't even there. Walked right past me, he did, with this little smile on his face, like he knew something I didn't. And then Jimmy came up from the shadows and pushed something in my hand, said that the drunk thinks I'm nothing, that I'm invisible. That I'm worthless..."

I glanced across at Holmes as Hoffmann's voice died away. I had seen subjects of hypnosis mentally travel back to earlier points in their lives and act as though they were actually there, but this was the first time I had seen someone act in such a manner of their own volition. Earlier I had thought that Hoffmann's voice had undergone a change, becoming less refined under the influence of whisky and fear, but this was altogether different. It was as though he had retreated to the point at which his future hung in the balance, the second in which his actions dictated the life he was destined to lead. Holmes, though, never took his eyes from Hoffmann.

"Did you kill him?" Holmes's voice was soft, but his eyes were like shards of grey slate.

"Yes, I did that. I took the knife Jimmy gave me and stabbed the old man in the neck. He sagged, like he was broken. I wasn't expecting that, so instead of holding onto him I let him fall to the ground. He was at my feet, curled up a little, with the knife still in him. We didn't rob him, even. We just ran. George was angry. He said I was kicked out of the gang, that I couldn't come back, that

I didn't belong in the Points. Even though I did what they wanted me to do."

"And so you returned home? You resumed your studies and, with no distractions, did well."

"Yes."

"The police never linked you to the murder?"

"No. They never arrested anyone for it."

"You got on with your life. You went to college, obtained your degree, trained to be a minister. You bought this fine house, in a good area of town, and forgot all about the crimes of a young man you barely recognised as yourself…"

"NO!"

Hoffmann's shout was loud enough to bring a knock on the study door, but the pastor speedily sent the concerned servant on his way.

"No," he repeated, more calmly this time, once he heard the servant's footsteps retreat down the hall outside. "I never forgot. I never saw Appo or the others again after that night, but I was always certain that I'd pay for what I did, one day. Sin exacts a price from us all in the end, Inspector."

"A wage, surely, Pastor," Holmes replied. "For the wages of sin are death, are they not? And James Donaldson has been paid in full."

I had missed the connection between Jimmy Donaldson and the murder victim whose home we had so recently visited, but Holmes had not. He sat now, his hands flat on the desk in front of him, his body hunched forward, all but willing Hoffmann to provide some useful information. His cigarette was forgotten, burnt down in a crystal ashtray in front of him, just as Hoffmann's third whisky lay untouched before him. This was Holmes at his best, using his powerful mind as a weapon to tease out the truth. Hoffmann had no chance.

"I read about Donaldson's death when it happened. I wondered if that successful man could have grown from the vicious boy I knew. No more than that, though. A casual interest born out of a shared name. I dismissed it from my mind almost at once and did not think about him again until Isherwood appeared at this very door with an envelope in his hand.

"Had Rawlins merely sent up a card, I believe I would have had him thrown out, but the envelope was to hand, and curiosity has always been a particular vice of mine, so I had Isherwood instruct my visitor to wait while I examined the contents. Inside was a letter, signed by Donaldson, which laid out in detail the events I have just described to you, though with a bias which suggested cold-blooded murder on my part. That was bad enough, but the rest…"

"The photographs, you mean?"

With a sob, Hoffmann buried his head in his hands. I had been fascinated to see that once he began to speak of current events, both his diction and vocabulary improved. I made a mental note to discuss the matter with Holmes later; perhaps there was something in the new ideas just beginning to come out of Europe regarding the link between lost memories and mental health.

After a minute or so, Hoffmann muttered an embarrassed apology and composed himself once more. "Yes, there were four of them. Photographs of James Donaldson, taken on the day of his death."

"You recognised Donaldson?" asked Holmes.

"I did, but even if I had not, the images would have sufficed to cause me grave concern and alarm. The first photograph was of Rawlins and Donaldson standing beside one another, holding a newspaper between them, with the date visible. The date, I was to discover, was that of Donaldson's death.

"In the second photograph, Donaldson was sitting on a chair with a sheet of paper held directly in front of him. I remember wondering if this was some form of foolish practical joke and, had it not been for the letter that accompanied the photographs, might have treated them so. Donaldson was holding the paper at an unnatural angle, but though I could not read it clearly, I had no doubt that it was the same letter I now held in my hand. The penultimate photograph though..."

Again, Hoffmann shuddered. His voice cracked as he repeated the words, then rushed to a painful conclusion. "The penultimate photograph showed Donaldson holding a gun in his mouth, Inspector, and the last, his dead body half in the chair, half on the floor, with Rawlins crouched beside him, the devil!"

"A devil, indeed, to kill a man merely for pleasure," Holmes remarked.

"For pleasure, Inspector?" The confusion on Hoffmann's face was unmistakable. "I would not have said that Rawlins looked as though he were taking pleasure in the act. The reverse, in fact. But surely Donaldson was killed in order to demonstrate that Rawlins would stop at nothing. Or perhaps as a hint regarding my own fate, should I fail to co-operate."

"Which is it then, Pastor? A demonstration or a hint? Rawlins must have told you, or there would be little purpose in either!"

"A demonstration. No, it was a promise. Or, no..."

"Come now, Pastor. These intentions you have suggested are identical in purpose, and thus you cannot claim distinction for them. But still, there is something here that I am missing. The blackmailer's stratagem with Donaldson was too wasteful. There must be something more in it, a greater goal served by this sacrifice..."

As Holmes's voice faded to a contemplative murmur, Hoffmann rounded on him in panic-driven and, I suspected, largely feigned outrage. "Wasteful, sir? You speak of waste when the topic is a man's very existence? You are a cold one, Inspector Lestrade, to casually consider the life of another human soul so small a trifle."

I expected Holmes to bridle at the accusation, but in this I underestimated my friend, who was just as capable of recognising feigned emotion as I. "Far from it, Pastor. I do the work that I do, in part at least, to prevent the loss of human souls. Yet I would also call Donaldson's death wasteful. As the fable tells us, one is unwise to kill the goose that lays the golden egg, and what else was Donaldson? He paid Rawlins's fee and told nobody, so far as we know. He would have continued to pay, too, rather than face scandal and ruin. His suicide makes that eminently clear. Even so, he was discarded in an especially bloody manner, thereby putting an end to his usefulness as a source of income."

He paused, distracted by a passing thought.

"A warning, yes – that I can see. *Pay what I ask or you will end your days like James Donaldson.* There is a utility in that which would be some compensation for the potential loss of Donaldson's future financial contributions. Though, did you not fear that you would be similarly treated, in the end?"

Only a fool could fail to notice the beads of sweat on Hoffmann's forehead or the way in which he blanched once again. I had no doubt that Holmes was on the right path. Rawlins had desired something more from Hoffmann than money, and the brutal staging of Donaldson's suicide had been intended to encourage his compliance.

But for all his fear, Hoffmann would say no more. Holmes asked for Rawlins's address, but it seemed that the pastor had reached the limit of his co-operation and he shook his head and looked away. I suspected that he retained the foolish hope that the entire affair would somehow fade away and his own involvement would be forgotten should Rawlins escape our grasp. Frustrated, Holmes stood up abruptly, as if the presence of Hoffmann offended him, grabbed the door key from the desk and swept from the room. The pastor silently watched him leave, ashen-faced.

I too was desirous of fresh air, far from the individual who sat before me. I paused only long enough to tell Hoffmann that we could be reached via Inspector Bullock, then followed my friend out of the study.

Chapter Thirteen

A s was so often my experience with Sherlock Holmes, any expectations I might have had about my friend's state of mind were confounded the second I caught up with him outside. I had expected to find him dissatisfied, rendered morose by his failure to elicit the name of the next victim from Hoffmann and despondent by the pastor's lack of moral fibre.

I was pleasantly surprised to discover that Holmes was far from downhearted. On the contrary, his mood was ebullient as he strode down the street, ignoring several cabs as they drove past.

"I feel the need to stretch my legs, Watson," he explained as he caught me glancing after one such rejected hansom. "I have too much energy to coop myself up in a cab – or to remain in the company of a man such as Pastor Hoffmann! And we have much to do, Watson, much to do!"

I was delighted to see Holmes in such splendid good humour, but at the same time I wondered what could possibly have engendered such an emotion in him. True, we had established that blackmail was taking place, and we had identified both the blackmailer and his mode of operation. But were we really any nearer to finding the imposter, even now that we had his name? And where were we to look next, in the absence of a fresh link in the blackmailer's chain, and with Hoffmann refusing to say where Rawlins now lived? I put both questions to Holmes.

"Nonsense!" he exclaimed. "We have the imposter's name – though it may, of course, be an alias, it does at least provide a further point of investigation – and that of his accomplice. Do not underestimate either of these things. More interestingly, however, we have a gap in the chronology of Mr Rawlins."

"A gap…"

"Pastor Hoffmann was the next victim after Donaldson. But the newspaper that Donaldson was holding was dated last February. How then can it be that the pastor only received a visit a few months since?"

I saw at once what Holmes meant. "An accident? It would be a simple matter to query local hospitals or check the newspapers. As you said yourself, the American press is extremely fond of such stories."

"An accident, Watson? Is that your answer to everything?" He laughed gleefully and clapped a hand on my shoulder. "Come now, ask yourself this. Where do criminals routinely find themselves that would mean they would not be seen around town for an extended period of time?"

Put like that, the answer was obvious. "Prison," I said.

For confirmation, all it took was a telegram to Bullock, asking him to check the records for Rawlins's presence in an American jail.

Though it took him most of the day, by the time we made our way to the station later that evening, he had obtained the information we required and handed over a thin manila folder, inside which were the arrest and imprisonment records of one Noah Rawlins.

Both documents made for interesting reading. Rawlins had been arrested for public drunkenness and assault of a police officer ten months previously and had been sentenced to six months' imprisonment in the colourfully named Sing Sing. The arrest record also contained a description of Rawlins and a photograph of a dark-skinned, slim man of about thirty, with hair combed back to reveal a widow's peak. Most intriguingly of all, the record listed an address for Rawlins – in a street in one of the better areas of the island, according to Bullock, who offered to take us there at our convenience.

Holmes consulted his pocket watch. "Too late for today, but shall we say ten a.m. in the morning?" Holmes was always happiest when he believed he was making progress in a case, and today was the most content I had seen him in weeks.

So many of the better type of New York home looked identical to my English eyes that I would not have been able to tell Rawlins's address from Hoffmann's if my life depended upon it. A wide street lined with trees, and a succession of high, narrow buildings welcomed us the next day as our cab turned the corner and deposited us near what Bullock assured us was the address on the arrest sheet.

The inspector led the way, as befitted his far more official status. He took the steps up to the door two at a time and, once we had caught up with him, rapped on it heavily with the back of his hand.

To everyone's surprise, the door swung open.

The interior was dim and cool. A postcard hand-addressed to "The Occupant" lay on the floor at our feet. Bullock picked it up and glanced at the picture of Buckingham Palace on the front, then flipped it over, but the reverse was blank. He handed the card to Holmes, who nodded as if confirming something to himself, before slipping it in a pocket.

The hallway extended the length of the house, with two doors leading from it on either side and a stairway that provided access to the first floor at its end. I had expected the house to be set up along similar lines to Mrs van Raalte's, with each door leading to one set of living quarters or other, but in fact it seemed that the entire building either belonged to Rawlins or was rented by him. Clearly, blackmail was a lucrative business. I was about to remark on this fact to Holmes when Bullock's cry from the first room on the left sent us running towards him.

The reason for his alarm was plain. Lying on the floor on his back was a man dressed only in pyjamas and dressing gown. A ragged hole in the fabric marked the point where, I had no doubt, a bullet had struck the dead man in the shoulder. That he was definitely dead required no great medical knowledge, however, for as I rolled him over, it was clear that a second bullet had struck the man under the chin, passing up through his mouth, and exited via the back of his skull. A gun lay near his feet, though it would require a more thorough examination before anyone could say whether it was the murder weapon or the dead man's own gun (assuming the two were not one and the same).

Holmes waited for me to conclude this briefest of exams, before moving into the place I had just vacated. He examined the corpse and its clothing for at least ten minutes, moving it as little as possible, but ensuring that he investigated every seam, pocket and stitch. I noticed that he spent some time on the fingernails, then examined the back of the corpse's neck and ears in detail, though he gave no indication as to his particular interest in those areas. Finally, he rose to his feet.

"So much for Mr Rawlins," he declared. "A single grey, almost silver, hair that does not belong to his head, but other than that, few points of interest."

I should have realised that the dead man and our quarry were one and the same. Now that Holmes had pushed his hair back, the resemblance to his police photo was clear, though I thought him a trifle tanned to play Holmes. I was struck by how insignificant he looked in death, in contrast to the mayhem he had caused in life. I wondered if Holmes felt the same, for an odd expression crossed his face as he looked up to ask Bullock to check the other rooms in the house, to make sure we were alone.

"Are you feeling quite well, Holmes?" I asked, as soon as Bullock had left the room.

Holmes's dismissive shrug was, I thought, as eloquent a response as I was likely to get. But in this I was wrong. Holmes was never likely to become the sort of man who speaks easily about his feelings, but on this occasion, he chose to explain himself a little.

"It is most peculiar, Watson. I know that I should feel a terrible rancour towards this man, who impersonated me for his own gain and rendered my name no more than a brand to be emblazoned on any handy shingle. He is certainly a blackmailer and possibly a murderer, to boot. And yet, I feel a curious and most unexpected sense of kinship for a creature, no matter how low in morals, who for a time was Sherlock Holmes." He smiled self-consciously in my direction and busied himself with closing the staring eyes of the dead man. "A foolish notion, of course," he concluded, as he pulled out his magnifying glass and commenced a minute investigation of the carpet beneath a shabby dressing table that stood, incongruously, in one corner of the room, where it took advantage of the natural light streaming through the window.

Rather than stand around watching Holmes, I made my way upstairs. The first floor mirrored that of the ground, with three doors on the left-hand side. I could hear Bullock in the nearest room, so I moved to the second door, which lay ajar. Inside was a small dressing room, with little space for furniture, excepting a large wardrobe with a mirror inset in its door that took up the entirety of the far wall. A chair and an ornate, if not actually gaudy, free-standing ashtray were the only other objects in the room. I sat and took note of the brands of cigarette in the ashtray, then carefully opened the wardrobe, with my hand gripping the revolver in my pocket, lest Rawlins's killer should leap out like some pantomime villain. Needless to say, no such event transpired, and I was able to examine the interior at my leisure.

In fact, there was not a great deal to examine. A collection of decent suits and reasonably expensive shirts hung on a rail. Directly beneath them two drawers contained a selection of ties and undergarments, respectively, tidily folded away. The drawers on the other side were almost empty, a single sock and a discarded cufflink their sole contents. I carefully searched the suits, and was disappointed in the first two, but I had better fortune with the third jacket. Crushed in the breast pocket was a much-folded piece of paper, which I fished out with some difficulty. I spread it out against the wall – and gave a small cry of horror as I realised I held a photograph of a corpse in my hand. From Hoffmann's description, this was undoubtedly the final image he had been shown, with Rawlins gloating over the body of James Donaldson.

Without delay, I hung the jacket back on the rail and was about to return to Holmes with the photograph when my eyes fell on a shoehorn hanging from the inside of the cupboard door. Where there is a shoehorn there are invariably shoes, and kneeling down I discovered a pair of brown brogues had been tucked neatly away.

The shoes were of good quality and appeared almost new, with few scuff marks to be seen on the leather. I turned them over to check the bottoms for wear and, to my surprise, two heavy objects fell into my hand. The first was a watch with a black leather strap. Though I was no expert, it seemed of solid manufacture. On the back were scratched the initials "HP". The second item was of equivalent quality – a gold money clip holding a bundle of hundred-dollar bills. I quickly pushed the shoes back in place and hurried downstairs to Holmes with my discoveries.

Bullock had already returned, bearing treasure of his own. As I approached, he and Holmes had their heads bent over a selection of documents, which they spread across a table. I recognised one of these as a British passport sheet, much like the one I had locked away in the safe at our hotel, and the others were of the same type, though not from the same country. I recognised stamps and flags from half a dozen European countries, plus another handful that, though strange to me, were obviously official papers of some sort.

"Most illuminating, Inspector," Holmes was saying as I took my place beside him and bent over the documents for a closer look. "This certainly renders our mute friend more interesting than was previously the case. Watson, what do you make of this?"

"Are they all passports?" I asked. "I know what a British passport looks like of course, and this one is the French equivalent, this one Dutch, but I cannot place many of the others."

"Yes, yes, Watson, that much at least is so obvious as to require no explanation, but there is another matter almost as plain which you have thus far wholly failed to identify."

Nettled by Holmes's dismissive words, I picked up each of the documents in turn and examined it in minute detail. I took some over to the window, where I angled them in the light, hoping thereby to illuminate a hidden message or the light scratches made by a pencil pressing through from another sheet placed above this one. I ran my fingers over others, searching for an inconsistency in the paper or the mark of a carefully concealed repair. I even held each sheet to my nose and sniffed, in case a perfume still clung to them. In each case I was forced to conclude that this was simply a collection of passports. Interesting in itself but of no greater fascination than that. I said as much to Holmes.

"At times, Watson, I wonder if perhaps you do not mock me when you look and look but do not see. Your observations contrive to miss the most vital fact to be drawn from even the most cursory of examinations."

He reached over and picked up the nearest sheet. "Height: six foot four. Hair: grey. Eyes: blue. Weight: one hundred and ninety-six pounds. Distinguishing marks: scar on left cheek." Pulling two more sheets from the pile, he read, "Height: six foot four. Hair: grey/brown. Weight: two hundred pounds. Three-inch scar across left cheek. And this one – height and weight the same as the first, thin scar on left cheek. And so on."

Holmes dropped the papers back on the table and indicated the entirety with a wave of his hand. "Each of these passports has been issued to the same man, Watson! A different name on each one, I grant you, but there can be no doubt that they refer to the same person."

"And that person is not the man now lying before us, Doctor,"

Bullock interjected. "At most he's five foot ten and wouldn't make two hundred pounds if he were soaking wet!"

There was no denying the truth of Bullock's statement. Nor could there be much doubt that the owner of the passports was the mute accomplice we had failed to apprehend in the Five Points. Holmes, however, was far ahead of me.

"The passports belong to Hans Piennar, of course. The descriptions match our knowledge of the man, and to whom else could they conceivably belong?"

"And then there's this," Bullock added, pointing to a small group of objects which I had failed to notice. A half-full ashtray, a fountain pen and some blank paper, and a well-used set of playing cards lay on the table, alongside a small notebook, which lay open at a pencil sketch of a man half-turned away, his face obscured. Although it was impossible to tell who the subject might be, I was struck by the oddest feeling that I knew the image itself, though I could not place it. I flipped through the book, which was full of such drawings, of the same figure in a variety of poses. On one page only did his face appear, and as soon as it did, I realised where else I had seen such sketches.

"*The Strand!* These are some of the illustrations that the editor prints alongside my narratives of our adventures together!"

"Exactly, Watson!" Holmes was triumphant. "Copies of *The Strand* illustrations of myself with, you will see, notes on some pages describing certain perceived characteristics of mine. I think we may safely assume that these were intended as *aides memoire* for the deceased. And done some time ago, at that."

Bullock was puzzled. "How can you be so sure of that, Mr Holmes?" he enquired.

"That these sketches were created to help Rawlins perfect his role, or that they were done some time in the past?"

"Both, if you'd be so kind."

"Watson has been omitted from those images that once contained us both, meaning there was no requirement for his impersonation. Why draw one of us when both were once included, if the intention is not to highlight the mannerisms and look of the sole remaining subject?"

"And the timing?"

"You will note that the book always falls open at the same page, indicating that it has remained in that position for some time. Additionally, the left-hand page is faded compared to the right, where it has suffered long exposure to the sun. Both indicate that the book has sat undisturbed for an extended period. Judging by the degree of fading and the length of time the window in question receives direct sunlight, I would suggest a period of six months at least has passed. The lack of actual copies of *The Strand* furthermore leads me to conclude that these sketches were prepared in advance and were discarded as soon as Rawlins had learned of me all he needed."

As we pondered Holmes's words, I recalled the items I had discovered upstairs and showed them to my two companions.

"Phew!" Bullock whistled as he fanned the hundred-dollar notes from the money clip. "There must be three thousand dollars here!"

I carried out a quick calculation in my head. "Six hundred pounds, give or take."

It was an impressive sum. Evidently, blackmail had proven a lucrative trade.

Holmes, however, appeared already to have lost interest in both money clip and watch. He gave each a cursory glance, but his real attention was focused on the photograph I had come across.

"You found this within a jacket, you say?" he asked as he held the photograph to the light.

"Yes, in a wardrobe upstairs. Presumably, Rawlins – or even the mute – had extra copies that they kept handily on their person, should their use be required."

Holmes frowned and shook his head. "Which pocket did you find it in, precisely?"

"The breast pocket."

"And already folded as we see it now? One long fold down the centre and several smaller ones, cutting across at angles?"

"Yes. But I assume–"

"Never assume, Watson. Especially when there is no need." He laid the photograph out on the table before him. "The photograph is rectangular, and yet the longest fold bisects it along its short side and not, as would be more natural, across its centre lengthways. Notice too that it falls into that position without encouragement. It has been stored in such a fashion for some time, obviously. Like this."

So saying, he unbuttoned his jacket and slipped the folded photograph into the inside pocket.

"Someone has carried it around like this for several days."

Put so plainly, it was difficult to disagree with Holmes. I did, however, raise one minor objection.

"But what of the other folds? They are not so clear, perhaps, but still, they do require explanation."

Holmes shook his head sorrowfully. "Come now, Watson," he said, "you hardly need that explained."

When I did not reply, he shrugged expansively and crossed the room to Bullock, with the photograph still held in his hand.

"If you would allow me, Inspector," he said, turning the man by the elbow so that they stood face to face. He gripped the photograph by one corner and placed his other hand on Bullock's chest. "Now, pay close attention, Watson," he said, and pushed the photograph with considerable force into the breast pocket of Bullock's jacket. "This pocket is not the obvious place in which to store such an item, you would agree? It is too large, for one thing, and would be difficult to extract when the jacket is being worn. But it is the only pocket easily reached by another person standing in front of the wearer. It is a reasonable supposition, therefore, that someone returned it to Rawlins in such a manner, making new creases in the paper as he did so."

"But who?" I asked.

"Impossible to say at the moment. Any one of his victims. Clearly he had forgotten about its presence or it would have been consigned to the fire long since."

As Holmes spoke his eyes strayed to the fireplace, and he strode over to it; with a soft exclamation he dropped to his knees and lifted a scrap of paper from the ashes. Further scraps followed, to be laid carefully at his side.

"Another passport, Watson," Holmes crowed, "or a section of one, at least. And something else…"

He gestured for us to crouch down beside him, the better to examine the papers he had uncovered. The section of passport comprised only a thin, tapering slice of ragged paper, where a fold in the sheet had fortuitously kept a few lines from the flames. The familiar request for "assistance and protection" could just be made out, as well as the name of the holder, Noah Rawlins. Little else remained legible.

The "something else" Holmes had mentioned was less simple to identify. I fancied that it was a telegram of some sort, though not an English one, nor American. In fact, I struggled to see how the tiny handful of fragments Holmes had rescued could help us at all. Only three scraps contained more than a single letter, for one thing.

"'MES', 'DON' and 'OAT'," Bullock read aloud. "James Donaldson, presumably?"

"It must be!" I exulted. "But what of the 'OAT'?"

"Oath, perhaps?" Bullock shrugged his shoulders expansively. "What do you think, Mr Holmes?"

Holmes cast a distracted look in the inspector's general direction. "Nothing occurs to me at the moment," he said shortly, as he stirred the fragments with his finger, then dropped them into one of the small paper envelopes he habitually carried with him.

Without another word, he scuttled around the room, completing his search. At one point he dropped to his knees and crawled beneath a dressing table where he scraped something into another envelope. A moment later he leapt up and, bending low over the table top, ran a finger down the back, behind the mirror. He sniffed at whatever he had collected, nodded and wiped his finger on his handkerchief. After another minute or so of seemingly random examinations, he seemed to have concluded his investigation and beckoned us over.

"I believe time is of the essence, gentlemen, so if you will forgive me, we will move swiftly onto my analysis, leaving your own comments until after. The murder of Mr Rawlins was not an event I had foreseen and I fear that it presages a new and unknown player in this game. But let us not get ahead of ourselves. First, we must establish what we know for certain. To begin with, though Rawlins is dead, his mute compatriot remains at large – and was here very recently. Bullock informs me that there are two bedrooms upstairs, both recently slept in. The ashtray too contains two different brands of cigarette."

Inspector Bullock had been a policeman too long to allow this to pass unchallenged. "It is possible that Rawlins wasn't choosy about his cigarette brand and simply smoked those that were cheapest at the time."

Holmes dismissed his concerns with a tut of disapproval. "The two brands were also each smoked in a distinct manner; one type was stubbed out half-smoked every time, the other smoked so low that they must have risked burning the holder's fingers. No," he went on, "I am sure that the mute was here recently, that he and Rawlins shared this accommodation, and that the former is now on the run."

"The clothes in the wardrobe!" I exclaimed. I quickly explained about the half rack of suits and the empty drawers. "It is as though the mute removed his own possessions and left Rawlins's behind. Could he have killed him and fled?"

Holmes was non-committal. "Perhaps. But why should he want to? They were colleagues in a lucrative enterprise in which Rawlins was a valuable, even unique, element. Can you really picture an excessively tall mute playing the part of Sherlock Holmes?"

"He may have had no choice. Perhaps Rawlins attacked him, and the mute killed him in self-defence?"

"By shooting him in the back and then administering a *coup de grâce* beneath the chin? Come now, Watson, do concentrate." He picked up the revolver from the table and flipped open the cylinder. "Four bullets remain in the chambers. This was definitely the murder weapon."

"Why would the killer leave his weapon, though?" Bullock interjected.

"Hmm?" Holmes was turning the gun over in his hands and

seemed barely to hear the question. "The killer believed that it could not be traced back to him, of course."

"Aye, that's believable enough, Mr Holmes. And when do you calculate Rawlins was killed, Dr Watson?" Bullock's question was a pertinent one. Without the equipment needed for a proper autopsy, I could not be as precise as I might have liked, but there were certain indicators that allowed me to suggest a rough time.

"The corpse is in full rigor, and liver mortis has covered almost the whole of his torso. If you will allow me a moment..." I squatted by the body and pressed down on the purple discolouration that marred the majority of visible skin. As I expected, only by leaning nearly my entire weight on Rawlins's corpse was I able to make any difference to that colour. "Lack of blanching is consistent with a body dead for a minimum of eight hours and, I would hazard, a maximum of twelve."

"Indicating that death occurred in the early hours of this morning?"

"That would follow, yes."

"So, if the mute murdered his partner, why then did he leave all of his money behind? The watch has his initials on it, we may assume the clip was also his. A man who has a whole night in which to pack and make his escape would be a fool to leave three thousand dollars behind. Indeed, why leave any evidence of his presence at all? It is far more plausible that the mute, returning home in the early hours, discovered his colleague already dead and, in a panic, burned what incriminating evidence he could, threw his clothes in a suitcase and fled, with no thought to the money."

Holmes's logic was sound. But if the mute had not murdered Rawlins, then who had? An unpleasant thought occurred to me.

"There is another possibility. What if Rawlins was killed in the belief that he actually was Sherlock Holmes? Your own life could be in great danger."

"I did consider such a possibility," Holmes replied calmly. "But while I have more than one enemy who would revel in my demise at home in England, I think it most unlikely that there are any such in New York. What we must ask ourselves is not why Rawlins was killed, but why he was killed at this moment, just as we close in on him. Once we know that, then we can proceed to the more specific matter of why he was killed at all."

"And do you have any answer to that question, Mr Holmes?" Bullock asked.

"Not entirely, Inspector," Holmes responded. "Or rather, none in which I have any conviction. But it does seem a great coincidence, does it not, that Rawlins should die the very day on which we discover his name from Pastor Hoffmann?"

"You believe we were overheard, Holmes?" I recalled the strange man who had approached us outside Hoffmann's house. "Followed, even?"

"Mmm." Holmes was too distracted by his own thoughts to hear what I had said. "I should like you to return to the pastor's one last time, Watson. It is tiresome, I know, but it may be that something will strike you. You may recognise a servant, or identify a means by which we were perhaps overheard in Hoffmann's office, which, you will recall, was securely locked throughout our conversation."

"Of course, Holmes. I'll leave right away."

"As will I," Bullock added. "I must get back to the station and arrange for the late Mr Rawlins to be collected and transported to the morgue. But what of you, Mr Holmes? Where might I find you, in need?"

Holmes was already in motion, pulling on his gloves by the

door. "I have a couple of small errands to run, Inspector: a trip to the telegraph office, then on to your much-admired Public Library. After that, time allowing, I will catch up with Watson at the pastor's or, more probably, return to the hotel. Leave a message there and I will be sure to receive it."

He adjusted his hat and picked up his cane, then turned back to me as a last thought occurred to him. "Look for new servants, Watson, those employed in the last six months. And ask where that speaking tube connects."

With that, he threw open the door and was gone.

Chapter Fourteen

My return visit to Pastor Hoffmann's home had proven frustrating. Having already upset their master once, I was conscious of a wariness amongst the servants as Isherwood escorted me not to Hoffmann's study, as before, but to an airy upstairs drawing room, where I was left to my own devices. The room was sparsely but well furnished, but there was no sign of a newspaper or periodical with which I might while away my wait. A handsome set of Shakespeare's plays were displayed behind the glass of an elegant bookcase, but a lock prevented my examining them more closely, leaving a whisky decanter and soda siphon the only available amusement. I poured myself a small drink and stood by the window, watching traffic in the street outside. Almost an hour passed in such a manner – straining my patience to near breaking – before I decided that good manners could only be maintained for a finite length of time. I strode to the door and wrenched it open, intending to demand an audience with Hoffmann immediately.

The drama of the moment was spoiled somewhat by the complete absence of onlookers outside. I looked along the corridor in both directions, but there was not a soul in sight to whom I might complain or from whom I might request direction. I might have stood there for another hour, feeling increasingly foolish, had a disturbance downstairs not caught my attention and led me to the banister overlooking the front entrance.

From my position, I had a clear view of the front door. Isherwood stood with his back to me, evidently preventing some unseen figure in the street outside from gaining access to the house. I heard him say that his master was not at home – which I hoped was simply a polite fiction intended to discourage the unwanted caller, else my own time had been utterly wasted – followed by a heated response as the unwelcome guest shouldered past Hoffmann's cadaverous butler and into the hallway. I had only a moment to stare at the unfolding scene before recognising Sherlock Holmes as the intruder, just as he registered my presence upstairs and shouted a greeting.

"Just the fellow I was looking for!"

With Isherwood trailing in his wake, he bounded up the stairs towards me. Up close, it was clear he had hurried here. His face was flushed and he panted with exertion as he approached. His voice, however, was as strong as ever as he glanced through the still-open door of the drawing room, then led me by the elbow inside, though not before shouting down to Isherwood that he would expect to speak to the pastor in the very near future.

As soon as the drawing room door was closed and Holmes was certain we could not be overheard, he invited me to be seated, while he lit a cigarillo and prepared to explain his unexpected presence.

"I have a great deal to tell you, Watson, for I have uncovered several points of interest in a very short period of time. First of all, after you departed, Bullock announced he would return to the station to arrange for Rawlins's body to be collected and, as I was travelling in the same direction, we shared a carriage part of the way. The inspector still had the revolver that was used to kill Rawlins in his pocket and while we were talking he pulled it out in order to remove the four remaining bullets from the chambers. The patterning on the stock happened to catch the light, and I was able to see that it was not entirely decorative. There were initials formed from the winding lines, spelling out 'HZC'."

My incomprehension must have been readily apparent, for Holmes hurried to expand.

"You have not heard the name of Henry Craggs before?" he asked. "I confess it was unfamiliar to me, too, though the case in which he is involved is not. Indeed, you yourself first brought that crime to my attention. You recall the newspaper you purchased when first we arrived? The article on a young socialite shot in the street, and her fiancé the prime suspect for the killing? That man is Henry Zachary Craggs. The police have been searching for him since the lady – Millicent Crane, by name – was slain, but not caught so much as a glimpse of him. But this is his gun, I am sure of it."

As an explanation it left much to be desired, and I own that I was almost as confused as before. "How then did it make its way to Rawlins's residence? What has Inspector Bullock to say on the matter?"

"He described it, if I recall correctly, as their first real progress since Miss Crane was killed. As to the other matter, I cannot say, for the moment. It is a fascinating conundrum, though, is it not?"

"It would seem so, certainly," I allowed. "You said that you had a great deal to tell me though? What else have you discovered in the mere two hours we have been apart?"

At this, Holmes's face fell. "I have acted like a fool, Watson," he admitted with a furrowed brow.

"An utter fool," he repeated and struck his hand on the wall in anger. "Remind me of this moment when next you feel I have become too cock-sure of myself. Rub this idiocy of mine in my face, should I ever give you the impression that I believe I know all there is to know. Sherlock Holmes is not infallible, and I would do well to remember that."

"Are you going to tell me what makes you such a fool, Holmes, or am I expected to guess?" It was never helpful to encourage Holmes in these moments of theatrical self-doubt; better by far to force him to explain himself, as proved to be the case on this occasion.

"After leaving Bullock with the gun at the station, I was left in the carriage with little to occupy my mind, save the list the inspector supplied that I had stuffed in my jacket pocket. You recall it – the list of all Rawlins's known clients? In re-reading it, I hoped that one or other name would leap out at me. If the mute did not kill Rawlins, then we must perforce construct a new narrative in which a furious former client – a victim of Rawlins's vile blackmailing business – decided to take his revenge on the man who tormented him, and so shot him dead. It was my belief that an examination of those very victims would, at the absolute minimum, allow us to narrow down our cast of potential murderers."

"And that has not proved to be the case?"

"Far from it, Watson! I have managed to rule out half a dozen people on the grounds they have alibis for last night and early this morning."

"In which case, what has prompted this bout of self-flagellation?"

Holmes made a pained face at my description of his activities.

"An unpleasant and inaccurate image, Watson. I say I have been a fool because I have. Inspector Bullock saw it, and even said so to me, but I failed to listen. It is only with the list before me that I recollected his words and realised what I had missed."

"Enough riddles, Holmes! What did you miss? What did Bullock say?"

"He said that one wealthy New York socialite is very much like another."

"And? That hardly qualifies as one of the great observations of our times, Holmes."

"But think of the implications, Watson. It is true that all socialites *are* much like one another – and unlikely to spare a glance for the Rawlins who first arrived in New York. So how did he identify his victims and ingratiate himself with them? Even if he had somehow stumbled across a single misdemeanour, that still does not explain how he so quickly identified the person he blackmailed next."

"Obviously you know the answers to these questions, Holmes. For once, might we not avoid the tortuous process of teasing that information from you?"

Holmes shrugged. "Society in New York is a small and enclosed world after all – like a series of overlapping circles, in which individuals come together in clubs, societies and numerous other social gatherings. In such a claustrophobic society, there is plenty of scope for people to discover one another's darkest secrets. I believe that just as Donaldson provided the name of Hoffmann, so Hoffmann in his turn supplied Rawlins with his next victim!"

Holmes's excitement was palpable and, as is often the way with such things, I found myself becoming more positive simply by being in his company. I quickly explained the situation I found myself in vis-à-vis meeting Pastor Hoffmann, and the hour-long delay to which I had been subjected. In return, he explained that he had rushed to the pastor's house as soon as he had recognised Hoffmann's potential new role in Rawlins's operation.

"I cannot help but think that everything we have seen so far is linked in some way. Pastor Hoffmann may have information that will shed light not just on the murder of Rawlins, but also on that of Miss Millicent Crane." He flicked the remnants of his cigar into the fire, favouring me with a small smile as he did so. "But time is short, and I would prefer not to have to explain myself more often than is needed. Shall we find the pastor, Watson?"

With that, he swept out of the room, already bellowing for Isherwood. There were few things, I reflected, strong enough to withstand Holmes in the full flow of an investigation.

Within five minutes, we were ensconced in Hoffmann's study once more, with the pastor glaring at us over the desk. There was no doubt that the passage of a full day had emboldened him, and the man who now coldly asked why we troubled him a third time more closely resembled the arrogant bully we had first encountered than the troubled man we had left the previous day. Even when Holmes attempted to wrong-foot him by asking, without preamble, about Henry Craggs, Hoffmann did not flinch, but continued – as he had since we first entered the room – to claim that we were wasting our time on a wild goose chase, that he had paid Rawlins, and had hoped never to hear his name again.

If my patience was wearing thin, Holmes remained utterly calm.

"Very well, let us put Mr Craggs to one side and concentrate on other areas of enquiry with which you may have more familiarity. You say that you did not follow Rawlins in your carriage after meeting with him in your study earlier this year? On the second occasion, when he left with a bag full of your money..."

"Exactly so, Inspector, as I have now told you several times. I paid the sum demanded and wished only to place the matter far behind me!"

Holmes nodded, as though Hoffmann had confirmed some important point. "Which is entirely understandable, of course."

Across the table, I thought I saw Hoffmann's shoulders relax a little and a more natural colour return to his face. If he thought that he had weathered the worst Holmes had to throw at him, however, he was soon to be disabused of that notion.

"One thing does still puzzle me, however. I wonder if you could help me with it?"

Hoffmann, his confidence rapidly returning, sensed no trap and murmured graciously that he would be happy to assist in any way possible.

"My query is this," said Holmes. "There was no need for Rawlins to kill Donaldson if all he desired from you was money. You would pay willingly to avoid a scandal – and he knew it. But he wanted something else in addition, did he not? Money in exchange for keeping your terrible secret, certainly – but the death of Mr Donaldson? That is a poor fit for such a scheme. Rawlins wanted something else from you, and used Donaldson's fate as a terrible warning?"

It was as though Holmes had struck Hoffmann a heavy blow. He sagged in his chair, his eyes darting from Holmes's face to my own, and back again.

"Yes," he said finally, in little more than a whisper. "There was more. There was a second letter, which Rawlins carried in his coat pocket. He showed it to me when I had him brought upstairs, after I had seen the photographs. It was a suicide note… written by Donaldson, which explained that he had been instructed to take his own life. The note was short, Lestrade, and failed to say what hold Rawlins had over him. Even so, there was no denying that Donaldson had been terrified enough to kill himself at the behest of the man who now stood before me in my study. And now that man wished... he wished..."

"He wished you to provide him with a new victim."

Holmes's words brought Hoffmann to a sudden halt. He flinched and stared across the desk at Holmes with what I can only describe as dread. "Yes," he sighed, "a new victim."

Even forewarned as I was, the leap from Donaldson's suicide note to Holmes's apparently accurate assertion was one I followed only with difficulty. Fortunately, a more comprehensive explanation was swiftly forthcoming.

"You appear perplexed, Watson," my friend said, cocking an amused eyebrow. "And yet my reasoning is straightforward enough. Why should Rawlins dispose of Donaldson, a man of substantial means, only to move on to the pastor, a man – and you will forgive me for saying this, I hope – of far lesser financial standing? The only logical conclusion to draw is that Donaldson was but the first link in a chain, an example with which to encourage others yet to fall into Rawlins's snare, who might prove less amenable to blackmail. And just as Donaldson handed the pastor's name to Rawlins, so he in his turn would be expected to provide a further link, another soul to be bled dry by Rawlins's infernal business." He turned his attention back to Hoffmann. "That is the way of it, is it not, Pastor?"

Hoffmann nodded and ran his tongue across his lips. "He said that people confided in their minister, even those dark secrets they would tell nobody else. And he said that if I did not pass on at least one of those secrets, he would go straight to the police and ruin me. How could I let that happen?" he asked plaintively. "I have responsibilities to my parishioners. Without me, who would guide my flock, not to mention the shock many would feel to their very faith, to see their minister brought so low?"

I knew that Holmes would usually give the benefit of the doubt to anyone who had fallen prey to a blackmailer, but the self-serving nature of Hoffmann's words was enough to eradicate any sympathy I felt for him. I could see Holmes frowning from the corner of my eye, and I knew that he too found Hoffmann wholly unsympathetic. His next words confirmed it.

"Be that as it may, Pastor, the fact remains that, in order to save yourself from public disgrace, you sacrificed another. Hardly the most Christian of actions."

Hoffmann began to protest, but I believe he could see the anger in Holmes's eyes and chose instead to forego whatever excuse had been on his tongue. "We will agree to disagree then, Inspector," he muttered bitterly.

Holmes, however, gave him no quarter. "Our disagreement will not make you any less wrong, Pastor. But that is of vanishingly small interest at the moment. You have still not answered my question – though, in truth, I ask more for my friend's sake than my own. *I* already know the answer. Even so, I ask again – did Rawlins demand you betray someone else into his clutches before he would allow you to go free?"

Miserably, Hoffmann nodded.

"And the name of this poor unfortunate?" Holmes snapped.

"That I will not tell you, Inspector Lestrade. Perhaps I have done wrong, but if I have I will not exacerbate the offence by inviting the police to involve themselves in his business. The gentleman in question has been visited by Mr Rawlins, has been shown the true meaning of terror and has paid the price of his indiscretion, just as I have. There is nothing to be served by raking the matter up afresh, or by involving you and your colleagues in his affairs."

There was cold fury in Holmes's eyes as he placed his hands on the desk and leaned in towards Hoffmann. "I should tell you now, Pastor, that my name is not Lestrade, and I am not a policeman, though I do work with them. My name is Sherlock Holmes. I believe you were kind enough to say that you had heard of me? Then you know that I am a consulting detective, and have doubtless additionally surmised that I am in the United States working on a case with my colleague here, Dr Watson. There is no reason, therefore, why you should not divulge the name to me. But you will not, will you? Instead you will remain in silence, protecting yourself at all costs. For I'd wager that whoever it was that you betrayed to Rawlins, he is unaware that you are his Judas. That, and no other, is the real reason for your refusal to speak, is it not?"

Hoffmann covered his face with his hands. Holmes repeated the question, and waited patiently for an answer. It quickly became clear, however, that he waited in vain. Hoffmann was a broken man.

In the end, Holmes rose to his feet and, above the sound of sobbing, addressed himself to the pastor. "I believe that answers all of our questions. The New York Police Department thanks you for your patience and assistance, as do Scotland Yard and myself. I do not think we shall have cause to trouble you again regarding this matter."

He moved towards the door, apparently keen to depart, but as he stood in the doorway, he turned back to Hoffmann and loudly asked a final question.

"Oh, I almost forgot," he said, "I have one last question. Your speaking tube – to where exactly does it connect?"

The question was sufficiently out of the blue that Hoffmann broke off his lamentations long enough to look up at Holmes as though he had taken leave of his senses. "Speaking tube? Where does it connect to?"

He stared uncomprehendingly for a moment or two, then collected himself enough to answer. "To the servants' hall. Downstairs. The other end is on the wall in an alcove off the kitchen."

"Splendid! Watson, give me two minutes to reach the other end of this tube, then stand here by the fireplace and speak for a minute or so, on a topic of your choice."

With that, he departed the room, leaving Hoffmann and myself in an awkward silence. I could think of no way to make Holmes's behaviour seem any less eccentric, so, in the absence of anything else to do, I took up position by the fireplace and, for the next minute and a half, recited a Burns poem I had learned at school.

I broke off as Holmes reappeared in the doorway, pleasure plain on his face.

"Weel done. 'Cutty-sark', indeed, Watson!" he exclaimed. "Pastor, one final matter, if I may?"

Hoffmann gave no reply beyond an indifferent shrug, which Holmes decided to treat as agreement.

"Very good," he said. "Would you object if we paid the shortest of visits to the kitchen staff on our way out? I should like to satisfy my own curiosity, if you have no objection."

Once again, Hoffmann's only response was a fleeting movement of his shoulders.

"Thank you," he said, as he and I left the pastor's study. The sound of sobbing followed us as we made our way towards the stairs.

* * *

There was only one servant who interested Holmes. He was a pale-faced young man of about twenty, engaged a half year previously as a general footman and answering to the name Jonathan Eales.

Holmes began by asking him about the speaking tube.

"Tell me, Eales, how long have you known that you might eavesdrop on your master, simply by listening through the speaking tube that connects the servants' area with the pastor's study?"

I thought Eales would say nothing, but after some thought he shook his head. "I knew nothing of that sort, sir."

Holmes affected exaggerated surprise. "Really? You have never noticed? It is a most striking effect, you know. Why, I myself have spent the last few minutes suffering through the worst reading of 'Tam o' Shanter' known to man, every word carried via that tube to the kitchen. Now what have you to say to that?"

The smallest of shrugs was the only sign that Eales had even heard Holmes.

"You intend to say nothing, then? Very well, I shall speak for both of us. Do stop me if you believe I have misrepresented anything. One, you are newly employed at Pastor Hoffmann's, the only new employee for several years. That is fact. Two, you are in the habit of listening in to your master's conversations via the speaking tube. That, I grant you, is conjecture, but conjecture with strong evidence at its back. Three, you made a little extra money recently by passing a name and address you had so overheard to an interested party, leading to the commission of a murder. *That* is cause for hanging." His brow furrowed with concern as he laid a hand on the youngster's shoulder. "Tell us what you know, Eales, and in return we will do all we can to intercede on your behalf with the police."

"You can't prove anything!" The words tumbled angrily out of the young man's mouth and were then bitten off as he retreated once more into dumb silence.

"Quite correct, though poorly expressed. We can prove nothing at the moment, but rest assured, that will not always be the case. And as soon as we *can* prove your complicity in the murder, any help we can give you will disappear."

"Come now, lad, help yourself." I added what weight I could to Holmes's plea, but if the words either of us spoke had an effect on Eales, he kept it close to his chest and would not be convinced.

"I'm saying nothing," he muttered, not sullenly or resentfully, as one might expect from a youthful miscreant caught red-handed, but almost proudly.

"Perhaps not," said Holmes, obviously realising he would get no information from Eales for the moment. "But that may not always be the case." He picked up his hat and gloves from the table on which he had dropped them. "Rest assured, Eales. We will be back."

In truth, there was little we could do to him. We would give his name to Inspector Bullock and, with luck, Bullock would arrange someone to watch him, but if he would not talk, all we had was supposition and conjecture.

"If we cannot convince Hoffmann to divulge the friend he sacrificed," he mused as we looked for a cab, "nor Eales to tell us to whom he spoke, then we must look elsewhere for a further avenue of investigation."

"You have something in mind, Holmes?"

"I do." Holmes shrugged on his jacket and ran a finger down the list of names in front of him. "If Rawlins's earlier victims remain a closed book to us, perhaps the last may prove less obstructive."

His finger rested upon the name typed at the very bottom of the list. "I think we should pay Mrs Elizabeth Lockhart a second visit," he said.

Chapter Fifteen

I was beginning to feel that we were unwelcome at every door in New York. Mrs Lockhart would, I believe, have refused us entry altogether had we not asked Inspector Bullock to accompany us. It was only the sight of his police identification card that eventually convinced her to see us, though even then her reluctance was plain.

"I was under the impression, Inspector, that I had answered all of your colleagues' impertinent questions when last they chose to invade my home, and yet now I find myself once again wasting time in idle gossip."

"Not idle gossip, madam," Bullock assured her. "My colleagues simply wish to clarify a single matter that has come to light since last they called." He gestured to Holmes. "If you would be so good…"

Holmes wasted no time in prevarication. He stepped forward and, ignoring Mrs Lockhart's sniff of disapproval, laid out his theory regarding Noah Rawlins's blackmail operation.

"Which is why," he concluded, "we find ourselves at your door for a second time, Mrs Lockhart. It is improbable in the extreme that you would have invited this man to investigate a simple matter of domestic pilfering, in light of his activities with every other client to whom we have spoken. Will you not make a clean breast of it, and in doing so help bring a dangerous criminal to justice?"

Holmes had not mentioned Rawlins's death, allowing Mrs Lockhart to believe that the criminal we now sought was he. Any hope we might have had that such a deception might render the lady more forthcoming, in fear that the blackmailer might yet return to her door, proved fruitless, however.

"Do you call me a liar, sir?" she exclaimed. "Do you dare to say so?"

She reached for a hand bell on her desk, perhaps intent on summoning the butler. Before she could do so, however, Bullock leant over and laid a hand over it.

"That won't do, I'm afraid, Mrs Lockhart," he said firmly. "We know that the man you spoke to, the man to whom you paid a large sum of money, is no detective. Furthermore, we know that he has carried out a campaign of blackmail against the good people of this city, and that you are numbered amongst his victims. Finally, you should know that he lies dead in the city morgue as we speak, murdered most brutally by persons as yet unknown to us."

Mrs Lockhart's hand remained poised over the desk, then moved to her mouth as the full import of Bullock's words hit her.

"Murdered?"

"The same. Shot to death in his own home. And thus we fear for the safety of those recently in contact with him, such as yourself."

Still the lady hesitated. I could easily imagine the mental struggle in which she was engaged. With Rawlins dead, perhaps she really was in danger. She had, after all, spoken to him very recently, and had paid him a substantial sum of money. Though on the surface of it, that should not make her a target, she could not be sure, and the protection of the police could prove key to her own survival.

Alternatively, with Rawlins dead, it might be that she had no more worries at all. The one man who knew her secret had been silenced, and if she had betrayed a friend to save herself, then it was best if that fact too was allowed to die.

The path she would have chosen remained a mystery, however, for Bullock was taking no chances. "I should make it very clear, Mrs Lockhart, that if you are unwilling to help us in this case, I shall be left with no choice but to march you from this house to the police carriage outside, in handcuffs, charged with obstructing the police in their duties." There was no hint of a smile on his face as he concluded, "Your friends in society would make hay with such an occurrence, I imagine."

The threat of public humiliation was enough to break down her reserves, though not her spirit. She glared with real hatred at Bullock as she made her confession.

"It seems I have no choice but to acquiesce," she began. "I trust it fills you with pride to threaten and browbeat a lady so. But you are all English, of course, so I should expect no less."

She drew herself even more upright in her chair before going on, the contempt in her voice heavy and unrelenting. "You are quite correct. I did not engage Mr Holmes to catch some petty thief. I did not engage him at all, if truth be told. Instead, he presented himself at my door, as bold as you like, and asked – no, *demanded* – to speak to me. I would have sent him on his way, had he not asked the maid to present an envelope to me before I made any decision. I do not deny that I am a curious woman by nature and, seeing no harm in it, I agreed to look at the contents. Inside…"

She faltered at that point, closing her eyes as she relived that moment.

"The envelope contained disturbing, even horrific, images?" Holmes prodded gently. "There is no need to go into details, if you would just confirm that what I say is correct."

To everyone's surprise, however, Mrs Lockhart shook her head. "Images? Sketches and the like, you mean? No, nothing of that sort. Inside was a sheet of paper, typed on both sides, relating... events from my life that I am not willing to discuss with you, even if that means I am to be marched from my own home like a common burglar."

I did not doubt that she spoke the truth. She would go so far in order to save face and honour, but no further, and we had reached her limit. Fortunately, we were not interested in her old sins, but only in the new.

"You need not say what was in the envelope, Mrs Lockhart," Holmes replied before Bullock could say a word. "That is a matter most properly left between yourself and your God, but there is one question that I must insist you answer, or the inspector will have no alternative but to arrest you. Will you answer this one question?"

Without looking in his direction, Mrs Lockhart gave the smallest of nods. "If I can," she said.

"What name did you give the blackmailer in return for leaving you alone?"

Like Hoffmann before her, Mrs Lockhart's defiance evaporated in the face of this simple query. "Henry Craggs," she said simply. "I knew his parents, of course. Back in the 'sixties, this was, and the two of them were idiots even then. So much in love, everyone said. Too much in love, perhaps. Certainly too much in love to wait for a minister to bless their union. She gave herself to him, the harlot, and he, like the rake he was, accepted her gift. Of course, they rushed to get married before the babe in her belly began to show, and when Henry was born, seven months later, there was much talk of premature births. But I knew, and I remembered when everyone else chose to forget."

"And you told the blackmailer when he asked?" Bullock pressed.

"I did! I would do so again too, if the situation were the same. I could not allow the contents of that sheet of paper to get out. I told the man that the second I read it."

"Thus removing the need to terrify her into submission with photographs of Donaldson's death," Holmes murmured to me in an aside, as Bullock continued his interrogation.

"You know the sort of trouble Henry Craggs is now in, Mrs Lockhart?" The inspector had made no bones before of his dislike of Mrs Lockhart, but now he seemed almost bemused by her. "You know he is accused of the murder of his fiancée?"

"I do. Even less reason for me to regret naming him. The man is obviously as morally corrupt as his father before him!"

"Whether that is true or not, is a matter for a jury to decide, Mrs Lockhart. I would advise you to confine your answers to matters germane to Inspector Bullock's questions, rather than wandering off in flights of self-justifying fancy." It was rare – indeed, almost unknown – for Holmes to extend any discourtesy to a lady, but he had evidently come to the conclusion that there was nothing to be gained by further pandering to our hostess. The two of them glared at each other, neither of them blinking, until Mrs Lockhart shifted her eyes away.

"Now," Holmes continued, "I would be grateful if you would tell us exactly what the blackmailer said when you offered him Mr Craggs like a sacrificial lamb."

In lieu of a direct reply, Mrs Lockhart turned to Bullock and addressed her remarks to him. "Do you imagine, Inspector, that a criminal takes his victim into his confidence regarding his future plans? He does not, I assure you. The sole thing he said to me was to thank me for being so helpful."

"A polite blackmailer," Holmes smiled, "that makes a pleasant change. But did he say nothing else? He gave no hint of his future plans?"

Mrs Lockhart was icy in her disdain. "None, sir. I would have said so, if he had. Now, if you will excuse me, I have a great deal to do and no time to waste explaining myself any further."

She had committed no crime, though her behaviour had been reprehensible, and so we had no choice but to bid her good day and make our way back outside onto the street. Bullock signalled for the police carriage, which had parked some distance down the road, and, while we awaited its arrival, quizzed Holmes.

"So, did you believe her, Mr Holmes?"

"That Rawlins told her nothing of his plans? Certainly. I asked the question from a desire to be thorough, and nothing else. Criminals do not, in my experience, regale their victims with the details of their schemes, else they would soon be captured. No, Mrs Lockhart told us all she knew, I'm sure."

"So where to next? We appear to have a growing number of corpses and fewer and fewer suspects."

I had been considering that very fact, and wondered if an earlier, rejected suggestion of mine might not find more favour now.

"Were we perhaps too quick to dismiss Algy Hinton from our thoughts?" I asked nobody in particular. Holmes had declared the love-lorn drunkard too short and unfit to move Mrs van Raalte's body, but I could not forget the venom in his diary as he wrote of Rawlins, and no physical prowess was required to fire a gun. "Perhaps he believed a genuine assignation had taken place between Mrs van Raalte and Rawlins and, in a drunken rage, struck her down? Later, he tracked down Rawlins – the man he blamed for many of the ills in his life – and shot him. He may have had assistance in disposing of Mrs van Raalte's body," I went on quickly, before Holmes could object, warming to my theme. "A handcart, an old blanket and a willing assistant are all he would have needed."

Holmes considered my theory for barely a moment before dismissing it completely. "'An angel in earthly form' and 'a veritable saviour' were the phrases Mr Hinton used to describe the lady, were they not? You met the late Mrs van Raalte, Watson. Did she strike you as especially angelic? A woman of many sterling qualities, I'm sure, but not one who would generally be compared to the seraphim, you would agree? Such a comparison would occur only to a man in love – and a man in love would never leave the body of his beloved in a stinking hovel, even if he had killed her in an unthinking and brutish frenzy."

Put like that, it did seem unlikely. I admitted as much as the police carriage pulled up alongside the pavement, and I would have said more on the subject had another two-wheeler not come round the corner at that moment, halting directly alongside us.

The newcomer's horse was lathered in sweat. The uniformed figure of a young policeman leapt from the driver's seat and hurried across to Bullock.

"Inspector Bullock, sir, I have been sent to inform you that Mr Henry Craggs has surrendered himself at the station and is now in custody awaiting questioning by yourself in the matter of the murder of Miss Millicent Crane."

His message delivered, the youngster stood at attention while we exchanged surprised glances. Finally, Holmes broke the silence.

"It would seem that your presence at least is required, Bullock. I hope you have no objection to Watson and myself accompanying you?"

Without waiting for a reply, he pulled himself up and into our carriage, where he sat, eager to be off.

Chapter Sixteen

H enry Craggs was not at all as I had expected. The brief
newspaper reports I had read, and the various descriptions
of his situation we had encountered, had led me to expect a
frivolous man, madly and foolishly in love. Instead, the figure
that presented itself at the police station was that of a man in his
late thirties, a fraction over six feet tall, who held himself with a
proud military bearing. The first flecks of dark silver peppered
his hair and neatly trimmed beard and matched the grey of his
eyes. I saw little sign that this was a man who had been on the
run for weeks; a slight reddening of the whites of the eyes and a
general paleness were likely caused by his recent lifestyle, but
beyond that he could easily have stepped directly from the Army
List. I felt instinctively that this was a man to be trusted.

Holmes too seemed to warm to him at once. As soon as Craggs
entered Bullock's office, Holmes offered our visitor a cigarette and
extended our condolences for his recent tragic loss.

"Thank you, sir. That is something I have rarely heard these past weeks." Craggs's voice was quiet but not timid. Bullock's character sketch had described a man of great self-assurance, as befitted a former army officer and self-made millionaire, but in many such men that assurance could shade into arrogance. Not so with Henry Craggs. Clearly control in everything was a quality he treasured.

Only when he spoke of his late fiancée did his resolve falter, affording us a glimpse of the inner man. "Millicent – Miss Crane – was a wonderful woman, everything a man could hope for in a wife. She was more than that to me, however. She was my greatest friend, also. Gladly would I have given my life for hers."

There was no danger of such a man descending into unmanly tears, but I fancied I heard the slightest of cracks in his voice as he described his betrothed, and his hand shook a fraction as he raised a match to his cigarette.

Under cover of lighting my pipe, I glanced over at Holmes, but for all our years of comradeship, I could no more read the look on his face at that moment than I could a statue's. His fingers were steepled beneath his chin, his eyes half-closed, and the merest hint of a smile played around his mouth.

"You are not here to confess." It was a statement, not a question.

"Not in the way you mean, no. I am here, in the main, because you continue to waste your time chasing me, rather than the guilty parties. I have done no wrong and no harm, least of all to Miss Crane, and would have you direct your investigation towards those who have. My fiancée has been killed, yet no man rots in your cells for the killing, nor does a rope beckon the killer to his end."

Craggs had an old-fashioned way of speaking, but his tone was as measured as his subject was grave.

"That is true, sir, but you must know that you have taken a grave risk in presenting yourself to us. Unless you can provide proof–" Bullock began, but Craggs was not finished.

"If you will forgive the interruption, Inspector, might I be granted a brief indulgence, the better to tell the whole of my story? I promise you, it will be worth the time you expend."

With that, he fell silent and stood before us, apparently willing to wait as long as it took to be granted permission to continue.

"Pray, be seated and carry on, Mr Craggs," said Holmes. "We would all, I think, be fascinated to hear your tale."

Bullock growled his own approval and, my permission not being required it seemed, Craggs sat and commenced his version of recent, tragic events.

"I would first impress upon you, gentlemen, that I am not a man one might expect to find in regular correspondence with the police, nor am I a man to flinch in the face of justified punishment. I was a United States Army officer for ten years before resigning my commission and going into business, my trade that of a supplier of goods to that self-same military force. I prospered – and do still, in that respect at least – making me a wealthy man before I was yet forty.

"Still, I was not content. I felt an absence in my life – an absence nullified by the companionship of Miss Millicent Crane, whom I met at a charity ball a year past January, since which time we have been inseparable. We engaged to marry in March of this year. Much of this I am aware that you know, gentlemen, and I have no intention of wearying you with the recitation of old facts. That said, I think it best to place each of the actors in this tragedy in their correct setting before the villain of the piece enters."

"The villain?" Holmes's eyes snapped open.

"The same, Mr Holmes. Two villains, in fact. One tall, in a good suit and boots, his hair brushed back much as your own, his accent English, his manner ingratiating and friendly. The other taller still, his suit less expensive, his features rougher, his voice silent entirely. They approached me as I went about my business, a month or so since, and fell in alongside me as I walked."

"Was either man known to you?"

"I had seen neither before, to my knowledge, but there was no doubting that they had knowledge of me. 'Might we stroll with you a while, Mr Craggs?' the first man said. In truth, I expected this to be but the preamble to a request for a charitable donation of some sort, but I agreed to accompany them to a nearby coffee house."

"That proved not to be the case, I presume?" asked Holmes.

"To my grave misfortune, no indeed, though for a time I continued to labour under that misapprehension. We took our seats and ordered coffee, before the smaller man made formal introduction of himself and his silent colleague; Messrs Holmes and Watson, he said, then placed an envelope on the table.

"Spying it, my heart fell, I admit it. To be frank, my main thought was one of concern that overmuch time would be wasted; often before have I been obliged, for courtesy's sake, to examine reams of documents, recounting this horror or that tragedy, and each designed to encourage the maximum contribution from any prospective donor. I feared the envelope contained something very like.

"To my surprise, however, Mr Holmes did not make reference to the envelope. Far from it, in fact. Instead, he asked after my parents – an oddity in itself, for they have been dead these two decades past, and neither man before me seemed older than myself. 'I am afraid they have long since passed over,' I said, thinking perhaps that they merely made polite conversation, but

Holmes laughed, and said that I misunderstood. I began to wonder if I had misread the situation, then he said something that I cannot repeat now but that rendered me speechless. A secret, sirs, that I thought dead and buried, but which these men sought to resurrect. I hope that you will not require–"

"Yes, yes, you were born out of wedlock, Mr Craggs. Take it as read that we are aware of this fact and move on, I beg of you." I could scarcely believe my ears as Holmes interrupted with a painful lack of civility, but Craggs seemed relieved that he would not himself have to speak the words.

"That is indeed the case, sir – my parents did not marry until two months after my conception. My primary consideration then, as now, was to consider the impact such a revelation, made public, would have on those closest to me. As I said, my parents are dead, and so beyond any shame in this life, which left only Miss Crane to be taken into account.

"You do not know her, of course, but perhaps one of you might have read of Miss Millicent Crane in the newspapers? The Crane family are supreme philanthropists, and she no different to the others. She is… she *was* a good woman, gentlemen, wise beyond her years and with a heart so large it could encompass the world. I knew that she loved me for the man I am and that her love would not be lost due to the misjudgements of my parents."

"And society as a whole?" Holmes asked. "Did you not fear their opprobrium?"

"No, sir, I did not. I am a man of means, beholden to nobody. If society – to the extent such a thing is entirely monolithic – rejected me but Miss Crane did not – as I knew she would not – then I would remain in every way the victor and they the losers. I told my two would-be blackmailers this and would have stalked from the coffee shop at once had the taller man not grasped me by the collar while the other whispered in my ear. 'Twenty-four hours,' said he. 'I give you twenty-four hours to raise our ransom. And do not worry. We will collect it from your home, though rest assured there will be no tongues set wagging by that. Nobody will think it strange that Mr Sherlock Holmes and Dr Watson should come calling.' But I was having none such and told him so. No Craggs has ever stooped so low as to entertain the threats of the criminal classes."

Only then did his voice truly break, the last few words indistinct and coloured by pain and loss. "It is not as though I were not warned unmistakably, and swiftly also. With the taller man, Watson, holding me in place, the other pulled something from his coat and pushed it across the table to me. 'Look at it,' he said, for whatever it was, it had been folded in two, in order, I supposed, to better fit the coat pocket. It was a photograph of a room I did not recognise. The man before me, the smaller, the one who called himself Holmes, was there, crouched down by the body of a dead man, his eyes glassy and unseeing in death, the pistol that killed him in his own hand."

While he had been speaking, Craggs's head had fallen lower and lower until by the end his chin all but touched his chest. As he described one of the photographs seen by Hoffmann, and discovered by me at Rawlins's house, however, he raised it again and caught the gaze, in turn, of each of us.

"I was warned so clearly and yet remained deaf. I scorned the image before me, and the men who presented it, and told them that I would be with the police within the hour if I ever saw or heard from either of them again. Indeed, to my eternal regret, I went further still. I grasped that revolting photograph and stuffed it into the breast pocket of Holmes's jacket. What was I thinking?!"

It took Craggs a moment to compose himself, but we could all see that he was desperate to tell everything he knew. "I know what you are all wondering," he went on. "Why did I not take myself to the police immediately, for a murder had been committed? All I can say is that I had a wedding to plan and no wish to become involved in an unwholesome investigation. I shall regret that decision until my dying day."

Bullock had been writing down everything that was said, but laid down his pencil as Craggs's voice descended to a whisper, racked with grief.

"Is this the picture you were shown?" he asked quietly, passing him the photograph I had discovered in Rawlins's breast pocket.

The shudder that passed through Craggs was indication enough, but he also nodded before handing it back to Bullock.

"How did you–?" he began, but Holmes held up a hand for silence.

"You were describing your regret at not reporting the threats you received to the police?" Had anyone stopped by Bullock's office at that moment, he would have struggled to identify the man accused of a terrible murder, so much compassion was there in my friend Holmes's voice. Craggs evidently appreciated it, for he gave a nod of gratitude.

"Within the hour, Miss Crane was snatched from the street. Within two hours, I found myself in possession of a note from her kidnappers, to say that my debt was now double the sum previously intimated, and that Miss Crane's life relied upon my keeping a good distance from the police and delivering the money twenty-four hours hence."

"Which you did."

"Certainly, Inspector. What assurance did I have that the police would even be able to help? None. But I did have the certain assurance of the death of my beloved if I so much as spoke to you or any of your people. So it was that I took myself to the dirt road mentioned in the note and, once there, awaited my tormentors. The evening was dark and storm-racked, the moon hidden by clouds and the lighting thus non-existent. I have the inclement weather to thank for my life, I think, though I can muster little enthusiasm for that particular mercy."

"You intended to pay the ransom?"

"I did, sir. And I had not long to wait – a matter of a few minutes at most. They appeared on the road in front of me. Watson held a lamp up high, casting a weak, yellow light that penetrated the rain only enough to illumine the heads and faces of the two men – and my beloved Millicent. She appeared unharmed – I remember thanking God – and so I approached, a bag filled with banknotes under my arm. 'Let Miss Crane go free,' I said, but, 'No,' said he. 'Throw the bag to us,' he shouted, and I – having little choice but to obey – did so."

Craggs brought his hands up to his face. We three sat around him watching his shoulders shake, for several long minutes, before Holmes coughed softly.

"Did they shoot Miss Crane before they collected their money?" he asked.

Craggs's eye snapped in Holmes's direction. "How–?"

"We know Miss Crane is dead. We have your word that you did not kill her. For that to be true, she must have been killed at this moment – had she been returned to you and killed later, you would have begun your tale closer to that point. But I am not certain, hence the question."

Over the years of our acquaintance, I have seen many people

struggle to accept Holmes's idiosyncrasies. His alleged lack of courtesy has often been the cause, but Henry Craggs gave every indication that he welcomed Holmes's plain speaking.

"Yes, then," he said simply. "I threw the bag containing the ransom across to them. I can yet see it hitting the wet ground, water spraying up around it, then toppling over and the rain hammering down on its exposed side, the whole scene lit by one flickering lantern. It feels like a dream brought on by a fever to me now. The fear in Millicent's eyes as I looked at her and smiled, hoping to engender some degree of reassurance in her. And the shattering bellow of the pistol shot, so unexpected…"

Craggs was looking at nobody now. His eyes had lost focus as he recalled the events of that evil night, and if he spoke to anyone, he spoke to himself – or the woman he had failed to protect.

"She fell," he continued. "One moment she was before me, though indistinct, the next, gone entire. In my confusion, I could not locate her. I believe I shouted her name, but for a time thereafter, all is blurred and unclear. I think I might have pulled out the pistol I secreted on my person, and run towards the two men, but the attempt was a vain one, for a white light flashed around me and all I can bring to mind is a great pain in my head and the sensation that I was falling…

"When I came to, it was morning. I lay in a tangle of dense thorn bushes, at the base of the steep hill along which the dirt road runs. With no way to easily climb back to the road, and no confidence that I would find anything even if I did, I thought it best to make my way back into town, there to report the events of the previous night."

"You failed to do so, however, Mr Craggs. Why was that?" I had all but forgotten Bullock's presence, but he had evidently been listening closely. He laid his pencil and paper to one side and repeated the question. "Why did you not report this terrible assault to the authorities at once?"

"Do you really wonder, Inspector, or do you merely sport at my expense? Have you not also seen the newspaper reports from that day? The very first place I stopped, hoping to find directions to the nearest telegraph office, there was a newspaper on the counter. 'Millicent Crane slaughtered. Fiancé accused,' it read, so I bought a copy. My Millicent had been dumped like an old rug on some waste ground, with my calling card crushed in her hand. There were no other suspects."

I would not say that Bullock was completely convinced by Craggs's explanation, but he took his pencil back in hand and gestured that he was ready to hear more. Craggs obliged, in a voice a little stronger now that he had moved beyond the recollection of that awful murder.

"My choices were limited. The police believed me a killer, my likeness was in every newspaper, and I did not know who had divulged the family secret that had started the chain of events whose culmination was the death of my fiancée. At first, I contemplated the sin greater than any other, but my spirits rallied when I thought to engineer a meeting with an old and trusted servant who, I believed, would know me to be no murderer."

"A servant?" Bullock asked, underlining a line in his notebook.

"Yes, Edwin Thomas, who had been with my family since a boy. I saw him leave my house as I skulked in the vicinity, and I followed him until there was nobody else to be seen and I could be sure we would be unobserved. 'Thomas,' I said, and he walked at once straight across to me, with a great smile of relief on his face. 'We thought you lost,' said he, 'killed by the same brutes as murdered Miss Crane.' You cannot comprehend the joy, gentlemen," he said, with the first smile we had seen on his face since his arrival, "to find that you are believed when you thought that never to be the case again. I took Thomas in my arms as if we were brothers, then went with him to a nearby house belonging to a friend of his, and there we made our plans."

"And what were those plans?"

Holmes had said nothing since asking about the shooting of Millicent Crane, but now it seemed that Craggs had entered an area of his narrative in which he had an especial interest. He lit a fresh cigarette from the stub of his previous one and leaned forward in his chair, almost willing Craggs to reveal something that would aid us.

Craggs, I think, sensed the change in Holmes. Until that point he had addressed his remarks almost exclusively to the scribbling Inspector Bullock, but now he shifted in his seat and spoke directly to my companion.

"My sole desire was to hunt down and slay the filth who had killed my fiancée. With that foremost in my mind, I asked Thomas to choose a half dozen of his most trusted fellows from within my household, and set them adrift, to seek out those friends and acquaintances employed in homes where previously this Sherlock Holmes had been seen. 'Find me these two men,' I said to Thomas, 'and bring me to them, and I will make you rich beyond the dreams of avarice.' But 'No,' said he in return, 'I will do this because it is right.' And so it was, and has been since then."

"Until a few days ago."

"Why do you say so?"

"One of your spies spoke to a Mr Jonathan Eales, currently in the employ of Pastor Hoffmann, and he reported that he had overheard his master speaking to Sherlock Holmes. That is true, is it not?"

"It is."

"And with that information you were able to ascertain an address for your quarry?"

Craggs nodded. "The coachman was happy to tell Thomas's man where he had driven Hoffmann in exchange for a few coins."

"And you went to that address and there killed Noah Rawlins!"

Bullock's intervention pained Holmes in the extreme. I could tell from the way in which his lips pursed that he judged it ill-timed and likely to lead to this promising line of evidence being summarily closed off. However, Craggs seemed once more to appreciate straight talking from his interrogators and showed no sign of displeasure.

"Rawlins? That is Holmes's real name, then? Yes, I went there *to* kill him; that I will not deny. Him, and his Watson also. I have wandered New York in beggar's guise for all this time so that I might have the chance to end their miserable lives. But when I arrived, someone had already robbed me of my prize. Holmes… my pardon, Rawlins lay slain upon the floor."

"And the other? Was the other man present?"

"He was not, Inspector. Though I waited half an hour, he did not appear, and seeing a policeman pause on his beat outside the house, thought it best to withdraw for the time being."

"At which point, you vacated the premises, though you left your gun behind."

"My gun?"

"Your gun, Mr Craggs. The murder weapon. It was found by the body."

"But I have missed that gun since that terrible night. I had it in my hand when I ran towards Millicent's killer, I know that, but I cannot even say if I contrived to fire it before I was shot down."

He pulled back the hair above the left side of his face, exposing a long, partially healed line of raw flesh that ran from just above his ear into his hairline and back out again beneath his collar. "Another half inch to the left and I should have been killed outright. In light of this, you will forgive me if I did not keep an inventory of my weapons and their eventual destination."

For myself, I did not doubt his sincerity, but Bullock had the scent in his nostrils. "And a hair matching your own was found on the body of the dead man. How do you explain that?"

As it turned out, Craggs was not required to explain anything further, for Holmes, who had been listening to the exchange with increasing impatience, chose that moment to intervene. "He has already said that he found Rawlins dead. Do you imagine that he came to that conclusion from across the room, Bullock? Obviously he bent low over the body in order to check for signs of life. A hair must have transferred itself during that inspection."

"Thank you for that reminder, Mr Holmes," Bullock said, though he sounded anything but thankful.

"Mr *Holmes*?"

Evidently, I was not the only one to have forgotten that Craggs had yet to be introduced to either Holmes or myself. Before Bullock could do so, however, my friend extended a hand in greeting and, after confirming his own identity, presented me to the prisoner.

"I wish that I were a writer such as yourself, Dr Watson. Only thus might I hope to lay out the sheer joy I feel at the involvement of yourself and Mr Holmes in my case. When I made the decision to give myself up to the police, I did so in the knowledge that I had failed to avenge Miss Crane and would likely never be able to do so. But if the stories told of your powers are correct, perhaps justice may yet properly be served."

Contrary to his own claims, Holmes was as susceptible to flattery as the next man and, though I had the sense that he had never believed Craggs to be guilty, there was no doubting afterwards that he wished to do the man only good. I had long since learned never to judge a book by its cover, yet I too struggled to believe that the decent man who stood before me was a murderer. It may be that a similar loss in my own past coloured my judgement, but my feelings were what they were, and I felt Henry Craggs was innocent. Inspector Bullock, on the other hand, continued to press him.

"If you found Rawlins already dead, as you claim, who'd you imagine killed him? After all, so far as the police are aware, you were the only person who knew where he lived."

Even Bullock knew this not to be true – Pastor Hoffmann at a minimum was also privy to Rawlins's address – but before I could point this out, Craggs spoke up for himself – and in so doing, entirely changed our perspective on the case.

"You are forgetting Rawlins's accomplice, the man I knew as Watson. Who better placed to carry out the deed?"

Bullock was scathing. "Do you believe us to be fools? The mute had no reason of which we know to kill Rawlins – and if he had, he would hardly have left behind the money we found in the house."

Unexpectedly, rather than continue to protest his innocence, Craggs was obviously puzzled by Bullock's words. "What mute?" he asked.

Chapter Seventeen

୧

" I have often had cause to remark that it is a capital mistake to draw conclusions based on partial information. It is extremely galling to discover that I am as guilty as the next man of such an oversight."

Holmes prowled about the office, his hands busy lighting his pipe while his brain turned over Craggs's startling revelation. If he were to be believed, the man we had assumed to be entirely mute had spoken several times at the time of Miss Crane's murder. Indeed, Craggs claimed that he heard Rawlins address him as Peter just before the fatal shot was fired.

"Why should a man pretend to a mutism from which he does not, in actuality, suffer?" Holmes stabbed the bowl of his pipe in the air as he considered the question. "Either to ensure that he remains unobtrusive, or because his voice is distinctive in some way."

"I fancy that the few words I heard Peter say had a Germanic tint to them," Craggs contributed.

"*Piennar*, I think, Mr Craggs. Hans Piennar is the man's name, though it would be understandable enough to mix *Peter* and *Piennar* in the conditions under which you heard it said. We almost had him in the Five Points, but someone–" Holmes glared across at Bullock, who returned the look with an irritated one of his own, "–interfered, from the finest of motives, however, and so the chance was lost. I assume that neither you nor one of your men have seen Piennar since that terrible night?"

Craggs glanced from Holmes to Bullock, as if he had reached an important decision. "In coming here, I thought myself to be admitting defeat, but now some measure of hope has been rekindled in my breast by the presence of you, Mr Holmes, and you, Dr Watson. In view of that, it would be churlish of me to withhold the fact that I have had men following you for some time, since the name of Sherlock Holmes was first mentioned in Hoffmann's house. I had to discover if you were the man I sought, you see."

"The man who stood and stared at you, Holmes!" I cried, remembering the odd encounter outside Hoffmann's home.

"Of course, Watson," Holmes replied impatiently. "Who else did you imagine it might have been? I suspect Mr Craggs is also responsible for the gentleman you followed when first we arrived. One very minor mystery is solved, at least."

"All well and good, Mr Holmes, but we still have a murder case on our hands, and evidence which points directly to this man." Bullock's irritation had been growing throughout the course of the interrogation, and I wondered if this was to be the moment at which it boiled over completely, but quite the reverse proved to be true. "I admit that I'm as yet unconvinced as to your innocence, Mr Craggs, but I've heard enough just now to detain you in one of our empty offices, rather than in a cell, while we decide what is to be done next."

Whether Bullock entertained serious doubts regarding Craggs's guilt or merely felt some sympathy for his motives, I cannot say, but I will not pretend that I was not pleased to see him escorted from Bullock's office to another, much the same but with a far stouter lock.

I was not sure where I myself stood as regards Craggs's guilt or innocence. Had this been a trial in a court of law, I suspect I would be obliged to say that he had killed Rawlins, but equally I would have recommended to the judge that mercy be shown, for the provocation was beyond that which any man should be expected to endure. That Rawlins and Piennar between them had murdered Millicent Crane was, I think, certain beyond any reasonable doubt, and Bullock and Holmes agreed with me that this was the single element of the affair that took priority.

We none of us had eaten all day, and so Bullock took Holmes and myself to the small, dingy restaurant we had dined in together some days previously. There, over turtle soup and glasses of Madeira, we discussed the revelations of the day and our plans for the next.

"We may assume that Piennar remains in the city," Holmes offered as a starting point. "He and Rawlins did not flee after the murder of Donaldson, nor after that of Mrs van Raalte or Miss Crane. It is ludicrous to think that the former would run after killing his partner-in-crime. At worst, he will be lying low, waiting for the public gaze to be fastened on Henry Craggs. Only then will he attempt to escape from New York. Added to that, we know he abandoned a portion of their ill-gotten hoard and so, short of funds, he has another reason for staying hidden for now. Our task is to flush him out, to drive him from cover…"

I knew Holmes of old. "No doubt you have a suggestion as to

how we might go about that?" I asked.

"Simplicity itself. All we need do is ensure the truth is given voice. Inspector, are you able to spread the news of Mr Craggs's capture? Let it be known that he has identified the killer of his fiancée and that the police expect to arrest the guilty party in short order. That should drive him out into the open."

Bullock grasped Holmes's suggestion at once. "Of course," he replied, draining his glass. "News of this development will be known by the whole of New York by tomorrow morning."

"Very good," said Holmes, "and in the meantime, if you could provide me with a trusted officer, who I might send on an errand or two?"

"I'll have Officer Hendricks report to you as soon as we arrive back at the station, Mr Holmes."

"That would be ideal."

Bullock proved true to his word. Within minutes of our arrival back at the station, a young officer presented himself at Bullock's office, which we had commandeered while the inspector saw to it that word of Craggs's capture was spread throughout the city. Hendricks was a tall, slender man of no more than twenty years, fair-haired and with a thin moustache which he rubbed nervously as Holmes invited him in.

The topic of their conversation remained unknown to me, for Holmes had asked me to check on Craggs while he gave the young officer his instructions. The prisoner was asleep, and I saw no reason to disturb his peace, but though I was gone only five minutes, by the time I returned Hendricks had departed and Holmes had already lit a pipe, which he smoked while slumped in

Bullock's chair. He gave no indication that he had registered my presence, and with nothing else to do, I took one of the other seats and settled down to wait.

Two hours passed in such a fashion, with Holmes lighting one bowl after another and I dropping in and out of an uneasy doze. The air was thick with smoke by the time a knock on the door jerked Holmes into activity.

"Come in," he instructed, knocking the ashes of his pipe into an ashtray and straightening himself in his seat.

I had expected our visitor to be Officer Hendricks, but in his place stood another officer and, by his side, a small, unkempt boy, dressed in torn short trousers and a jacket several sizes too large for him buttoned over a ragged shirt, once white, now stained a dirty grey. His feet were bare and filthy and he was painfully thin, but other than that he appeared to be in reasonable health.

"Sherlock Holmes?" he asked as the officer pushed him into the room, holding out a folded sheet of paper to my friend.

"The same," Holmes responded, reaching out and taking the paper, which he spread on the desk before him. Whatever information it contained clearly proved satisfactory, for he smiled with pleasure and handed the boy a small coin for his troubles. As the officer led the boy from the room, he folded the paper again and slipped it into his pocket.

"Have you any objection to a short trip, Watson?" he asked, already rising from his seat.

"None whatsoever," I replied. "Do you have a particular destination in mind?"

"I do. I think now would be a good time to revisit the dockland area. Something tells me that Mr Piennar may be found there this evening."

* * *

The docks at night were a very different affair from the bright and bustling scene we had witnessed on our arrival. Much of the area was entirely in darkness, with here and there islands of sulphurous light marking the location of an office yet open or a gang still hard at work. A rain shower just prior to our arrival had slicked the cobblestones and made them treacherous underfoot, adding to the sensation that this was not a welcoming place.

Holmes, however, advanced into the gloom with no hesitation, making directly for a derelict shed from beneath whose ill-fitting door a dim light could be seen. I followed with my hand tight around my revolver and an eye on every shadow.

To reach the shed that I was now convinced was Holmes's destination, it was necessary to cross a long, flat patch of hard earth. A wooden fence, broken in sundry places, enclosed the space, an open gap with rusted brackets for a gate providing the only entrance. The shed itself sat at the far end of this enclosure, surrounded by darkness that had been rendered no clearer even by ten minutes blundering about. I stilled my breathing and listened carefully, but except for the tread of Holmes's boots in front of me, I could hear nothing out of the ordinary.

Even so, I was not relaxed, and it was this tautness that allowed me to swing the butt of my revolver across the temple of the dark figure who reared up from the ground as we passed through the gap in the fence. My assailant fell back while I fumbled with the gun, but before I could twist the weapon round to bring it to bear on the swine, I felt strong arms around my midriff and a voice in my ear saying, "For pity's sake, Watson, must you assault everyone you meet?"

I shrugged off Holmes's arms with irritation and not a little confusion, keeping my gun in hand, as the door of the shed creaked open and a not unfamiliar voice requested that we hurry inside. The man I had struck struggled to his feet and returned to his place by the gap in the fence. He was a guard, I surmised – set to check any man approaching the shed. This supposition was confirmed by Holmes, who whispered, "It's quite an impressive set-up, wouldn't you say, Watson – a base complete with troops," leaving me reassured and confused in equal measure. I had no time to query Holmes, however, before we slipped inside the shed and the door closed softly behind us.

Inside, a lantern on the floor illuminated three men sitting round an upturned barrel that they were using as a table on which to play cards. I did not recognise the two men sitting to the left and right, but as the man directly in front of me turned in his seat to watch us enter, I realised that the voice that had asked us to hurry belonged to Bob Peters, the seaman Holmes had saved from the noose on our voyage over.

He touched a forefinger to the brim of his cap as the other two men vacated their seats, and invited us to take them. They disappeared out into the darkness, leaving Holmes, Peters and I alone.

"Good evening to you, Mr Peters," Holmes said cheerfully. "I hope you have some success to report?"

"I do, Mr Holmes, sir. The lad you're after is bunked up on the *Patricia*, a German ship bound for Marseille."

In contrast to the last time we had met, Peters was confident and clear-spoken. I was at a loss to explain his presence here, but plainly he was expecting us, for once we were seated, he reached into a tattered bag at his feet and pulled from it a scrap of paper on which I recognised a description of Piennar in Holmes's handwriting.

"Weren't hard to find him neither," the sailor said, his mouth stretched in a wide grin. "There ain't many even in New York look like that big brute."

"I am obliged to you, Mr Peters. If you will point my colleague and me in the direction of the *Patricia*, we will take a police officer – possibly more than one – and effect an arrest."

"Best make it several more, Mr Holmes. Thon's a big lad, so he is."

In reply, Holmes clapped the man on the shoulder. "Never worry. Watson here has a revolver with him, and Inspector Bullock would be only too happy to provide further men, if required. I'm sure we shall manage somehow, if you would be so kind as to arrange for someone to run to the inspector's station and alert him to our need of assistance."

I did not doubt that Holmes spoke truly, but even so I was not unhappy to see Peters frown, then, having come to a decision, march across to the door of the shed. He carefully pushed it open, then said something quietly into the darkness. The other two seamen followed him back inside, closing the door behind them.

"I've sent a lad to speak to Bullock, but I'd not forgive meself if anything unpleasant was to happen to you, Mr Holmes," Peters said. "So I think it'd be best if me and a couple of the boys kept you company, just in case."

"There really is no need, my dear–" Holmes began, but got no further, as Peters interrupted politely but firmly.

"I'd be sitting in the condemned cell today, Mr Holmes, if I weren't already done for, were it not for you. You'll allow me to repay that debt a little, won't you?"

Holmes did not insult the man by claiming there was no debt. Instead he gave a single sharp nod of gratitude and agreed that we should leave at once, with Peters and his friends to accompany us. I had hoped that Holmes would explain himself before we set off, but there was no time to waste, according to Peters, as the ship on which Piennar was stowed would set sail later that night. He grabbed a pickaxe handle from behind the door and led us all out into the darkness.

Emptiness is the defining quality of a dock bereft of working men. What is all bustle and noise during the day is quiet as a churchyard at night. So it was that we made our way – Peters in the lead, followed by Holmes and me, with the two other sailors guarding the rear – across open ground, our every step potentially visible to any sharp-eyed observer on the ships that lined the docks.

In the end, either nobody looked or the dark was enough to hide us, for we arrived at our destination unmolested and, I thought, unobserved. A wooden gangway, wide enough for two men to walk abreast, stretched from the dockside to the entryway of the *Patricia* herself. The ship moved as the water moved, rising and falling in a rough rhythm, though never enough to concern even a land-loving soul such as myself.

The only light came from a lamp flickering atop a pole attached to the gangway. We made sure to remain in shadow as Peters brought us to a halt and whispered that he and his friends would briefly board the ship to ensure that the man we sought was still in his cabin. They slipped soundlessly up the gangway and were soon lost to sight.

I took the opportunity, while Holmes and I were alone, to ask for some explanations – how he could possibly have known that Piennar would head for the docks chief amongst them.

"Really, Watson, that particular deduction does me little credit. As soon as we knew that Piennar was not the mute we had thought and thus was hiding some identifying factor in his speech, I wondered what that might be. Once Mr Craggs mentioned his belief that he had heard a Germanic note in his pronunciation, I realised that an Afrikaans accent might easily be mistaken for a Teutonic one. A native German speaker might hide for some time amongst his émigré countrymen in the Five Points, but an Afrikaner, forced by his need of assistance to speak and so reveal his true origins? I thought not, and so asked the inspector to post men at every road out of the city, while I sent word to Peters and requested that he seek out any Boer looking for passage to Europe or Africa. There are plenty of captains in these waters who would be happy to hide such a man on board until they were ready to sail. Fortunately, there is a brotherhood amongst sailors, and Peters was swiftly able to identify a huge Boer with little by way of luggage and a pressing need to be somewhere other than America."

Holmes's speech raised far more questions than it answered, but before I could quiz him further, Peters returned and, from the top of the gangway, waved that we should follow him.

Quickly we ran across and onto the ship itself, where Peters waited in the shadow of a doorway. "This way," he said, "and mind how you go. It's darker than you'll be used to."

Sure enough, what light there was inside the ship was widely spaced and untrustworthy, consisting mainly of smoky oil lamps that swung this way and that with the motion of the ship. We clambered down grimy ladders and through seemingly identical murky corridors for several minutes, moving slowly, with an ear for any legitimate crew who might detain us, but even such slow progress soon brought us to our destination.

Peters halted before one door much like every other, a painted wooden slab with a brass handle, but no other markings.

"Your man is inside, Mr Holmes, sir," Peters whispered. He held his pickaxe handle in one hand and now, with the other, he reached into his jacket and removed a length of metal piping from within. "You best take this, sir," he said to Holmes, handing it over, then, "Doctor, you have your revolver with you?" he asked. I held the weapon out silently in confirmation.

"Good. Stay behind me and the lads then, when we get in there." He turned to the other sailors. "In three, lads," he said, before holding up three fingers, each of which he lowered in its turn. As the last finger folded in on itself, he nodded and, with a cry of "NOW!" kicked the door with all his strength, sending it flying back on its hinges. We pushed our way into the room behind him, ready for anything, our various weapons held out before us, violence in the very air.

The room was empty.

A bunk holding a disordered heap of dirty linen stood directly in front of us, taking up most of the back wall. By its head, a small metal cabinet sat with its door ajar, and at its foot a wastepaper basket. There was no other exit, and though Peters dropped to his knees to look under the bed, no place to hide. It seemed that somehow our man had absconded.

"I was under the impression that you had checked whether Mr Piennar was within this room?" Holmes asked, making an admirable, if obvious, attempt to keep any note of recrimination from his voice.

"We did, Mr Holmes," Peters replied unhappily. "He was here not five minutes since, I promise you."

Holmes moved inside the room, wordlessly brushing past the

three sailors as he glanced inside the metal cabinet and poked in the wastepaper basket with the metal pole Peters had given him.

"He has certainly been here recently," he said after a moment's thought. "See here: a crushed pack of the brand of cigarette we know he favours and…" he laid a hand on the bed sheet, "…the bed is still warm. There is a little money in the cabinet, so we may assume he will–"

Whatever he was about to say was lost, however, as a gasp from behind warned me in the nick of time that our quarry had returned. I had a moment in which to duck and attempt to bring my revolver to bear before a blow like an iron bar descended on my arm, striking my wrist and causing me to let go of my grip. The gun spun into the darkness as I found myself face to face with Hans Piennar.

He was as large as we had been told, six and a half feet tall and almost as broad, with the thickest neck I had ever seen on a man and hands the size of my head. He swung one of those ham-sized fists at me while I was still reeling from the pain in my arm, and though I twisted to avoid it and so was spared a direct hit, his knuckles glanced off my chin with sufficient force to knock me backwards, where my head crashed against the wall. I tried to stand but my legs had lost all utility. I was forced to remain seated, the pain in my head competing with that in my arm and my jaw, and all attempting to send me spinning into unconsciousness at any moment. Piennar stepped past me, and I reached out a hand to stop him, but there was no strength in my arm and he easily brushed me off – though not before I noticed that one shining brass button was missing from the greatcoat he wore, a match I was sure for the one Holmes had found on Mrs van Raalte's body.

For the next several minutes I was obliged to take a spectator's role in proceedings. My compatriots turned as one and engaged the man, but he was too strong and pressed them back, allowing them no time to come at him en masse. One of the sailors went down under the impact of a ferocious double-handed blow, and Piennar quickly stooped and grabbed the fallen man's weapon, a short, metal-tipped stave, which he swung before him.

I could see Holmes pushing against the men in front of him, frustration plain on his face.

"Take him alive, if possible," he shouted over the others' cries. "I have questions I should like to ask him."

Taking him in any fashion seemed unlikely, however. As Holmes spoke, the second of Peters's comrades was brought to his knees, then dispatched with a savage uppercut. I felt consciousness threatening to leave me too as I watched the unfortunate man strike the back wall, then fall, eyes open but unseeing, on the bunk. I tasted blood in the back of my throat and felt it running over my eyebrow and down my cheek.

By the flickering light of the single lamp outside the cabin, I made out Peters pushing forward to thrust a blade deep into Piennar's shoulder, and I wondered if this marked the turning point in the fight. If it did, though, it was not as I would have hoped, for the huge Boer simply pulled the knife from his flesh and returned it to Peters with the full force of his strength. He buried the blade to the hilt in our friend's chest, then allowed him to drop to the floor.

Holmes was alone with Piennar now. He held the metal pole he had been given, extended before him like a rapier, and bounced on the balls of his feet as the Boer kicked Peters's body out of the way and advanced. Piennar's own stave hung loosely at his side, as though he had no intention of using it, as though his superiority was so clear he could kill Holmes with his bare hands. I pushed myself up against the wall, ignoring the waves of dizziness and nausea which washed over me, searching for my revolver, but the room spun and I fell back.

I refocused my eyes just in time to see Holmes lunge forward and Piennar brush off his attack with no more exertion than a man would show when swatting a fly. Holmes's weapon flew from his hands and clattered away, and Piennar's massive hands closed round my friend's throat. I tried again to stand, crying out Holmes's name as I watched him turning purple then blue in the face, and managed two steps in his direction before my legs gave way once more. I had strength enough left to turn my face, to bear witness to my dearest friend's final moments, as the life was throttled from him.

And then, as unconsciousness finally overcame me, I fancied that I heard a loud bang and saw Piennar jerk and loosen his hold on Holmes's neck. Another loud retort caused my head to ring. Just as my eyes closed I thought I saw him slump to his knees and blood bubble from his mouth.

I could not be certain, however, and without another thought, darkness claimed me for its own.

Chapter Eighteen

When I returned to consciousness, I found myself lying in a hospital bed. My head ached and my arm was securely bandaged, but otherwise I felt myself undamaged though curiously light-headed, even giddy, a sensation I laid at the door of the morphine I could feel dulling the pain. Holmes was seated to my left, hidden behind a newspaper, obliging me to cough loudly in order to gain his attention.

"Good morning, my dear fellow," he beamed, folding the newspaper and laying it in his lap. "I had begun to think you intended to sleep the entire day away!"

His voice was rough and cracked, and as I pushed myself into a seated position I saw a bandage around his throat.

"We have both been in the wars, it seems," I said, with some concern, but Holmes would have none of it.

"In common with your doctors, I have been more concerned with the nasty blow you took to the head than with my own trifling injury," he said. "Besides, I have only myself to blame, and you to thank. Had you not given the alarm when you did, we might all have been killed. As it is, one of Peters's companions broke his neck when thrown against the wall, and Peters himself remains in some pain from a knife wound to his chest. He is expected to live, however, for which he also has you to thank."

"And thank you he shall, when he can!"

Bullock's voice carried from the doorway of my room, where he stood alongside two uniformed policemen.

"We've just come from his room and taken his statement. Not that it matters specially, not with Rawlins and Piennar both dead."

"Piennar is dead, then?" I asked. "I thought that I saw him fall when I heard gunfire, but I could not be sure. Your work, I take it, Inspector?"

"Not I, Doctor. We have a deal to tell you, it seems, but to start with you should know that the shots that did for Piennar were fired by Henry Craggs!"

Bullock could not keep a wide grin from his face as he made this revelation. "The clever bugger picked the lock of the room we'd put him in, removed his gun from the drawer of my desk and followed you and Mr Holmes to the docks. By the time we arrived, he'd shot and killed Piennar, and was sitting, quiet as you like, with Mr Holmes. You were still out for the count, of course, and missed all the excitement."

"Craggs killed Piennar?" I said, turning to Holmes for confirmation.

He nodded and whispered, in a voice so quiet that only I could hear him, "And so his revenge was complete," before raising it to address Bullock. "He did indeed, the poor, unfortunate man. But who can blame him? The fact that he saved the lives of both myself and Dr Watson notwithstanding, he had seen the woman he loved murdered in the most brutal fashion, and had then been forced to flee for his life, suspected of that same hideous crime. What man would not desire vengeance in such a case?"

"That's as may be, Mr Holmes, but we can't encourage people to take the law into their own hands, no matter the provocation." Clearly, Bullock had some sympathy with Holmes's words, even if his position made it impossible for him to admit that fact. "You should know that I'll speak up for Craggs at his trial. He'll not suffer overmuch for his actions last night."

"I am delighted to hear it, Inspector," said Holmes. "I suspect that Watson and I will have left these shores by the time Craggs is in court, but once I place the documents we discovered in Piennar's cabin into the hands of the British government, I believe I can safely say that they too will wish to intercede on Mr Craggs's behalf."

"Documents, Holmes?" My head remained heavy, but there was a tale to be told here, one to which I was not as yet privy.

"In his suitcase, Watson. In code, but of undoubted interest to the British Cabinet. But it would perhaps be simpler if I were to start at the beginning, rather than commencing my explanation at the end?"

"Certainly, Holmes, do as you think best. Though I warn you that I am still a little woozy, and so may need you to repeat yourself later."

In answer, Holmes crossed to the door and firmly closed it. He asked Bullock to move his chair closer to my bed, and did the same with his own. Only once he was completely satisfied that we could not be overheard, did he begin to speak.

"Almost from our arrival in New York, I have suspected that the whole notion of a duplicate Holmes was but a ruse designed to lure me from England. The work I have been doing for my brother, Mycroft, is important enough that more than one foreign power might think it profitable to do whatever they must to achieve that goal."

I had never pried into Holmes's work for Mycroft, but now that he had broached the subject himself, I felt confident that I should do so. "You believe that the entirety of this affair has had as its sole aim absenting you from London?" In relation to any other man, I would have dismissed such a claim as the wildest and most self-aggrandising fantasy, but I knew Holmes too well even to consider drawing such a conclusion.

"I do. I had suspected as much even before leaving England, but the instant I saw Rawlins's mocked-up office, I knew that I was correct. The detective business was an obvious sham, and that being the case, I had to ask myself why."

I believed I had spotted a flaw in Holmes's logic. "But if the goal was simply to divert you, why also bother with blackmail?"

"I cannot say with certainty, but I imagine initially as a source of income. Our own government has encountered problems in the past in keeping our agents surreptitiously in funds. Why not turn to blackmail to top up their coffers?"

Bullock had listened to these exchanges with a growing air of confusion. Now, as he considered Holmes's words, he pounced upon two of them.

"*Our agents*, Mr Holmes? What d'you mean by that, if I might ask?"

Now it was Holmes's turn to look confused. "Why, surely you have realised by now that Piennar was an agent of a foreign power? More specifically, he worked for the so-called Free States in southern Africa – the Boers."

I understood now my friend's caution in securing my hospital room from intruders. The Boers were a ruthless and violent people, self-proclaimed freedom fighters who, in reality, were revolutionaries determined to destroy anything that did not meet with their satisfaction, regardless of right or law. We had fought one war against them some twenty years before, and it had become plain in recent months that they were itching for another conflict. If Holmes had been investigating them then he had been swimming in deep waters indeed.

"And Rawlins? Was he also a spy for these Boers?"

"As I said to Watson a few days ago, Rawlins was obviously glib and convincing, with an easy manner and a gift for ingratiation. In other words, he possessed every talent of the professional confidence man. It occurred to me at the time, however, that an actor would equally well find the description a neat fit. Then, when we discovered Rawlins's body, I found minute traces of greasepaint under his nails, left there when he removed the make-up that hid his sun-reddened skin and rendered him sufficiently pale to pass for an English detective. He had been punctilious in removing his make-up, even remembering to wipe behind his ears and the nape of his neck, but he had forgotten that fragments would be trapped beneath his nails as he cleaned himself. A burnt hair pin – such as is used to darken the eyebrows and hair for the stage – dropped behind his dressing table heightened my suspicions, but it was only when I checked a variety of actors' journals at the library that I found mention of N. Rawlins, a jobbing – and not entirely successful – English actor working in the western United States."

"You think Piennar hired Rawlins to play you, Mr Holmes? And this in order that you be cajoled from London to New York, the better to allow your enemies to scheme against you?"

"Against England, rather, but essentially, yes, I believe that to be the case. Mr Rawlins had the added advantage to Piennar, of course, that as a hired hand with no idea of the wider picture, he was utterly expendable. I would suggest that our own investigations indirectly caused his death, in fact. As we closed in, Piennar panicked and was forced to kill Rawlins to ensure his silence, then fled for home.

"That would also be the reason Piennar left so large a sum of money behind him after murdering Rawlins. He planned to take this ship back to Europe but had no way of knowing how close we were on his heels, or if we suspected him at all. What better way to confuse matters than to leave the money behind? A frightened underling might take only the clothes he required and flee, leaving his superior and their ill-gotten profits behind."

"You remain convinced Piennar killed Rawlins, Mr Holmes?" asked Bullock.

"I do. Just as he killed Mrs van Raalte, once her usefulness was at an end, then attempted to dispose of her body where it might remain hidden until he was safely away. Each was a loose thread that needed to be dealt with before Piennar could leave the country."

"You make a convincing case," Bullock responded thoughtfully. "But there's one thing that continues to niggle at me. Craggs's gun. Why leave it by Rawlins's body, when Piennar must surely have believed him dead?"

"Ah, but remember, Piennar thought the police unaware of Mr Rawlins's demise. Furthermore, he believed that they still favoured Craggs as the killer of his own fiancée. What better way to muddy the waters than to bring that name into play? If the police were busy hunting a dead man, they could not also be looking for Piennar, leaving him free to flee in safety."

Perhaps it was the effects of the medication I had been given, but I was conscious that Holmes had omitted some detail from his retelling. Had I been more myself I would, I think, have said nothing, but the morphine in my system made me loose-tongued.

"You have not told us what exactly you were being lured *from*, Holmes," I said. "On what vital task did Mycroft have you working?"

Even in my befuddled state, I could tell that Holmes was not pleased by this question. His eyes flicked to Inspector Bullock, then back to me, as he considered how best to answer. Before he could do so, however, Bullock spoke up.

"I think it might be a good idea if I now absent myself, gentlemen," he said, fixing his hat firmly on his head. "There's a great deal still to be done at the station, and if I'm not there... well, it'd be best if I were anyway."

"That would be very... understanding of you, Inspector." The appreciation in Holmes's voice was genuine, I thought. "There are a number of matters that I need to discuss with Watson, after which I shall return to my hotel. I wonder," he concluded with a smile, "whether you might join me for dinner this evening? At about eight, say?"

The two men shook hands and Bullock left, closing the door quietly behind him.

"Really, Watson, you do make things unnecessarily difficult at times!"

Holmes rounded on me as soon as Bullock was gone, but there was affection in his scolding. All I could do was apologise, and ask again regarding his recent travails on his brother's behalf.

"This is not exactly the most secure place to have such a discussion, but the doctor informs me that they are likely to insist that you remain in your current position for at least another day, and I would hate to impede your recovery by keeping you in suspense for too long." He paused, seemed to consider for a moment, peering at the ceiling apparently rapt in thought. "Oh, very well," he said, finally, with a wide grin, "make yourself comfortable and I will tell you the entire story, in the strict understanding that none of this is intended for publication."

Needless to say, I hastily agreed and he, who had, I assumed, always intended to tell me everything, took a seat once more and began to speak.

"I will not bore you with the background to my recent endeavours for Mycroft, both because you would find it tedious and because I did not, in truth, pay a great deal of attention to it myself. Instead, I have lately focused tightly on the immediate task at hand – which, for the past few months, has been to ensure the safety of certain American individuals who have periodically visited England to engage in talks pertaining to the present Boer situation in Africa.

"Each of these men has his own bodyguard, of course, and naturally our own police have provided more general protection, but I was asked by Mycroft to check the location of every meeting in advance, to ascertain the whereabouts of known agitators – the usual grubby, difficult and unrewarding work with which Mycroft likes to punish me, in fact.

"Notwithstanding that, I may say that I have proven singularly successful. To date, no visitor has been molested, and several Boer agents have been apprehended. Last month, however, I received word that I would be required to arrange a safe meeting place for two personages of far greater prestige than had heretofore been the case. I had just finished making the arrangements when the letter – sent, of course, by Piennar – arrived that set this affair in motion. I should, perhaps, have remained until the meeting was concluded, but there seemed little purpose in doing so, and I cannot deny that I was sorely in need of rest."

I confess I was aghast to hear Holmes so blithely speak of neglecting his duty in order to pursue a personal matter. Holmes must have read the ire on my face.

"In my defence, I had no reason to suspect that I was being hoodwinked, but I cannot deny that I was at a low ebb mentally and physically when the letter arrived and so, perhaps, was more malleable than would normally have been the case. A few days in New York, with an interesting intellectual puzzle to divert me, seemed both harmless and potentially even invigorating. I admit that my error of judgement could have cost England dear. That it did not was a consequence of a handful of indicators left by Rawlins and Piennar which, fortunately, I was able to read in time."

"Thank the Lord!" I said with feeling. "But having realised that Rawlins – that the duplicate Holmes – was merely a ruse, when did you know about the rest? Please tell me that it was in time to protect the important meeting to which you referred."

Rather than reply, Holmes reached down and opened the door to my bedside cabinet. He extracted a newspaper, which he laid in my lap with the front page uppermost.

"Halfway down the far right column," he instructed.

The headline read "FOREIGN AGENTS APPREHENDED", with beneath it a few lines establishing that two agents of an unspecified foreign country had been arrested the previous night, near the Carlton Hotel, London.

"And also, here," Holmes went on, indicating another small piece further down the page. The header on this occasion was slightly larger and comprised just three words, "US–BRITISH TALKS".

"'A confidential meeting took place last night between Lord Robert Cecil, the Prime Minister of Great Britain, and the United States Ambassador to the Court of King James, Joseph Choate.

Early reports indicate that a rapport was quickly reached between the two men, a fact which augurs well for both countries'," I read. "By God, Holmes! The Prime Minister…"

"I was able to telegram Mycroft in plenty of time, thankfully, and the meeting was moved from the Carlton at the last minute. The capture of the two men sent to disrupt the meeting was, I must admit, an additional and very welcome bonus."

"Does that not come perilously close to a guess, Holmes?" I chided him. "True, you were correct that the Boers intended to attack the meeting, but you could not know for certain. What if they had dragged you overseas not to keep you from your duty, but in order to murder you, far from the protection of Scotland Yard?"

Holmes instantly bridled, as I knew he would. "Scotland Yard? *Scotland Yard?* The day that my safety depends on their protection is the day I retire to a life of sedentary bee-keeping! Have you not noticed, Watson, that I am a hard man to kill?" He did not wait for a reply. "In any case, there was no guesswork involved. Do not tell me that you have already forgotten the scraps of burned paper we found at Rawlins's home? 'MES', 'DON' and 'OAT' they read, if memory serves, and the inspector made the natural assumption that the reference was to James Donaldson, Piennar's first victim. I, however, saw something else. *Holmes*, *London* and *Choate*, I surmised, and contacted my brother without delay."

A nurse bustled into the room at that point, and Holmes fell silent while she fussed around me, straightening my pillows. I was due a further dose of morphine too, which she administered with a reassuring degree of skill, before warning Holmes that he had but five more minutes remaining of his visit.

"If Dr Watson is not allowed to rest, his recovery will never be complete," she said as she closed the door behind her, and as she did so her words reminded me of something Holmes had said earlier.

I felt the morphine smothering me in its warm embrace as I called Holmes's name. My mouth felt as though it belonged to someone else as I beckoned him over.

"You said that Henry Craggs's revenge was complete when he killed Piennar. But you told Bullock that Piennar killed Rawlins..."

My voice trailed off and I felt my eyelids closing as the drug took effect. Faintly, as if he were far across the room, I heard Holmes's voice, though it took all of my concentration to make sense of his words.

"There I may have gone too far," he was saying. "Did you not wonder that Rawlins and Piennar held onto a weapon which could only incriminate them in the future, and that solely on the off-chance that they might be able to use it to frame a man who they believed already dead by their hand?"

"So Craggs..."

"...is guilty of double murder, yes. His arrival at Rawlins's home was just a little too convenient, his explanation too pat. I would suggest that he was given the address by the servant Eales, who was, of course, in his employ. He went there at once and, having surprised Rawlins somehow, shot and killed him. Piennar must have arrived soon afterwards and, with no idea who might have killed Rawlins, decided discretion was the better part of valour. I suspect he left the money deliberately, for the reason I gave the inspector, but the money clip and watch? Forgotten in his panicked flight.

"But none of this matters. I can prove nothing because I choose to seek out no proof. The man has suffered enough, lost enough, without losing his freedom too. Perhaps I have gone too far in doing so, but I do not blame myself, Watson. Sometimes, it is better not to speak."

He may have said more, but if he did I was unaware, for the seductive power of the morphine finally overcame my resistance, and I found my eyes would remain open no longer. As I slipped into sleep, I could hear the soft voice of my old friend, murmuring explanations in the gathering darkness.

About the Author

STUART DOUGLAS is the author of numerous short stories and novellas, including the Titan Books Sherlock Holmes novel, *The Albino's Treasure*. He is one of the founders of Obverse Books, and the Features Editor of the British Fantasy Society journal. He lives in Edinburgh.

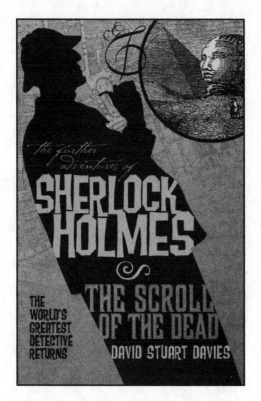

THE FURTHER ADVENTURES
OF SHERLOCK HOLMES

THE SCROLL OF THE DEAD

David Stuart Davies

In this fast-paced adventure, Sherlock Holmes attends a seance to unmask
an impostor posing as a medium. His foe, Sebastian Melmoth is a man hell-
bent on discovering a mysterious Egyptian papyrus that may hold the key
to immortality. It is up to Holmes and Watson to use their deductive skills
to stop him or face disaster.

ISBN: 9781848564930

AVAILABLE NOW!

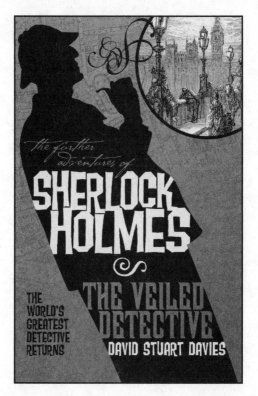

THE FURTHER ADVENTURES
OF SHERLOCK HOLMES

THE VEILED DETECTIVE

David Stuart Davies

It is 1880, and a young Sherlock Holmes arrives in London to pursue a
career as a private detective. He soon attracts the attention of criminal
mastermind Professor James Moriarty, who is driven by his desire to
control this fledgling genius. Enter Dr John H. Watson, soon to make
history as Holmes' famous companion.

ISBN: 9781848564909

AVAILABLE NOW!

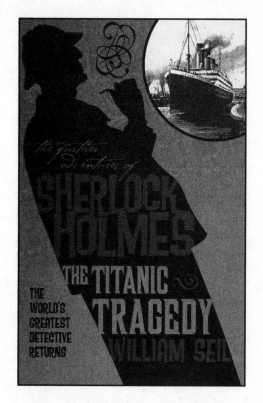

THE FURTHER ADVENTURES
OF SHERLOCK HOLMES

THE TITANIC TRAGEDY

William Seil

Holmes and Watson board the Titanic in 1912, where Holmes is to carry
out a secret government mission. Soon after departure, highly important
submarine plans for the U.S. navy are stolen. Holmes and Watson work
through a list of suspects which includes Colonel James Moriarty, brother to
the late Professor Moriarty—will they find the culprit before tragedy strikes?

ISBN: 9780857687104

AVAILABLE NOW!

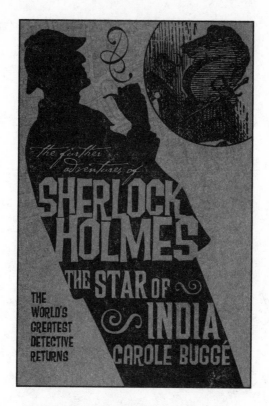

THE FURTHER ADVENTURES
OF SHERLOCK HOLMES

THE STAR OF INDIA

Carole Buggé

Holmes and Watson find themselves caught up in a complex chessboard
of a problem, involving a clandestine love affair and the disappearance
of a priceless sapphire. Professor James Moriarty is back to tease and
torment, leading the duo on a chase through the dark and dangerous
back streets of London and beyond.

ISBN: 9780857681218

AVAILABLE NOW!

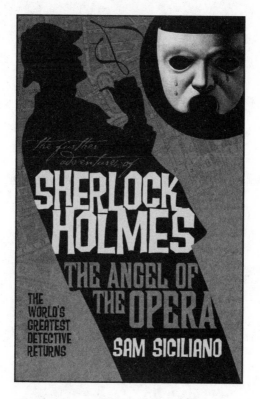

THE FURTHER ADVENTURES
OF SHERLOCK HOLMES

THE ANGEL OF THE OPERA

Sam Siciliano

Paris 1890. Sherlock Holmes is summoned across the English Channel
to the famous Opera House. Once there, he is challenged to discover
the true motivations and secrets of the notorious phantom, who rules its
depths with passion and defiance.

ISBN: 9781848568617

AVAILABLE NOW!

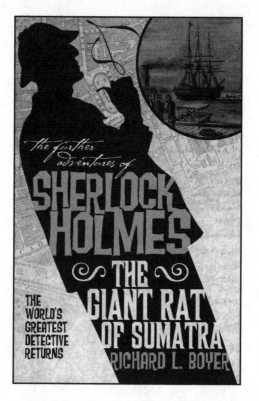

THE FURTHER ADVENTURES
OF SHERLOCK HOLMES

THE GIANT RAT OF SUMATRA

Richard L. Boyer

For many years, Dr. Watson kept the tale of The Giant Rat of
Sumatra a secret. However, before he died, he arranged that
the strange story of the giant rat should be held in the vaults of
a London bank until all the protagonists were dead…

ISBN: 9781848568600

AVAILABLE NOW!

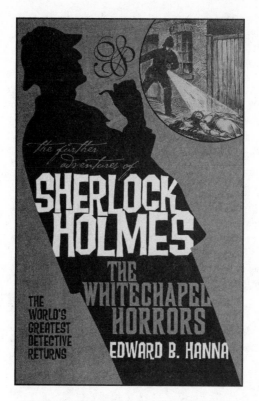

THE FURTHER ADVENTURES
OF SHERLOCK HOLMES

THE WHITECHAPEL HORRORS

Edward B. Hanna

Grotesque murders are being committed on the streets of Whitechapel.
Sherlock Holmes believes he knows the identity of the killer–Jack the
Ripper. But as he delves deeper, Holmes realizes that revealing the
murderer puts much more at stake than just catching a killer…

ISBN: 9781848567498

AVAILABLE NOW!